Best Frenemies

max monroe

New York Times & USA Today Bestselling Author

Best Frenemies

Published by Max Monroe LLC © 2023, Max Monroe

All rights reserved.

Editing by Silently Correcting Your Grammar
Formatting by Champagne Book Design
Cover Design by Peter Alderweireld

Dedication

To the way real life can sometimes be stranger than fiction.

To how this book got one of us pregnant.

And to Tiffany, otherwise known as "the cottage cheese and mustard girl" on TikTok. This book was powered by your super strange but oddly satisfying meal recommendations. Though, we can't deny our families think we're nuts whenever they see our plates.

Author's Note

Best Frenemies is a full-length romantic comedy stand-alone novel that's jam-packed with the kind of enemies-to-lovers vibes that will consume you.

And since this book is so fun, so sexy, and so damn hilarious, we can't let you start it without an important warning.

Due to the hilarious and addictive nature of this book's content, the following things are *not* recommended: *reading on the subway, reading on a first date, reading while you're in line at the grocery store, reading on your wedding day, reading during the birth of your child, reading at a family dinner, reading while eating and/or drinking, reading at work, reading this book to your boss, and/or reading while operating heavy machinery. Also, if suffering from bladder incontinence due to age/pregnancy/childbirth/etc., we recommend wearing sanitary products and/or reading while sitting directly on a toilet.* It might seem like a long list of places not to read, but we assure you, if you do it in the right setting, it'll be worth it.

Happy Reading!

All our love,
Max & Monroe

Chapter One

Friday, March 18th

Mack

Mark Twain once said, *"Eat a live frog first thing in the morning and nothing worse will happen to you the rest of the day."*

I don't know about tasting squishy guts from a biology project literally, but I *am* an expert in the exercise metaphorically. I've been training with Claude O'Connor at Shamrock Boxing Club first thing in the morning for the past five years, and I've yet to leave his gym without at least two new and mysterious pains.

You'd think that would be reason enough to stop going, but I've always been an addict for anything that challenges me on a physical level and gets my heart pumping with adrenaline. As a rule, aches and pains are normally a consequence of that.

To be honest, aches and pains and inconveniences are a huge part of *life*. With over seven billion people in the world, it'd be pretty impossible for everyone's everything to go to plan.

My sister Lizzy says my outlook is the result of a privileged upbringing—one she likes to remind me was shockingly different from her own, despite the same set of parents. But when Randy and Beth Houston had me in their forties, everything about their world view shifted.

Suddenly, it wasn't about the recommended milestones and keeping up with the Joneses—or anyone else, for that matter.

My mom said I was an unexpected gift, and come hell or high water, she wasn't going to let any of us waste it. And since my dad defers all of his opinions to his wife, my life has been pretty fucking special.

I proudly march to the beat of my own drum, even if my march has a limp on my way to the subway entrance at 59th Street.

With my AirPods in my ears and the sweet sounds of Led Zeppelin providing the soundtrack for my early morning, I scan my MetroCard and step on to a nearly empty train with my gym bag and a drink carrier filled with three meticulously planned Starbucks coffees.

The morning rush hour has yet to commence, but that's mostly because it's so early—not even six thirty yet—and the people who actually care about sleep are getting in every last wink they can.

For me personally, the world's full of too much stuff to spend any more time than I have to looking at the insides of my eyelids.

Just as the subway takes off for its next stop, my phone buzzes with a text. It takes a juggling effort to free it from my pocket and check the screen, but at this hour of the day, I'm too curious to let it go without looking.

My inbox has three unread messages, and after scrolling past the two from last night from *Mary-Jamba Juice* and *Callie (Whole Foods Columbus Circle)*, I click the one I've just received from my larger-than-life cousin.

And trust me, I know the way I save women's numbers in my phone might make me sound like a total dick, but what can I say? Sometimes, it's hard to keep track of who is who. I'm a single guy who likes to date around. I love women and I love spending time with women, but that time usually ends after one or two dates.

Thatch: Got a favor, cuz. Need you to help Gunnar get home from school today. Both Cass and I are slammed with work. Ace will be home when you drop him off, though, so you and your dick can hopscotch right back into your bachelorhood without too much delay.

Thatcher Kelly is my eldest cousin from my mother's side of the family—his mom and my mom are sisters—and I'm the youngest at the ripe old age of thirty-one. Ace is his eldest son and currently in his first year of high school, and his youngest son Gunnar goes to the private elementary school where I'm a music teacher.

I love both of his kids, and I'm more than happy to help his smallest wild child get home today, but that doesn't mean I can't mess with him a little before I officially agree. Quite frankly, as I'm sure you can tell by the tone of his message, he'd be disappointed by anything less.

Me: What's in it for me?

Thatch: My undying love and anything you can pilfer from my pantry.

Me: That's it?

Thatch: I'll let you get in a few good punches the next time I fit in a session at Shamrock, so you can know what it feels like to be a real man for once. I know you normally have to put your thumb over the tip of your vagina to pee like you're spraying a hose, but maybe if you get a few hits on me, your dick'll swell enough to let you hold it.

A few times a month, when he's not too busy running his bajillion-dollar financial empire or keeping up with his unpredictable wife Cassie, Thatch joins in on my training sessions with Claude. I'd like to say he's full of shit about "letting me get a few hits in," but he's a big motherfucker—and that's saying a lot, considering I'm 6'2". Boxing with him is like boxing with a tree that punches back.

Me: Meh. My boyish charm is one of my strongest attributes, and I use the hose as a party trick. Got anything else to offer?

Thatch: Name your price, Macarena. I can't get Gunnar myself, and I'll be spraying a hose with you if Cassie finds out I didn't get coverage. You've got my dick over a barrel, and you know it. Let's just cut to the chase.

The thing is…I would get Gunnar home without payment anytime. I'm not a parent myself, but I know well enough from my older sister that childcare isn't the kind of shit that falls off trees. But it's not that often that I have something to leverage against my wealthy AF cousin, so I'm not going to waste the opportunity.

Me: Okay. I need you to get the ball rolling on some potential investors for me.

Thatch: Finally ready to take that little music project seriously, huh?

The little music project he's talking about is actually a music foundation that I've been trying to get started for the past two years. Music education is always the first thing that goes when schools have to cut budgets, and this foundation will help avoid that tragic situation that I've seen occur far too many times. Especially in the under-resourced inner-city schools that are struggling for funding in the first place.

And since Thatch has a lot of money *and* he has a lot of friends with a lot of money—and I've had no luck raising funds on my own in the last two years—getting help from him seems like the absolute best place to get it.

Me: I've been taking it seriously. Money just doesn't take an elementary school teacher seriously.

Thatch: Well, woof woof, dude. I mean, have you seen yourself? You look like a badly styled Matthew McConaughey.

Me: I don't see what my unique sense of style has to do with getting funding for innocent kids.

Thatch: Jeez, fine. Turn down the Sarah McLachlan music, would you? I'll help.

Me: And I'll make sure Gunnar gets home today.

Thatch: You might dress like a clown, but you deserve to be the Mother Teresa of music education. I mean, I don't think Mother Teresa wore Chuck Taylors and used to be the drummer in a band called Armpit, but the whole "help those in need" thing really fits.

I do love wearing Chucks, and I did, in fact, drum for a band called Armpit when I was a wild and crazy college kid at NYU. But while music is still in my blood, I've given up the live music scene. There's something about having groupies and teaching elementary kids that doesn't go well together.

Me: Armpit was kick-ass. Even you can't deny that.

Thatch: Kick-ass? You were all right, but you were never gonna get anywhere with Butthole Billy as your lead singer.

He's not wrong. Billy Lanser sounded a lot like Celine Dion if she had laryngitis and forgot how to sing on-key. But he had all the gig connections, and in our misguided youth, the rest of us just wanted to be onstage—even if Billy got us booed.

Me: Sometimes you've got to put some lipstick on a pig so you get an invitation into the barn.

Thatch: If this is your idea of poetry, you'd better stick to music. I'll work on setting up a meeting just as long as you promise not to say any more dumb shit like that when we have it. These guys are billionaires, for fuck's sake.

I click out of our text thread just as the subway rolls to a stop at 79th Street, and I slip my phone back into my pocket.

With a slight grimace thanks to a throbbing thigh, I adjust the gym bag on my shoulder and the drink carrier in my hand and head off the train. It's only a short walk to the entrance doors of Calhoun Elementary, and once I'm inside, I aim straight for the front office. It's my daily routine—one of the only things I actually plan rather than doing it on the fly—to check my mailbox for anything important while schmoozing the ladies who run this place before heading downstairs to the gymnasium's locker rooms for a quick shower and change.

Betty and Carol, the nice secretaries who work the reception desk, and Mona, the school nurse, are gossiping behind the front counter when I walk through the door, and their faces light up with smiles the moment they see me.

"Morning, ladies," I greet and flash a wink as I hand them their regular Starbucks orders I always pick up on my way in on Friday mornings because I'm smart.

I help them get their daily caffeine fixes, and they help me with things like organizing field trips, contacting parents, and sick kids. All three of which are pretty much the bane of my existence.

"You're a lifesaver, Mack," Betty chirps and greedily takes her caramel macchiato from my hands.

"Thank you," Carol mouths silently with a newly answered phone pressed to her ear.

"You're the best," Mona says and pats me on the shoulder. This kind of praise isn't new, but I'll tell you, it never gets old.

"Hey, Betty, can you make sure Gunnar Kelly is waiting here for me after school? His dad asked me to help him get home today."

"Sure thing, honey," Betty agrees readily, the smoothness of her caramel macchiato dulling the normally sharp edges of her personality.

I'm just about to ask Mona for the latest tea when a grating voice trills from behind me.

"Mr. Houston, is there a reason you're in a crop top and a backward baseball cap like some kind of teenage influencer this morning?"

Principal Dana Harris is standing behind me, her right shoulder resting on the doorframe of her office. I glance down at my post-gym attire—black shorts, sneakers, and a black *tank* top that reveals nothing but my biceps. I think me baring my midriff might be wishful thinking on her part.

"Principal Harris, if I were a teen influencer, I'd be in Costa Rica riding the waves this morning instead of talking to you."

She narrows her eyes at me.

"I fit in a workout every morning before I come in," I explain further. "I've tried doing it in a parka, but I passed out thirty minutes in."

"You're like this every morning?"

"He also brings us Starbucks on Fridays," Mona inserts on my behalf. "So don't start messing with our Mack Daddy, Principal Dana. We finally got him trained to be a good boy."

I laugh at that. Mona is sixty years old, happily married with kids and grandkids, and one of the cougar-iest women you'll ever meet. She's nice, but she'll eat you up, Hall & Oates style. You know?

"I also shower and change in the locker rooms before classes start," I add, and Principal Dana just purses her lips. "I'm aware of the dress code, and more than willing to—" I pretend to cough "—*loosely* follow it."

"You're lucky you have good hair and no split ends. If Barry tried to pull this at seven in the morning, I'd fire him. That man's hairline makes me cringe."

Barry—otherwise known as Mr. Koch—is one of Calhoun's history teachers. He's fifty-five and the proud owner of an OG dad bod and receding hairline. He's a suit kind of guy. No tank tops or crop tops or any other tops besides ones he can accessorize with a tie are part of his wardrobe.

"You know, Principal Dana, I know I have great hair, but I don't think it's considered professional to threaten to fire anyone who's not so fortunate," I state through a knowing smile.

"You know, you're right," she responds and crosses her arms over her chest. "It was very inappropriate of me, and I think you need to call the actual principal of this school and let him know so he can take proper action."

My smile is big and uninhibited, and the ladies behind the desk don't bother to hide the roll of their eyes either.

Dana Harris is our *temporary* principal here at Calhoun Elementary. Her father, Donald Harris, had to take a medical leave of absence after he suffered a heart attack a few months back. He's on the mend now and doing very well, but he had to put his daughter Dana in charge, despite her desire to *not* be in charge. She's been trying to get fired ever since.

It might seem like a real nepotism type of situation, but in reality, no one else wanted the job either. All of the staff and teachers are happy with their current positions and aren't looking to take on any extra responsibility. Our salaries are decent already—livable in New York, at least, which is truly saying something—and the Harris family is known for taking care of their employees by respecting workload, classroom size, and giving us the autonomy to make our own lesson plans. It's a teacher's dream. Which is why the turnover rate here is so low.

And since Calhoun Elementary is a privately funded institution in New York City, and has been in the Harris family for generations, Donald was able to handle things how he wanted, which included keeping the principal position in-house until he's able to come back next year. This ensures his school will keep running the way he intended, without undergoing changes from some hotheaded, big-egoed new guy.

Though, I don't think Dana was his first choice. She's thirty-eight, used to be the administrator over our support staff, and has a long history of putting things like facial appointments above work. Not to mention, last year, she took night classes and graduated from cosmetology school because she'd planned to officially switch careers and follow her passion for hair.

Her father's unfortunate medical emergency combined with her administrative certification really fucked up her plans.

"I don't think we need to bring Donald into this," I tell her with a little grin that I know will piss all over her three months of efforts to get canned. "Honestly, if I had a conversation with him, I could only express how fantastic of a job you've been doing. You're a true asset to Calhoun. I hope we never lose you."

Betty snickers. Carol nearly chokes on her coffee. Mona is long gone, but Dana, well, she glares at me.

"Now, if you don't mind, I'm going to get moving so I have time to take a shower and get ready before the bell rings." I finish getting my mail out of my mailbox and offer a sweet smile as I head for the door. "Have a wonderful day, ladies."

"Mr. Houston," Dana calls out just before I can exit. "Before I forget, I need you to meet me in my office today during lunch. I have something important to discuss with you and Ms. Dayton."

"Me and Ms. Dayton?" I question with a quirk of my brow.

Dana smiles proudly. "I have something I need you to work on *together*."

Together?

Katy Dayton is one of my fellow teachers, and the woman doesn't like me... *at all.*

It's been like that since we both started in our teaching positions the same year and never really got off on the right foot. Honestly, if she has a secret voodoo doll of me that she sticks pins in every night, I wouldn't be surprised.

Last year, Principal Donald put us in charge of organizing the big fall carnival, and it only took one meeting for Katy to kick me off the planning committee.

"Oh, and please let Katy know about the meeting," Dana instructs with the kind of smile that whispers the word *checkmate.* "I haven't had a chance to talk with her yet."

Sadly for Dana, thanks to Claude's frogs and a laid-back personality, I've got a steel fortitude against being messed with.

Whatever she's plotting to get under my skin isn't going to bother me nearly as much as it's going to bother pretty little Katy Dayton.

Chapter Two

Katy

As Mr. Carter, Calhoun Elementary's PE teacher, guides my first-period third graders from my classroom and toward the gymnasium, I snag my cell phone from inside my desk drawer to text the one person I've been dying to yell at all day.

Anna, better known as Ms. Franklin here at Calhoun Elementary, is my best friend and runs our art department. I've known her since our Columbia University days, and for the last five years that I've worked here, we've spent the morning before the toll of the bell gassing each other up for another day of little brains and sticky fingers.

But today—of all the days in the universe and beyond—she decided not to show up, and that leaves me freaking the hell out.

We're supposed to leave for a much-needed, week-long spring break vacation together tomorrow on a seven a.m. flight out of JFK, and Anna Franklin is missing in action.

Me: Where the hell are you hiding today? Do you LIKE making me anxious?

Anna: No, actually. That's why I've been avoiding talking to you altogether. So I don't have to tell you the thing I don't want to tell you.

Me: What don't you want to tell me, Anna?

Anna: See, when you say my name like that, I get even more likely to ghost you.

Me: ANNA.

Anna: My classes have a sub today because I'm sick as a damn dog. Apparently, I have the freaking flu.

Me: Seriously? You got sick twenty-four hours before our flight takes off? Didn't I tell you to sanitize at least twenty times a day? Now what are you going to do? Mask up for the flight?

Anna: Technically, no. Technically, I'm going to not mask up and, instead, stay within the confines of my apartment. Technically, I've been instructed to quarantine my contagious ass for the next seventy-two hours.

Me: Are you just saying technically a lot to try to make this news seem less awful???

Anna: Is it working?

Me: NO. Anna, I can't believe this! I'm just supposed to go alone? How did this even happen?

Anna: Oh, I don't know. Maybe it's because I teach art classes to a bunch of germinators.

I can't believe she's not going to be able to go on our vacation. We've had this planned for months. And now…I'm just supposed to go by myself?

Me: Maybe you'd feel better in the Florida air.

Anna: Katy, honey, I'm running a 102 fever, sweating like I just did hot yoga, and my cough sounds like it's coming from the depths of hell. I don't think 99% humidity is going to help this situation.

Me: Ugh. I'm sorry you're sick. Do you need me to bring you anything?

Anna: Dude. I can feel your insincerity through the screen right now.

Me: I'M SORRY. I CARE, I DO. But come onnnn. We've been waiting on this vacation all year. Maybe I should just stay here, and we can daydrink in your apartment.

Anna: KATY, YOU BETTER GO TO FLORIDA OR I'LL KILL YOU.

I roll my eyes and send her one final text when I spot Mrs. Ross standing at my door with my next class of second graders waiting impatiently behind her.

Me: Relax, I'm going to go. I was just offering to stay to make you feel better. Alma is giving me the stink eye right now, so I'll call you later.

I shove my phone back into my desk and offer a polite smile toward my fellow Calhoun teacher, Alma Ross, knowing darn well it's not going to have an effect. Alma's crotchetiness is unmatched.

"Good morning, Mrs. Ross. Bringing the class yourself today?" I question. Normally, her aide does it.

"Not by choice. Olivia's out today," my seventy-year-old coworker grumbles. "Otherwise, I wouldn't be standing here trying to ignore the bunions on my feet while you dilly-dally on your phone, dear."

Alma's the oldest teacher here at Calhoun, and she runs our English Department. From my interactions with her alone, I'd be inclined to understand why the normal retirement age is what it is. But for all the guff she gives the rest of us, she does manage to keep her students engaged and excited to learn. I don't know how, but I guess the only soft spot she has left inside her grumpy body is for the kids.

"I'm so sorry about that, Mrs. Ross," I apologize. "I was just checking in on why Ms. Franklin isn't at school today. If I would've known Olivia wasn't here, I would've come and gotten the students from your room."

"Too late for that," Alma mutters and gestures for the group of second graders to file inside. She barely offers me a wave goodbye before she turns on her black orthotics and shuffles her way back to her room at the end of the hall.

I don't bother waiting around to see her make it there and, instead, step into the waiting room of excitedly wiggling bodies. Second graders, as it is, don't have any still bones whatsoever.

"Good morning, class," I announce with a smile once my students are semi-settled into their desks. "How's everyone doing today?"

"I've been better," Jimmy Lucas says through a deep sigh that's worthy of a man who just got off a twelve-hour shift working construction in one-hundred-degree temperatures.

"Oh no…" I bite my lip to fight the urge to laugh and force a sympathetic smile to my lips. "I'm sorry to hear that, Jimmy. Is there anything I can do to make today better for you?"

Before Jimmy can answer, Seth Brown is quick to chime in. "You probably just need a wine cooler, Jim. My mom says wine coolers make her feel less stressed."

Here we go.

If there's one student I can rely on to get a class *way* off course, it's Seth Brown. He's adorable and even sweet to his core, but he's practically a professional distractor.

Throughout this school year, I've had to contact his mother Sammy numerous times and have had several parent-teacher meetings with her because of Seth's penchant for disruption in the classroom.

"What's a wine cooler?" Jimmy asks, and a rocky future of angry emails from concerned parents about alcoholic beverages being encouraged in my class as a coping mechanism for their seven- and eight-year-old kids flashes before my eyes.

Quick as a whip, I jump into the conversation. "A wine cooler is an alcoholic beverage that only adults can have and is *not* approved by any official agency as a way to deal with stress."

The words just barely leave my lips and Melanie Morris's hand shoots up like a rocket from the fourth row.

"Yes, Melanie?"

"What's a alkalolic beverage, Ms. Dayton?"

"My mom says they're delicious, and she loves—" Seth Brown starts to put in his unneeded two cents, but I quickly cut him off.

"Seth," I state firmly and meet his eyes. "You know the class rules. If you have something to say or a question to ask, you need to raise your hand."

"Sorry, Ms. Dayton," he says sheepishly, his part-time Opie persona in full effect.

"Now, we have gotten way off track here," I announce and walk toward the front of the classroom. "And it's important that we get back on track. Today, we're going to take a timed addition test."

"A stinking test? On a Friday?" Seth groans from the third row, clearly forgetting about the whole raising his hand during class thing in a record amount of time.

"Yes, Seth," I respond. "A short test to see what we've learned these past few weeks."

"Yes!" Caroline, one of my most motivated and well-behaved students, cheers from her spot in the first row. "I love timed tests!"

"Of course, you do," Seth mutters under his breath, but Caroline hears it and she's quick to respond.

"Shut up, Seth!"

"That's enough," I hop in without hesitation. "Everyone, settle down. Unless you want to spend your recess with me doing *more* addition problems, there will be no more outbursts, okay?" I look around the classroom, meeting each of my students' eyes to ensure they know I mean business.

Luckily for my sanity, they listen.

"Thank you," I announce and stop right in front of my desk to grab a stack of freshly printed-off papers. "Now, today's timed addition test will be a little longer than you're used to. You're going to have five minutes to complete as many addition problems as—"

I stop mid-instructions when raucous laughter roars through the wall behind me, and then what sounds like a semitruck rams straight into it and shakes the floor. *For the love of everything.* I twist my torso to face the offending direction—through my room's wall and to the other side where Mack Houston's classroom sits.

Mr. Music Man.

Mr. Fun Time Bobby (without the booze).

Mr. Giant-Thorn-in-My-Side.

Basically, all my work-related problems come from *Mack Houston*. His classroom is always loud, always boisterous, and always on the verge of being out of control, and since he's right next door, my students' and my ears never miss a moment of the chaos.

I teach mathematics for first, second, and third graders at Calhoun Elementary, but with Mr. Houston's boisterous classroom right next door, most days, I feel like I'm trying to teach advanced calculus to grad students in the middle of an amusement park.

The onslaught of noise dulls slightly, and after heaving a deep sigh, I turn back to my students to continue giving them directions. A timed addition test might not seem like such a big deal, but I always try to make sure I give my kids specific instructions before a test, as well as a healthy dose of encouragement to get them in the right state of mind.

Sure, I might be a little type A when it comes to organization and how I run my classroom, but I feel strongly that it's my job to decrease stress and confusion. Calm and relaxed and clear expectations—that's the ambiance I'm always trying to provide.

"You will have five minutes to complete as many addition problems as you can," I announce as I walk around the classroom and set the tests on their desks. "Keep your papers facedown until I start the timer and tell you to begin. The problems do get a little harder as you go, but I promise they are all addition problems we have gone over lots of times together." I offer a little smile toward my students. "I know you've got this. You know the material. I am so proud of each and every one of you. You have worked so hard over the past few weeks to learn these new problems, and I know you can rock this quiz."

Caroline raises her hand, and I gesture toward her with a friendly hand. "Yes, Caroline?"

"Ms. Dayton, can we…" Unfortunately, after the first couple of words, a loud round of pandemonium breaks out again next door, and the only information little Caroline manages to relay is that she has the ability to move her lips. It's a regular mime show in here, and I haven't made a dime off admission.

"Man, I wish I was in Mr. Houston's class right now!" Seth hoots, and a few students don't hesitate to agree with him.

"I know!" Jimmy nods several times. "It sounds like they're having a party over there!"

I swear, the disruptions never end—drums and screams and kids sliding by my door in the hallway like Tom Cruise in *Risky Business*. All thanks to Mack Houston, the good-time guy, who just happens to teach music at the same school as me. And his obnoxious teaching style—if you can even call it teaching at all—*always* comes at the expense of my classroom.

God help me. I can't take this anymore.

"Class, I need you to stay in your seats. Leave your test papers facedown. I'll be right back." I hold up one finger to the class at large and stalk toward the door like a woman possessed. Out my door and around the small divider between our rooms, I march right through *his open door* to the noisy classroom and raise my voice over the din to get his attention.

"Mr. Houston!"

The entire time, I continually glance back toward my open door to make sure my students remain safely in their seats and that no one is peeking at their papers.

His classroom is filled with another second-grade class, and they are running around like banshees with drums. Literally. I wouldn't be surprised if his instructions were, "*Embrace the female Gaelic spirit inside you and streak across the room with these drums.*"

They bang and yell and whoop, and I have to curve my hands around my mouth to make a megaphone and try again.

"Mr. Houston!" I repeat, finally catching his attention. "May I speak with you for a moment, please?"

Every student's head whips in my direction, but I only have eyes for one man—*the menace*. Mack Houston.

His smile is so wide it's almost lopsided, and two big dimples crater into the center of his cheeks. His sun-highlighted brown hair curls haphazardly around his ears, and his green eyes shine bright. If it weren't for the manly, muscular body that sits beneath his far-too-casual attire, I'd think he was less than half of his actual age. As it is, the only real explanation I can think of is some kind of Tom Hanks in *Big* situation.

I sigh as Mack jogs my way, his cheesy smile aging so much it might as well be cheddar from Wisconsin. He holds up a hand to his class, tossing a pair of cymbals to the boy behind him just beforehand, remarking, "Make yourselves busy, guys. I'll be right back."

His ruffled hair bounces as he quickly closes the last few feet between us, and I have to actively work not to roll my eyes. Him telling his class to work without him is an absolute joke—*the man doesn't have them work while he's there.*

"What can I do for you, Katy?" he asks informally as he guides us into the hall. Once we're there, his laid-back approach to everything never wavers as he leans against the wall and crosses his khaki-pant-clad legs at the ankle. Black Chuck Taylors stick out from the bottom of his pants.

"Do you have any idea how loud your class is being right now?" I question back.

He tilts his head to the side, and a smirk crests one corner of his mouth. "Well, that depends. What kind of scale are we working with? Decibels? Hertz?"

I shake my head in frustration. I don't have time for him to be playful. The period feels like it's already half over, and I have zero time to waste. "We're trying to take a test next door. A little deference to my students would be nice."

"A test?" he retorts with a laugh. "On the Friday before spring break?" He shakes his head. "I think I found your first mistake, Katy Cat."

Katy Cat? Sheesh. If I had a nickel for every time this guy has made me roll my eyes, I'd be a lot richer than I am right now. As it is, all I can look forward to is the upcoming week of vacation which, thankfully, includes seven whole days *without* his classroom making my ears bleed and my nerves frazzle.

Just get through today, Katy. Just get through today, and then it's rest and relaxation time.

"Can you keep the volume down or not?" I ask, cutting straight to the point.

"Sure," he agrees easily enough, drawing a wrinkle of suspicion between my eyebrows. "We were just about to head out to the rooftop terrace for our first water balloon fight of the year anyway."

Water balloon fight? Is he for real?

It's situations like this that make me wonder how he's still drawing a paycheck as a flipping educator. I get the motivation to keep learning fun for your students, but his version of mixing fun and education is on another level. A level that always appears to include very little educating.

"What exactly do water balloons have to do with music?"

"Ah!" he hums, shaking a dramatic finger between our faces. "What *don't* they have to do with it, Katy Cat?"

I sigh at both his riddle-like answer and the ridiculously annoying nickname he gave me a year and a half ago and shake my head. "Never mind. I better get back to my classroom so my students don't have to wait any longer than they already have."

"Gotcha," Mack taunts with a wink, strolling back in through his door, only to lean back out into the hallway dramatically, not quite done with me yet. "Oh, we'll be on the rooftop terrace if you get done with time to spare. Bring your kids out to play. We've got plenty of balloons."

I shake my head again and smile sarcastically, enhancing the expression with an over-the-top thumbs-up. A deep, throaty laugh jumps from his lungs and makes the strong cords of his neck flex, and my chest tightens.

I don't know how on earth someone so annoying can be so attractive, but I know one thing with certainty—I can't wait to be free of work, *and him*—and on the beach for a whole week.

"Oh, by the way. I almost forgot to tell you," he adds. "We have to meet with Principal Harris during lunch today."

"What?" I scrunch up my nose. "Why?"

"I don't know."

"You didn't ask her why?" I quirk my brow, and he just shrugs.

"Didn't see the point. She'll tell us at lunch." And then, he turns on his heel and heads back into his classroom.

Seriously?

Any sane, normal human being would have asked her, but *no*, not Mack Houston. That man just skates his good-looking ass through life without a damn care in the world. I, on the other hand, will be overthinking this meeting for the next two hours.

Good grief. I loathe him so much it's physically painful.

Now, I just have to make it through the rest of today, *including* the meeting I apparently have with Principal Harris, and then, it's *sunny Florida, here I come.*

The end-of-day dismissal bell can't come soon enough.

Chapter Three

Mack

The lunchroom is rowdy as I drop off my class at their assigned table and give high fives on my way through the others. One enthusiastic child throws an Uncrustable at me in hopes of bringing me to a stop, but I just rip it out of the package as I walk and turn back to look him directly in the eye while I take a bite.

That's the thing about young kids—you can never give them an inch, or they'll take a mile. And in order to be the Fun Teacher like me, you *have* to maintain control. Fun without control would just be pandemonium. And despite what Katy Dayton thinks, that's *not* what's going on in room 216.

Sandwich lesson instilled, I head toward the front of the school for the "big meeting" with my two biggest fans.

Several teachers stop me to say hello, and Mona even pops her head out of the nurse's office at the sound of my voice.

Eventually, though, I make my way into the reception area and offer Betty and Carol a smile and a wink while sliding by them on my way to the principal's office at the back.

"Well, well, well, Mr. Houston, it's so nice of you to join us," Principal Dana greets when I step through her office door. Katy is already sitting down in one of the chairs across from her desk, and the scrunched-up look on her pretty face makes it apparent she is not any more thrilled to see me now than she was two periods ago.

"Am I late?" I question innocently, already knowing that I am. Schmoozing the staff as I walk takes time.

"Only ten minutes," Katy mutters under her breath. "But that's nothing new."

Principal Dana smirks and pulls out a nail file, loving every second of Katy's disdain for me. I think she's hoping if she gives Katy the space, she'll do the legwork of eating me alive.

But this isn't the first time Katy and I have been in this office together, and I'm sure it won't be the last. Ms. Dayton's not shy about airing her grievances about me and my classroom as regularly as possible.

This year, the only thing standing in her way is that Principal Dana rarely agrees to meetings. Something about them getting in the way of her "self-care" time.

I sit down in the seat beside Katy, and I swear to God, she moves her body away from me on instinct. With her long legs crossed and her shoulders pointed away from me, it's like her entire being revolts against my presence.

She sees us as straight-up rivals. I see our battles as a pastime. One thing is for sure—we are not built the same.

Truth be told, I've always had a bit of a thing for her. Maybe it's her unattainable nature that calls to me—most women aren't a challenge—but she's also beautiful and complex. A little uptight, sure, but she's got these big blue eyes and flawless skin and an almost majestic shade of brownish-copper hair that makes her feel a little otherworldly.

And she's a good teacher too. I've heard that more than a hundred times from just as many students. Which, considering she teaches math, is a pretty big fucking feat if you ask me.

Her students don't mind that she's firm or that she makes them work in class. She's patient and she's kind, and apparently, my guts are the only ones she hates.

"Now that we're all here," Dana begins and stands up from her chair, hitching one mauve-pant-covered hip on her desk. "We can get this meeting moving. It should be noted I have to leave by 12:45 for a hair appointment that I cannot miss. And seeing as it's already 12:15, let's keep the questions to a minimum, yeah?"

I suck my lips into my mouth on a near snort. Oh yeah, whatever this meeting is about is obviously *very* serious. Katy doesn't let Dana's tone stop her from acting as though it is, however.

"If you're leaving at 12:45, who is covering your recess shift?"

"Sounds like you're on top of it," Dana responds without hesitation.

"But—" Katy starts to refute, but Dana just barrels right over her words.

"As for why you're here, I've decided to put the two of you in charge of Career Day."

"But we've never done a Career Day before." Katy jumps in, resigned to recess duty and on to the next problem. But that's Katy Dayton for you. *Everything* is problematic.

"I know. But my father was adamant we add one this year, and we're running out of time."

"You want us to plan it?" Katy's jaw looks like it wants to unhinge itself from her face. "*Together?*"

Clearly, I am a demon, and Katy's desperately searching for the number for an exorcist.

"Yes," Principal Dana responds. "We need volunteers in the community to come in and talk about their careers to our students. So, the two of you will have to pick a day between now and the end of the year for an assembly, find our guest speakers, and get the event organized."

"I can handle this on my own."

I almost chortle. Katy Cat sure can cut to the point if the point is cutting me out.

"I'd actually like to be involved," I interject, stirring the pot beautifully.

"Oh, come on," Katy says with a groan. "You do *not* want to be involved in this."

"Sure I do, Katy. Why wouldn't I? I happen to know several people with careers who I think would enrich the hearts and minds of the students here at Calhoun."

"That is such bullcr—"

"Ahem." Dana clears her throat. Angry, Katy flops back into the structure of her chair and narrows her eyes with frightening focus.

"Are we trying to highlight any specific careers?"

"Well, it's safe to say we're not trying to convince our students to start OnlyFans accounts when they graduate high school," Dana says with a sigh. "But I'd say most of the world at large is your oyster."

I have to bite my lip to fight my laughter. And I can't stop myself from putting on my most serious face to ask, "What's an OnlyFans?"

Dana glares at me. "You and I both know what an OnlyFans is, Mr. Houston."

"Actually…" I feign confusion, even tapping my chin for good measure. "I don't think I do. Can you elaborate?"

"It's a sex subscription site. Kind of like pay-per-view for porn," someone chimes in from behind, and all three of us look toward the door to find Alma Ross standing at the threshold.

"Mrs. Ross, is there a reason you're interrupting this meeting?" Dana asks, and Alma just shrugs.

"Just being nosy."

"And you don't think you can be nosy somewhere else?"

"Not really." Alma shrugs again and settles herself in the chair beside the door. A few seconds later, she has yarn in her hands and starts knitting what looks to be a scarf.

The woman has officially settled in for the show, and even our temporary principal knows it's not worth the fight.

"So, it's settled," Dana continues. "You two will handle planning our first annual Career Day this year. And you'll keep the careers to things parents won't send me angry emails about."

I raise my hand. Dana ignores me completely.

"Katy, do you have any questions?"

"Where we will be hosting it?"

"The auditorium."

"And how many speakers should we invite?"

"As many as you want as long as they don't go over two hours. Anything more than that, and we can't count the day as a full curriculum."

Katy starts to open her mouth again, but Dana is quick to cut her off. She's done humoring anything other than an overpriced latte and a two-to-three-hour transformation into a new-haired woman.

"So, we're good? You guys got this?"

"Um…" Katy pauses and glances at me out of the corner of her eyes. "Actually, I really think it would be best if I handled the planning myself. Mr. Houston is *very* busy planning water balloon fights."

"Oh, Ms. Dayton, I'm wounded," I say dramatically and hold a hand to my chest. I look directly at Principal Dana. "She doesn't like me. I'm pretty sure she hates me."

"He's not wrong," Alma says without shame. "Mack's definitely on this one's voodoo board."

"I don't hate him," Katy is quick to retort. She looks at Dana. "I don't hate him. I just…we just…we don't work very well together. Our teaching styles are very, *very* different."

"Speaking of teaching styles," Principal Dana states, and immediately, her eyes go to me. "Water balloons?"

"I think it's pretty obvious," I answer with a guffaw. "Water balloons are hyperelastic, as are sound waves. Put simplistically, the force-to-breakage coefficient of a water balloon is intensely similar to the effect sound barriers have on—"

Dana holds up a hand. "You can stop now. I assume you got parent permission?"

"From all three periods that engaged in the balloon fights." *All thanks to Betty's and Carol's help.*

"Okay, then. Moving along."

"Wait…" Katy's voice pipes up. "That's it?"

Principal Dana moves her eyes to her. "You have a problem, Katy?"

"Honestly? Yeah." Katy glowers. "I'm still having issues with Mr. Houston's class being disruptive to my class. It's like trying to teach math while the circus is in town. And quite frankly, I don't care if the elephants do a fantastic job of teaching the ear frequency or whatever line of crap you have cued," she adds, turning to me directly.

Principal Dana looks at Katy. She looks at me. And then, she glances at the watch on her wrist and lets out a deep exhale. "Since it's already twenty till one, we're going to have to find another time to work out these issues when I'm not on my way to self-care. I have to get going."

"She's in her Taylor Lautner era," Alma chimes in, still busy knitting whatever it is she's knitting.

And yes, she means Taylor Swift, but this is a hilarious constant with Alma Ross. She always confuses celebrities' names, and it's one of my favorite things. Frankly, I'm not the only one. The sheer joy in Dana's eyes is proof of that.

"Taylor Lautner?" Katy asks. "Isn't that the—"

"I think what Katy wants to say—" I quickly cut her off before she can ruin something that brings constant entertainment to my work life "—is that we fully support you focusing on your self-care, Principal Dana. And I will make a point to work out my issues with Ms. Dayton."

"Thank you, Mr. Houston."

I don't miss Katy's scowl or the fact that she rolls her eyes. If there is one thing that is certain, it's that Katy Dayton *really* dislikes me.

Principal Dana looks at her watch again. "Okay, great meeting, everyone." Within ten seconds, she's logged off her computer and has her purse in her hand. "Keep me updated on how the Career Day planning goes. But, like, bare minimum updates, okay? I'll see you all after spring break."

And then, she's gone. Leaving Katy, Alma, and me sitting there in her office.

"I can't wait to see how this goes down," Alma mutters to herself as she shoves her knitting shit back in her bag.

But Katy doesn't say much of anything. Instead, she gets up from her seat and heads straight for the door.

And I can't blame her. She's been the loser of every verbal battle between us today, and her perfectionistic ego probably can't take any more.

Me, though? I'd happily go a few more rounds.

Is it bad if there's a part of me that's looking forward to getting back from my spring break trip so I can get to Career Day planning with the woman who can't stand me?

Chapter *Four*

Saturday, March 19th

Katy

After a three-hour flight and a twenty-minute Uber ride, I have officially arrived at my vacation home away from home. I gently kick the condo door shut behind me and walk straight to the kitchen area to set down my bags of groceries on top of the counters.

My long, relaxing spring break week has officially started.

No class. No students. No late-night marathons of grading papers. *No thinking about the disaster that will be Career Day planning with Mack Houston.*

I am a free woman ready to enjoy my vacay.

Hallelujah!

Cute, beachy, Florida-themed décor dots the kitchen of my rental. Seashells and plastic flowers intermingle with a teal table runner that showcases ivory-colored napkins and gives way to wicker and glass beneath them.

Everything may be a bit kitschy, but I can't deny it's all perfectly designed to frame the floor-to-ceiling windows on the back side of the condo.

Outside of those windows? *Heaven*—otherwise known as miles and miles of crisp white sand and bright-blue Gulf water that makes my heart skip atop itself in my chest.

I can't believe I'm finally here. *Man, I really needed this.*

I haven't had a vacation of any sort since last spring break, an entire year ago. I thought I might do something for Christmas break—one of the other major times a teacher can plan these things other than summer—but I ended up having to go back home to Savannah, Georgia, to help my mom take care of my dad as he recovered from knee surgery.

You might assume that he injured himself doing something simple like yard work or cleaning out gutters. You know, normal things that a parent of an almost thirty-year-old woman might be doing. But those and any other guesses you might have would be wrong.

My dad, Kai Dayton, is one of the craziest SOBs you'll ever meet. He's lived his life in the fast lane, and wherever he's gone, my mom hasn't been far behind. But I suppose that's bound to happen sometimes when you get pregnant with your only kiddo at sixteen.

Don't get me wrong, I respect the hell out of both of my parents for making something out of our lives. But I cannot say in good conscience that we escaped without any consequences. See, my dad was a professional motocross rider up until five years ago, and he hasn't lost an ounce of craziness in his retirement.

He goes hard all the time, and occasionally, that means he has to go home… and sit his butt on the couch because he shattered his patella after gunning a huge jump on his backyard course.

And since my mom Melissa is squeamish about injuries, it left me to take on the temporary caregiver role. A role I stepped into a lot while growing up in a house with two wild and crazy parents. But it's not just that—out of the three of us, I've always had the oldest soul. Hell, in high school, rather than partying with friends, I was my parents' designated driver.

Needless to say, these seven days to myself are about as essential as air to breathe. And I'm grateful fellow Calhoun teacher Kimmie Ward's parents decided to rent out their Florida beachfront condo this year and that they were able to accommodate me during spring break week of all weeks.

Shoulders sagging with long-delayed relief, I tuck my groceries away into one of the cabinets and finger the sweet note left on the counter. *Enjoy your time!*

I know Kimmie's parents themselves didn't leave the note—they're in Pennsylvania. But the fact that their cleaner or condo manager or whoever did is still nice. Turning to my Neoprene wine sleeve at the other end of the counter, I take out the very expensive bottle I've been saving for a special occasion and set it next to the note. It's not like it cost a million dollars—more like sixty—but for a single elementary school teacher without a trust fund, it's a huge splurge. And since the moment I booked this stay, I've been looking forward to drinking it while my toes are in the sand and the calm waters of the Gulf roll in before me.

Though, I figured I'd be sharing it with Anna.

The mere thought of vacationing without my best friend has me pulling my cell phone out of my purse and sending her a text message.

Me: I have officially arrived in Destin, and I still feel bad I'm here without you.

Her response is instant.

Anna: Don't be stupid. Enjoy your vacation. You deserve it.

Me: I said I felt bad, not that I wasn't going to enjoy the time, regardless. LOL

Anna: Is that…Katy Dayton…being sassy???

Me: I can be sassy.

Anna: Really?

Me: I can!

Anna: I guess we'll just have to find a way to fit in a summer trip so you can show me. But I expect to see you shit-faced and partaking in debauchery.

Me: I can get on board with that.

I mean, once we're on the trip, she won't be able to do anything about it if I'm not quite as loosey-goosey as she's expecting.

Me: How's the sickness going? Any signs of death or dismemberment on the horizon?

Anna: I dismembered my right lung earlier by coughing it up, but other than that, I'm good. Currently bingeing The Office and sucking on cough drops like they're my sole source of nutrients. Now, go do the damn vacation thing. And I don't mean be boring and read a book on the beach. I mean, go find a big, muscly, meathead that you can bring back to the condo and bang for me. It's what a good best friend would do.

Me: That might be the weirdest, most disturbing thing you've ever said to me.

Anna: Don't be a prude. You need to enjoy this vacation for both of us.

Me: Yeah, okay, weirdo. I'll be sure to film the banging and send it to you.

Anna: Perfect. Use Cinematic Mode! You've got that fancy iPhone for a reason!

On a snort, I slip my phone into the back pocket of my jean shorts and finish unpacking my groceries.

Once I'm satisfied with my unpacking job, I fold up my reusable grocery bags and stack them together so I can tuck them into the drawer next to the sink. Everything looks completely in order, just as when I arrived.

Yes, I am the proud owner of a type A personality, but I can't help it. I think the wild, unpredictable, and impulsive lifestyle of my parents forced me to become this way out of survival.

I grab my suitcase and peruse my way down the hall toward the two bedrooms at the end. Photos dot the walls, mostly abstracts and landscape-style shots of the beach, but a braces-sporting shot of a middle-school-aged Kimmie Ward pulls me up short and makes me smile.

Back in motion, I pad my way down the hardwood floor and peek into the first bedroom I reach. It's the smaller of the two, I remember from the website listing I booked on, but is perfectly quaint enough for a weekend at the beach. What the listing didn't show, however, is the mini Kimmie Shrine, full of photos and medals and trophies.

Photos of a teenage Kimmie in a *wrestling onesie*, mind you.

Oh boy. That's *something…*

Man, I wish Kimmie and I were closer. This would be the perfect opportunity to send her a text message and tease her a little about her parents' nostalgic décor.

But I don't have her phone number, and even if I did, I probably wouldn't use it. I'm not the bold type who texts casual acquaintances teasing things. I'm the overthinking type who thinks them, types them, and then swiftly deletes them.

I'm also the type who keeps my friends circle small and intimate. Which is why Anna is the only person I feel compelled to send a snapshot of Kimmie's bedroom.

Her response is instant.

Anna: Am I high on cough syrup or is that Kimmie in a wrestling leotard?

Me: You are experiencing both at the same time.

Anna: For the love of everything, don't bring our meathead back to that room. He'll never come with that in his field of vision.

Feeling a little uncomfortable now that Anna has mixed coming into the conversation with Kimmie Ward's childhood and apparent love of wrestling as a teenager, I pull the door shut, pass the hallway bathroom, and head to the bedroom at the end.

A magical light filters through the huge windows on the ocean side of the room, and wispy white curtains float in the soft breeze drifting in through the screen.

Instantly, I inhale the addictive aromas of salt water and fresh air that are wafting in from a cracked-open window.

I love the ocean. I always have. That was one of the perks of growing up in Savannah, Georgia. Hilton Head and the Atlantic Ocean were only a fifty-mile drive away.

Don't get me wrong. I love living in New York, but I can't deny there's just something about the Gulf waters and white sand beaches that speaks to my soul.

"Yes," I whisper joyfully, releasing my grip on my suitcase and performing a spin.

The huge four-poster bed in the middle of the back wall is covered in bright white linen, and the walls are a cheerful blue-gray that make the room seem like it goes on forever.

"Oh *yes*," I moan when I spot the bathroom on the left side of the bed. The glittering white tile in the gargantuan walk-in shower stands out like a beacon. A nice hot soak under the rain showerhead is exactly what I need after the three-hour flight from New York.

Gently, I lift my suitcase onto the bed and start digging through my clothes and setting them into the drawers of the dresser. It doesn't take me more than five minutes to get all my things organized, and the water of the shower heats up just as quick.

And once I step under the spray and inhale a deep breath, I know I'm exactly where I need to be.

Yep. I'm pretty sure this is heaven.

Chapter Five

Mack

With the wind of the open road still burning on my cheeks, I turn my Jeep rental into one of the open parking spaces for the condo complex I'll be calling home for the next week and shift the engine into park. After my flight from NYC was delayed and the car rental place was packed to the brim, I've still managed to make pretty good time.

The Florida sun is bright and beautiful, bouncing its rays off everything around me and heating the air to a perfect eighty degrees.

There are a ton of other cars here, but with forty other beachfront condos and a weekend as picturesque as this, it's no shock that it's starting to fill up on a Saturday afternoon.

My loud music cuts off dramatically with a turn of the ignition key, and thanks to riding topless with no doors, jumping out is a breeze. I reach easily into the open back and grab my duffel and my paddleboard before bleeping the locks with my key fob.

The sidewalk through the center of the condo complex gives a view to the beach ahead, and the smell of the salty ocean air beckons. Since I've lived in New York my whole life, I don't get to the ocean nearly enough, but when I do, everything else disappears.

Though, if I'm honest, I live a pretty stress-free life, and I do it with intention. Too many people get caught up in the peskiest little day-to-day shit, and I don't have time or energy for it. At least some of that, I'm sure, is because of the way I was raised.

As a "surprise baby" who came fifteen years after my sister, I had a fifty-fifty chance of being my family's greatest joy or biggest resentment. Lucky for me, my family went with the former, putting me at the center of their world and finding absolute elation in all my growth and milestones. My sister Lizzy was like a built-in second mother when needed, and the rest of the time, a champion and friend.

Frankly, my family is the reason I teach music. They didn't complain when I picked up an instrument and taught myself to play—and let me tell you, in the beginning, my musical aspirations were to the detriment of their ears.

And they didn't balk or judge when I said I wanted to make a career out of music. They made an effort to encourage, which shaped me into a teacher who wants to be a support system for his students. A teacher who keeps an open mind and always tries to inspire a love for learning. So many of my kids who show a real interest in music and the arts don't have the kind of support I did growing up, and I feel it's my duty to give them that when they're in my classroom.

Once I reach the end of the sidewalk, I stop at the front door of my condo rental, set my paddleboard against the outside wall, and punch in the code from the emailed rental instructions.

After the knob clicks open, I gingerly push my way inside.

I wouldn't say I'm a cautious kind of guy by nature, but over the years, I've learned to hasten my bull-in-a-china-shop ways. Basically, there've been a few occasions I've gotten a little overzealous in an environment I didn't know and knocked over a valuable or two, and it goes without saying that no one wants to take the chance on having to pay damage fees on a rental.

Clear of hidden dangers, I step through the rest of the way and close the door behind me, tossing my bag on the floor and strolling inside. The kitchen is big and inviting with bright white cabinets, and the light marble countertops are sleek and clear of clutter. Only one vase of flowers sits on the corner and a bottle of wine on the island.

I step forward to the bottle, checking out the label and whistling audibly. The price sticker is still on the bottom, proclaiming a cost of $69.99. *Dayum, that's a pretty good bottle of fermented grape juice.*

Right beside the wine sits a note scrawled in black Sharpie that reads, *Enjoy your time!*

Well, well. *I think I will.* When in Rome, you know?

I scoop up the bottle from the counter and round the island, opening each of the cabinets until I come to the one with the glasses. I don't bother holding out to find a fancy wineglass—it won't hold nearly enough anyway—and settle on a red plastic cup that reminds me of my college days.

I only have to dig through three drawers before finding a corkscrew, and the sound of the cork popping is so satisfying, my smile climbs all the way to my eyes. *Oh yeah. The sweet sounds of vacation.*

Once crimson liquid rises up the sides of the glass and reaches three-quarters of the way full, I place the bottle back on the counter and take a swig. "Ahh," I hum. It's a little too rich for me, but seeing as I'm not that big of a wine guy, I'm not going to be picky. It'll do just fine for getting me in the mood to relax.

Boozy fruit juice in hand, I stroll away from the counter to the living room and admire the view of the ocean through the windows. It's amazing how expansive the world seems at the coast. How much it reminds you of your exact insignificance in the universe.

Using my toes for leverage, I kick off my Converse and dig my bare toes into the plush carpet. It feels like a sensory tease for the sand that's to come.

Moving along, I make my way down the hall and stop at a closed door.

Immediately, I'm intrigued, so I test the knob. It turns with ease, and I grin as I push my way inside. Bright-yellow walls give way to a daisy-comforter-covered bed and a bench seat window with a view of the beach. It's a cute little girlie setup, and my gaze travels the space smoothly, but a pause is all but inevitable as I reach a wall of much...*interest.*

Trophies, medals, and photos of fellow Calhoun Elementary teacher Kimmie Ward in some sort of manly-looking spandex getup litter the space, and my eyebrows shoot up to kiss my hairline.

Oh man. Talk about a weird and wonderful discovery.

Kimmie is at least twenty years younger than present in the photos, but that doesn't do anything to lessen my enjoyment.

Good God. I cannot fucking wait to razz her about this shit.

I don't even pause before taking my phone from my pocket, snapping a quick photo of the wall of Kimmie, and sending it off with a text message.

Me: Sweet unitard, girlfriend. I'm going to suggest Principal Harris relaxes the dress code on Fridays even more so you can wear what you're comfortable in.

Her response is instantaneous and only heightens my enjoyment.

Kimmie: SHUT UP! Why did I forget you were going to my parents' condo this week?

Me: Because you foolishly removed me from the center of your world? Understandable, I guess, given your relationship with Jim and all, but still…

Kimmie: Jim is my husband.

Jim is, in fact, Kimmie's husband, and he's an awesome, big-ass, burly dude whom I've gotten to know over the years while attending various school functions.

Me: Exactly. And it really unbalances the universe when more than one spouse loves me, and since Jim's already called dibs on fanboying, I figure this is for the best.

Kimmie: You're ridiculous.

I tuck my phone back into my pocket with a laugh and smile, but not before snapping a couple more pictures of the Kimmie Shrine for, you know, future reference and such.

I guess staying at a friend's family's place is going to be even more fun than I thought it was.

I walk back into the hall, leaving the door open to let some of the beach light into the hallway and peek briefly into the hallway bathroom. A final closed door sits at the end, beckoning me, and I take a swig of wine from my glass as I open it.

The bedroom is big and sunlight shines in through every window, and I silently hope the curtains have enough blackout properties to keep me from waking up at the crack of way-too-early. Pretty nice digs, though, even if they're bright.

After a couple moments of no movement, the sound of rushing water makes my eyebrows pull together, and a sudden sense of urgency lights a fire under my feet.

Shit. Did a pipe burst or something?

The previously cracked en suite bathroom door bangs open with a crash when I hit it at a run, and a shrill, frightened scream shatters the air.

"Ahhhhh! Oh my God!" a wet woman cries from the walk-in shower at the top of her lungs. "Who are you?!"

It's uncontrolled chaos for several moments as she gets louder and louder, and my body fights to make sense of what's happening. My defenses are alert, and my grasp on reality is shaken.

Is that… Could that be Katy Dayton…naked?

No fucking way.

Her hair is wet and soapy, and her body is covered in a sheen of water as the showerhead continues to spray toward her.

I mean, it really looks like her…but *how?*

She turns and whips her arms across her chest, and her forehead creases in the center with uncontrolled disgruntlement. It's a look I know well from experience and one I can't mistake when it comes to her. She's the only woman I know who can make a stink eye look downright beautiful.

Sweet Mary, mother of Jesus, it's her. And she is, in fact, naked.

Holy shit. My eyes are bugging harder than a '90s cartoon character.

"Why are you in here?!" she screams again, and the shrill volume is enough to yank me out of my dazed state of mind.

I turn around as quickly as I can, but I have to admit that the vision of her bare—*perky and perfect*—right breast will likely be burned into my brain forever. If it weren't for the tile half-wall on the bottom of the ornate shower blocking my view of the lower half of her body, I might be dead right now, in all honesty.

Sure, she's freaking out now, but I have a feeling she'd be freaking out even more if she suddenly had a corpse to deal with.

"Katy, it's okay. It's okay. Calm down, it's me. Mack. Mack Houston," I ramble, my back still to her, and I hold my hands up above my shoulders in some sort of weird message of innocence.

"Mack?!" she shouts at the top of her lungs, louder than she did when she reacted like I was an ax-murdering intruder.

"Yes. That's me."

"What in the h-e-double-hockey-sticks are you *doing* here?"

I almost laugh over the fact that she can't even curse under these circumstances. Always proper and professional, that's Katy Dayton for you.

"I'm—"

"You know what?" She cuts me off before I can explain. "Never mind. Just get out. Get out. *Get out!*"

I throw a thumbs-up over my shoulder. "Getting out right now. I swear. You come find me when you're done, and we'll sort this out."

"*Get out!*" she shrieks again, making my feet fall into a jog all on their own.

I grab the edge of the bathroom door and swing it closed behind me as swiftly as I can but stop there before going any farther.

My coworker. Katy Dayton. Naked. In the bathroom of my vacation rental.

Man oh man, I'm betting she hates me even more now.

I swig the wine and head to the kitchen to finish off the rest of the bottle. I'm pretty sure I'm going to need the lubrication for the ass-fucking she's going to give me over this one.

Chapter Six

Katy

Mack Houston is here?! In my freaking rental?!

What kind of fresh hell of a nightmare am I living in right now?

And come *find* him when I'm done? Why is that even a thing when I'm over one thousand miles away from home on a vacation that was only supposed to include me and Anna before she had to bail for fluish reasons?

Not to mention, he saw me *naked*. Not completely naked, I hope, but considering we're coworkers and he's also the bane of my existence, he definitely saw *far too much* of me.

Lord help me.

This whole situation is a mental mindfuck, and I can't keep myself in the shower long enough to wash the soap out of my hair. I need to figure out why in the hell he's here, and I need to do it *right now*.

Frantic, I jump out of the shower, and shampoo drips from my hair and onto my forehead. My feet miss the mat in front of the glass door completely, and I play slip-and-slide on the tile.

"Owww, shit," I yelp, my knee hitting the hard surface and slowing my descent into the buck-ass splits. If the Dallas Cowboys went pornographic, this move would be right on brand.

"Frackkk," I groan, twisting my hip and squirming on the floor to get my feet back under me. My skin is wet and aggressive against the tile, and my hair smacks me in the eye and deposits shampoo. "Gah!"

All thanks to adrenaline, I'm a one-woman vaudevillian act of disaster.

I use one palm to put pressure on my lava-filled eye and the other hand to pull myself up off the floor. Once I yank a towel off the bar, I wrap it around myself haphazardly and use a corner of it to wipe off my face.

My dripping hair is officially cutting a river through this condo like the Colorado through the Grand Canyon, but I don't care. As long as my tits and bits are covered, figuring out how in the *hell* Mack Houston ended up in my vacation rental with me seems like the priority.

I've always been heavy-footed, but my everyday gait's got nothing on the thunderous sound of my progress across the hardwood floor as I burst out of the master bedroom and head toward the kitchen.

Of course, Mack just stands untroubled at the counter, his ankles crossed and a stupid smile in place on his face. Instantly, my rage spikes from an eight to an eleven. *How can this man be so calm right now?*

It's only after my boiling blood rises to the whites behind my eyes that I notice the glass in his hand and the corkscrew on the counter and *my* bottle of now-opened wine.

No. Flipping. Way. *No flipping way!*

A gasp flies from my mouth. "Are you drinking *my wine?*" I shriek as months and months of saving that bottle for a special occasion flash before my eyes.

"This?" He tips his chin down to the glass in his hand and studies the liquid. "Is it yours?"

"Yes, it's mine!" I yell, much louder than I expect. To be honest, the volume actually makes me startle myself a bit. I clear my throat to get my bearings and lower my voice back to normal. "What on earth made you think you had a right to drink it?"

"It was sitting with a welcome note," he protests, jerking his chin toward the counter. "I assumed it was a gift with the rental."

I follow his gaze to the note and bottle on the counter and bite my cheek to stop the evolving sting in my nose. I do not want to cry in front of Mack Houston over a bottle of wine, so help me God. But I'm on the emotional brink. I scrimped and saved and sold my soul to the devil to be able to afford this week in the first place, and now it's one giant freaking catastrophe.

"This is unbelievable! I cannot believe this is happening!"

"Relax, it's not that big of a deal."

"Not that big of a deal?" My jaw drops. "I've been counting down the days to this vacation, and now I'm here and not even an hour into my getaway and *you* show up out of nowhere while I was in the shower!"

"Uh." He scrunches up his nose. "*Wow.* That 'you' was said really distastefully, Katy Cat."

"No, it wasn't."

"Yeah, it was," he answers with an infuriating smirk. "It was one step away from you just saying 'Ewww.'"

"Forget what I said." I heave a deep sigh. "Why are you here? *How* are you here? This has to be an April Fools' joke. Clowns have to jump out of the corner at any moment now, right?" I glance around the kitchen maniacally. "I swear on everything, I'll stab you with that corkscrew if you've somehow managed a stupid candid camera prank."

"First of all, April Fools' isn't for another few weeks, and there are no clowns or cameras. At least, I don't think there are." He winks, and I hate that my eyes mistake it for sexy. *Stupid, stupid blue orbs.*

It doesn't matter that he's muscled to an eleven and bearing arms beneath his shirt in the most scandalous of ways. This is Mack Houston, and we *hate* him.

I glare, but I'm not entirely sure who I'm angrier at in this moment—him or my rebelliously pulsing vagina. "Then why are you here?"

"Because I rented this place."

"What?" My chin jerks back. "No, you didn't."

"Yes, I did."

"You didn't. You couldn't have. Because *I* rented this place. I secured the reservation several months ago."

His face morphs into amusement, and his voice is one hundred percent confident. "So did I."

I shake my head. "No, you didn't."

"Listen, I know you keep saying that over and over, but it's not going to make it true," he responds, still infuriatingly unfazed over the whole debacle. "I talked to Kimmie about renting her parents' house on the beach right when we came back from Christmas break."

"So did I," I retort. "I confirmed the rental through RentBNB, too. Did you? Or did you just assume talking to Kimmie made it so?"

"I'm not an idiot, Katy Cat. I booked it on the website, just like you did."

"How?" I cry.

Mack shrugs, the laid-back, nothing-fazes-me bastard. "I guess they double-booked us or something. Technical glitch, I don't know. I'm as clueless as you right now."

"We have to call Kimmie. We have to sort this out right now."

"Okay. Call Kimmie, then."

"I can't call Kimmie," I say through gritted teeth. "I don't have Kimmie's number. You call Kimmie."

His shoulders straighten and eyes narrow pointedly. "Well, I hate to break it to you, but I don't have Kimmie's number either."

"You don't?" I could have sworn he was friends with her outside of school. He's freaking friends with *everyone*, and now he doesn't have a relationship with the one person I need him to?

"No." He shakes his head. "Why do you seem so shocked by this?"

"Because you're Mr. Popular. Your classroom is the fun zone, and you're the head ringleader of the entertainment circus. You know everyone, and everyone knows you, and they all fawn all over you constantly."

His amused smile is infuriating. "I think maybe you've done a little bit of judging when it comes to me that's not fact-based."

This is so not the time to get into all the things I've judged this guy for. It would take wayyy too long. This is the time to sort this out and get back to my relaxing vacation.

I snag my phone from the kitchen counter and send a text to someone who might actually be able to help me.

Me: Do you have Kimmie's number?

Anna: Seeing as I accidentally groped her AND her husband in the same night at that teachers' night out thing you missed...no. I deleted it for my own safety. Why?

Frackety frack frack!

Does Kimmie Ward even have a freaking phone? I mean, how does no one have her number?

I hesitate over the screen as I decide whether I want to open this can of worms with Anna via text, but I quickly choose to depose her on this debacle at a later time, you know, when I'm not standing in a towel with shampoo in my hair while my archnemesis looks on.

"Forget it," I mutter to myself and click out of my messages and go straight for the confirmation email I received. "I'll call RentBNB customer service."

"Right now?" Mack questions lightly, his eyes widening at the sight of me.

"Right. Now."

I'm cold and wet and soapy, but I'll be damned if I do even one dang other thing before I get this sorted out.

Chapter Seven

Mack

I know it wasn't great of me to pretend I don't have Kimmie's number, but sweet Katy and I have been on the wrong foot since the day I grew them in the womb—or at the very least, the day we started at Calhoun Elementary together five-plus years ago.

Even Cosmetology Star Dana is aware of our issues—it's exactly why she put us together for Career Day planning.

I sigh as Katy paces the living room in her towel, silently wondering how a woman with shampoo in her hair and a scowl on her face and a giant rod that far up her ass could still manage to be this fucking beautiful.

She chats animatedly with the customer service line for RentBNB, and I try really hard not to notice how sexy her legs look beneath the white cotton material of her towel. She pauses briefly and turns to me, lifting a hand to her other ear. "You think maybe you want to get on the phone with customer service too?" she whisper-scolds, making me suck my lips into my mouth to keep from laughing.

As if both of us on the phone with customer service is going to do anything but cause more confusion.

"Nah." I shrug. "Looks like you've got it covered."

Glowering, she turns back to face the windows again and continues her politely toned tirade.

"Yes, I understand that it's an automated system and that it's never been double-booked like this before, but it's double-booked now, and I'm currently looking at the other double-bookee standing across from me in the living room. Inconvenient, yes. But probably not as inconvenient as it was ten minutes ago when we were looking each other in the eye while I took a shower, wouldn't you say?" She laughs. "Yes, that's exactly what happened." She pauses. Listens intently. Then adds, "Okay… So, what are we supposed to do now?"

I take another swig from my glass of wine and smile to myself when I realize she's *still* pacing the living room, in her towel, with shampoo still matted to her wet hair.

The woman is so worked up over this whole mix-up that she didn't even finish her fucking shower.

If only Katy Cat would let me be the one to help her relax…

"No, that's not acceptable." She shakes her head. "That's not what either of us booked. We thought we were getting a place to ourselves, and we paid a price tag that suggested the same. This isn't an episode of *Married at First Sight*, and I'm too young to be a cast member on *Three's Company*."

She glances over her shoulder at me briefly and then turns back to the window, her voice lowering to a murmur. "Listen, we're not technically strangers because we work together, but I don't think you're understanding how much I do not want to be here with this person. The two of us are like oil and water. We don't mix."

Ouch. I mean, listen, I know the woman isn't fond of me, but hearing her say it aloud hurts a little more than expected. She whispered at least, clearly trying to spare my feelings, but I heard her, nonetheless. And it's surprisingly wounding. I've never really had anyone truly not like me before. Maybe I need to tone it down just a little…give her a chance to see another side of me.

"Yes, I'd say a refund is warranted." She pauses and turns, and the corners of her mouth flex down. "Okay. Yeah. Thanks. You too. Bye." She sighs again, pulls her phone away from her ear, and touches the screen to end the call. She looks downright despondent and doesn't take her eyes off the view out the window. I give her a moment to gather herself—it's abundantly clear I'm not her favorite person, but as much as it might seem like it to her, I'm not out here trying to shit all over people—and then do my best to breach the awkward silence.

"So…"

Good job, Mack. Smooth delivery.

Her back straightens suddenly, and my eyebrows draw together. Something is happening; I'm just not entirely sure what. And evidently, she's not ready to give me a clue yet either. Instead, she turns to face me, crosses her arms over her chest, and a sassy attitude emanates from her stance.

"They're refunding us?" I ask, hoping innocent questions don't incite her inner beast.

"Yes. RentBNB is going to take the loss for the huge inconvenience their system caused."

"And, what? We're both supposed to leave?"

She shakes her head. "They said it was up to us to figure it out, as with this short notice, they wouldn't be booking it again anyway."

"That's great," I say with a smile, perking up. "Free vacation for both of us."

"Uh, *no*." Her eyes go so wide they consume her pretty face. "No way. Not for both of us. One of us, *maybe*. But not both."

My eyebrows draw together. *Jeez. Does she really dislike me so much that she'd give up a free vacation?* "So, what? You're leaving, then?"

"What?" She narrows her eyes. "I never said I was leaving. And considering I was here first, you should leave. Not me. Plus, my flight isn't until Saturday."

I roll my eyes. "I don't think vacation rentals follow 'shotgun' rules. You can't 'call it' or race me to the front seat of a beachfront condo. And my flight isn't until Saturday either."

"I've already showered here, Mack. I've been on the bed. I've put my stuff away. The place is basically broken-in for me. Therefore, I should be the one to stay."

"Having showered here is the criteria we're basing this on?" I ask with a scoff, thoughts of a truce and toning it down long forgotten.

"Yes." She doubles down.

"Fine."

Her head jerks back. "Fine?"

"*Fine*," I repeat, guzzling down the rest of my wine, setting the glass on the table, and then heading straight for the hallway bathroom. With a hand between both my shoulders, I strip off my shirt before I reach the door, and the air conditioning pebbles goose bumps on my freshly exposed skin.

Immediately, Katy comes unstuck from her place in the living room and starts chasing after me.

"Hey! Where are you going?" Her voice is a screech. "What are you doing?"

"I'm showering."

"Oh no, you're not!"

"Yes. I am," I disagree, unbuttoning my shorts and shoving them to the floor so I can step out of them as I walk.

"Oh my God!" she yells behind me. "You just took off your pants!"

"Very astute, Ms. Dayton. You should be a teacher."

"Shut up, you lunatic. Stop taking off your clothes!"

"I really don't want to shower in my clothes," I contest, doing a little spin in my boxer briefs to give her a grin. "All that wet fabric freaks me out."

"What?" she yells, annoyed with my nonsense.

"I have a thing about wet clothing."

"No, you don't." She scoffs. "You literally had a water balloon fight at school yesterday!"

"Ah, but you only get wet if you lose."

"What are we even talking about? Stop trying to change the subject, and *stop taking off your clothes!*" she commands on a scream, her volume and panic escalating notably as I step into the bathroom, grab the waistband of my boxer briefs, and start to shove them down as well.

"Sorry," I say without turning around. "Can't."

"Oh my God, that's your ass. I see your ass!"

"Bare asses are usually involved in showers, Katy, but I think the biggest question here is, why are you staring at my ass?"

"You're a total psycho, you know that?"

I look back over my shoulder and wink.

I also laugh when I take in the shocked look on her face, and she lets out a cry of animalistic proportions. "Oh my God, this isn't funny!"

"Trust me, Katy Cat, it's funny," I call over my shoulder as I step into the shower and turn on the spray. "Anyway, if you want to finish up with your shower, don't be afraid to come in here. I, personally, am not scared of a double-booking," I tease, working her up even further.

Katy might not like the idea of getting into a shower with me, but I wouldn't mind even a little. Something about her attitude gets another—*ahem*—part of me excited.

Roaaar. Wildcat.

Chapter
Eight

Katy

When Mack finally comes out of the hallway bathroom, I've managed to rinse the shampoo out of my hair and throw on some clothes from my bag. Luckily, I've also succeeded in washing away *some* of the bad feelings too.

I'm not saying I'm feeling a sense of camaraderie and am ready to sing "Kumbaya" around a campfire with him, but I'm not wielding a pitchfork either.

That said, it might be because I didn't have the foresight to pack one in my luggage.

His hair curls around his ears, beads of water still clinging to the strands, and his bright-green eyes shine with an intangible mix of mischief and good nature. I don't know what to make of him—I never know what to make of him. But in this environment, without the pressure of professionalism, it's as if the power of his smile is a little—okay, *a lot*—more potent.

I'm so annoyed with the situation we're in—and with the abysmal way he's handled it—but for whatever reason, all I can think about is the way his bare ass looked when he dropped his drawers in the middle of the hallway. Tight and toned and...*juicy.*

Sweet Jesus. I'm losing it. It's been wayyy too long since the sun has shone on the Prideland, if you know what I'm saying.

Since the flower has been watered. Since the pipes have been cleaned out. Since…I've had an orgasm from something other than myself and a vibrator.

I suck my lips into my mouth as he comes over to the couch I'm sitting on and takes a seat on the other end. I chew on the inside of my cheek and pull my knees up to my chest as he crosses his ankle over his knee and smiles a downright gorgeous smile at me.

Handsome freak.

No wonder everyone loves him so much…

"Listen…" he starts, holding up his hands almost nervously. Almost contrite—a different look from him entirely. "I feel a little bad. We've gotten off on the wrong foot here. We shouldn't be bickering. We should be making the best out of this free vacation, you know? I don't want to be your enemy, and I don't intend to get in the way of your fun." He meets my eyes, and his lips bend down slightly at the corners. "I shouldn't have been so flippant about getting in the shower when I knew you were upset. I'm really sorry about that, Katy."

His words completely disarm me, and a soft sigh escapes my lips as I search the depths of his green eyes to gauge his honesty.

I expect games and jokes and facetiousness, but all I find is an obvious genuineness. A certified truth.

No red flags. No obvious tells. Just straight-up facts.

I flit my eyes away from the strength of his mesmerizing gaze and stare down at my hands.

As annoyed at him as I am, and as easy as it would be to keep fighting…he's right. I don't want to be stressed the whole time I'm here, and I *don't* want to leave. I want to go to sleep without my always-tension-filled shoulders touching my ears, for God's sake. And watching him strip himself on the way to the shower is so ingrained in my thoughts at this point, I can't even pretend to complain about it.

Although, there's no way in hell I'll let him know how affected I was by it.

So, I keep my response simple and focused. No discussion of sexy, toned butts, whatsoever.

"Okay, fine," I agree and meet his eyes. "I'm willing for both of us to stay here this week…but only if we establish boundaries first."

His smile is back in Mack Mode—downright playful. "Boundaries?"

I nod seriously, showing my yin to his yang right out of the gate.

"And what kind of boundaries do you have in mind?"

"Well, for one, no getting naked in the hallway would be a good start." *It would surely help my sanity, that's for damn sure.*

Unbidden, a visual of his toned ass and thighs pops into my mind, and a sharp heat migrates to my cheeks.

Stop it. Stop it right now. Think about anything else but that. *Politics, slow cooker recipes, the smell of urine in the subway tunnel…anything else but that.*

All the while, Mack searches my eyes and my face, the hint of a smile making one tiny dimple appear in his right cheek.

Casseroles. Expired milk. The smell of Barry's fish sandwiches in the teachers' lounge.

"Okay," he eventually responds. "No getting naked in the hallway. I can handle that. What else?"

"Um…" I pause and try to think through all of the possible things I need to survive this vacation without murdering him. *Or jumping his bones out of desperation.* "No eating my food or drinking my wine unless I offer it to you. No annoying me on purpose. Clean up after yourself. And…you sleep in the guest bedroom. I get the master bedroom because I was here first, and my stuff is already in there."

"Wait…I have to sleep in the room with Kimmie's trophies and wrestling spandex pics?"

"Yes. This is your consequence for drinking my wine and making me do all the work with customer service." I nod, resolute. "And if you can manage these terms, then I think we can officially call a truce and put down our pro-verbial weapons."

"You're the one holding a scythe, Ms. Dayton. I'm holding a paddleboard."

"Fair enough. I'll stow my war chest as well."

He nods. "Okay, Katy Cat. I agree to the terms."

"One more thing," I add with narrowed eyes. "Don't call me Katy Cat."

He laughs. "You don't like the nickname?"

"Hate it more than Harry Potter hated Lord Voldemort, actually."

"Okay, *Katy with the smooth Potter references*," he says and holds out a hand in solidarity. "I agree to all of your terms."

"Perfect." Dutifully, I shake on the deal and try not to think about how much softer the skin of his hands is than I ever imagined it'd be. "Now, I think we can successfully find a way to enjoy this vacation, while giving each other some peace and much-needed space."

Instantly, he winces a little and then laughs.

"What?"

"Oh, nothing. I just… Well, I was going to invite you to come down to the beach while I paddleboard. Kind of the opposite of giving you some space. But if you want to be left alone, I get it."

I consider the options carefully—staying alone in the house or going down to the beach…*and secretly watching his juicy ass play in the water in board shorts.*

A giddiness sizzles in my chest that's wholly unfamiliar. Sad as it sounds, I haven't been this excited about the idea of something in a long time.

Careful to be casual, I shrug one shoulder. "I guess I could come down to the beach and read. I was thinking of doing that anyway."

"Yeah?" he asks, and if I'm not imagining it, I could swear he almost sounds hopeful.

"Yeah," I agree. "It's not like you're going to be chatting my ear off while you're in the water."

"Even if I tried to chat your ear off, you won't be able to hear me." He smirks and lifts his eyebrows playfully. "So...the beach?"

It takes me a surprisingly small amount of time to respond.

"Sure. I'll come."

"Fantastic. Let's go," he responds, jumping up from the couch with a spryness I can only dream of.

"Now?"

Mack laughs. "Yes, now."

"Oh."

"What? You need time to prepare or something?"

"No, I just didn't realize when you asked that you meant now."

Mack grins so big, the tops of his cheeks touch his bottom eyelashes. "Well, since today's already half gone, I figure there's no use in wasting any more time, you know?"

It will take me less than five minutes to get ready and I almost agree, but there's something inside me that forces my mouth to pump the brakes. I'm not a jump-and-do person. I'm a plan-and-plot person. Since this wasn't my idea, it's feeling a little out of control in a way I'm not used to.

"How about you head down there now, and I'll be right behind you after I get in my swimsuit and put on sunscreen."

"You don't want me to wait for you?"

"No use in you losing any more daylight hours while I'm doing girlie things." I hop off the couch and head toward the master bedroom. "I'll see you down there!" I call over my shoulder.

And then, I shut the bedroom door and lean up against the wood, even letting the back of my head fall against it with a soft thud.

I've got girlie things to do, all right.

I've got to freak the frack out.

An entire week with Mack Houston. In the same condo.

Holy hell. I'm in trouble.

🍎

By the time I get to the beach, Mack is already out in the water, paddling across the surface with precision. I hate to say it, but even from a distance, he looks good.

Really good, actually.

It's like the sun's whole purpose today is to highlight every tight and toned surface of his body.

In all the time we've worked together, I've never seen him without his shirt on. Barely even seen any skin below his collarbone, to be honest. But today, I've seen his bare ass and his impressive chest and abs, and if you put it all together, that's almost an entire peep show.

If I'm going to survive this vacation, I'm going to have to make a pact of epic proportions with myself—I do *not* need to see the...ahem...*missing puzzle piece.*

Sure, he's attractive. Like, beyond attractive, but archnemeses normally are. It's a whole part of the story arc or something.

I won't let myself get distracted by his perfect chest and flexing biceps.

We're oil and water, baby. We don't mix.

Once I get the beach chair that I found inside the condo's utility closet set up, I plop my white-bikini-clad ass down into the seat and grab my phone and the book I plan to read out of my beach bag.

Now that I'm finally done hyperventilating, it's time to fill my best friend in on the situation at large.

Me: Well, I'm here, but be glad you're not. Our condo got overbooked!

Her response comes in record time.

Anna: What? What do you mean "overbooked"?

Me: I have a roommate.

Anna: You're rooming with some stranger??? Katy, what the fuck? Do you have some kind of Dateline fantasy you've never shared with me?

Me: He's technically not a stranger, but I'm not sure I wouldn't have been better off with one.

Anna: Listen, honey, I'm on an unhealthy amount of DayQuil, so you're going to have to spell it out for me or else I'll just chalk this up as hallucinations.

Me: Mack Houston is technically my roommate. Mack Houston is technically not a stranger. Mack Houston is technically in more danger of me strangling him than the other way around, I think.

Anna: SHUT THE FUCKING FRONT DOOR.

Me: Yeah.

Anna: How in the hell did that happen?

Me: I have no idea! They overbooked the condo somehow!

I can hear the sound of my whining voice in my own head as I type.

Her next three texts come in at a rapid-fire pace.

Anna: They overbooked the condo with the one person in the whole wide world you can't stand? You're the math person…what are the statistics on something like that happening?

Anna: HAHAHAHAHAHAHAHAHAHAHAHAHA

Anna: You and Mack Houston? In the same condo? I'm sorry, but I can't stop laughing!

A deep sigh escapes my lungs as I type out a response.

Me: It's not that funny.

Anna: I'm sorry, you're right. It's not funny. It's FUCKING HILARIOUS.

Me: You're the worst best friend, you know that?

Anna: So, what's the situation? Are you both staying??

Me: I can't believe I'm saying this, but yes. Customer service refunded us, so it'd be insane for either of us to give up a free vacation.

Anna: Man, when I told you to bang someone on vacation, I certainly didn't think it would end up being Mack Houston.

Me: I AM NOT GOING TO BANG MACK HOUSTON.

Anna: I wouldn't blame you if you did. That man is a serious treat. He's like a muscle-clad sundae with hot fudge and whipped cream and cherries and sprinkles on top. I'd bet my right tit he has a big cock and he's REALLY good with his mouth… 😏

Me: Being one-titted is a hefty bet to make on something you have no idea about!

Anna: Oh, I know. I just have a sense for these things. And Mack Houston isn't just a pretty face, honey. He knows how to make a woman come.

Me: I think you need to lay off the DayQuil.

Anna: And I think you need to get up close and personal with our coworker and let me know if my suspicions are right. Come on, it's perfect. Finally, you'll have an outlet for all that pent-up aggression. You don't have to be best friends…just be best frenemies!

Me: Best frenemies? Jesus.

Anna: That's right, baby. Hate fuck the shit out of that hot man and then come back to school like nothing happened. It's genius! The ultimate revenge for the years of torture you've received at his hands.

Me: I'm just realizing our brains work veryyy differently. How are we best friends?

Anna: Because when the nitty gets gritty, your bestie has to get real. Now, get in there and get some man meat, Katy.

I send her back the eye-roll emoji, lock my screen, and shove the device back into my beach bag. Obviously, Anna is currently off her rocker at the hands of DayQuil and can't be trusted right now.

I mean, I wouldn't get up close and personal with Mack Houston if he were the last man on earth. The fate of humanity could be on the line, and I still wouldn't do it. We'd all just crumble into oblivion if that kind of responsibility were on my shoulders.

You're such a liar.

Okay, fine. If the fate of humanity depended on me, I'd consider it. But other than that, it's a big hell no.

With my mind in such a scary place, I force myself to focus on the book in my lap. A whole new world without the dilemmas of frenemies with potentially big penises.

This is why I'm here. To relax. Enjoy the beach.

Unfortunately, I only get two pages into my reread of my favorite trilogy— *The Shadow Brothers* by Brooke Baker—before a group of college-aged girls rob my book of my attention.

There are three in total, and if I tried really hard, I think I could sew the material from their three string bikinis into the material of one normal one. We're talking perky boobs, round butts, and long legs covered in dental floss.

They giggle and chat as they lay out their beach towels and put on the kind of tanning lotion dermatologists warn you about. And even though they can't be a day over twenty, they pop open White Claws from their cooler and chat about what bars they're going to hit tonight.

"There's no way I'm going back to the Crazy Crab," the blonde in the neon-yellow bikini says as she flips her hair behind her shoulder. "There were way too many creepers there last night."

The brunette in the pastel-pink bikini laughs. "You say that about every bar we go to."

"Whatever. I don't care. Pick another place."

"What about Frankie's?" the other brunette, wearing a flowery bathing suit with both butt cheeks out, suggests. "They have a DJ."

"Yeah, okay. I'm down for Frankie's," the blonde agrees.

I try to tune out their ongoing conversation about bars and spring break and college courses, but something the blonde says catches my attention and holds it hostage.

"Who is that guy?" she questions, and I look up from my book to glance at them out of my periphery on instinct.

And when I discreetly search for the guy in question, my roomie, Mack Houston himself, is the only man I find. He's still paddleboarding across the water, his large presence undeniable.

"*Dayum*. He's someone I certainly want to know," Flower Bikini purrs. "The body on that man. I volunteer as tribute."

Pathetic or not, this is the norm when it comes to Mack Houston. Women fawn all over him. Hell, I've seen both moms *and* dads of students flash flirtatious looks in his direction at all the school functions.

But I don't normally have a front-row seat to the inner workings of people tripping all over themselves.

Out of the corner of my eye, I analyze the state of his new groupies. All three women have that familiar slack-jawed look as they stare toward him, and their mouths move a mile a minute as they pick apart his presumed situation manically. Unfortunately for me, my ears don't miss a single word of their conversation as it continues.

"*I bet he's early thirties.*"

"*You think he's that old?*"

That old? Holy hell. I roll my eyes so hard it threatens to give me a headache.

"*You think he's married?*"

"*I sure as hell hope not. But honestly, if he is, I don't kiss and tell.*"

As they laugh and snicker about their moral emptiness, I climb from my chair and drop my book in my bag, destination anywhere but here.

Any more of this conversation and I might start to lose brain cells. *Or get chest pain.*

Without wasting another second of time, I grab my beach bag, dust off the bottom of it, and walk as far away from Mack Houston's fan club as I possibly can.

Is it just me or does it suddenly feel like this is going to be one long-ass vacation?

Chapter Nine

Sunday, March 20ᵗʰ

Mack

As I finish brushing my teeth and doing the usual morning bathroom routine, my already sun-kissed face staring back at me in the mirror, I make a decision.

Today, I'm going to get in Katy's good graces. For real.

I can dial up the charm and spin back the tendency to instigate, and I can get to know Katy Dayton on a *genuine* level.

Because, at this point, I think I have to.

Yesterday, by the time I got in from paddleboarding and took a quick shower to wash off the sea and sand, Katy was already in her room with the door closed and the lights out. It wasn't even eight yet, and she'd officially called it a night.

And the only reasonable conclusion is that it's me. I mean, I have a hard time believing this is her norm. I know some people like sleep more than I do, but what grown-ass adult goes to bed before the sun even sets?

It's because she truly loathes you…

No. I shake my head. *Not anymore.*

Today, I fix it. Because there's no reason that woman should be going to bed before old people hit early-bird dinners in the name of keeping her distance from me.

I leave the bathroom and head for the kitchen, "Determination" my newly christened middle name. I'm ready to rebuild bridges and balm wounds and cover myself with olive branches.

The only problem is that Katy is nowhere to be found.

I glance down the hallway and note that her bedroom door is open, a fair sign that she's not in there, and if she's not there, I don't think she's anywhere in here. This condo is spacious, but it's not massive. If she were in here, I'd have seen her by now.

There's half a pot of still-warm coffee in the coffeemaker on the counter, though, so I don't imagine she's been gone for long.

I open the fridge to all the groceries Katy bought. The old me would have grabbed one of the yogurts without thinking anything of it—because if the roles were reversed, I wouldn't mind at all.

But Mack "Determination" Houston has the self-awareness to realize that I already drank her wine yesterday and agreed to an explicit rule about not consuming her food and drink without permission not long after.

My phone vibrates inside my board shorts pocket, and I pull it out hoping it has some kind of clue about her location. Not surprisingly, I'm not signed up for the Universal Notifications Subscription Plan.

Instead, it's my cousin Thatch.

Thatch: I have three possible investors lined up for you already because I'm THAT good. We can all meet Wednesday. Lunchtime. My office. Don't dress like a douche.

I'm quick to respond.

Me: I appreciate your hustle, T, and in this case, am even willing to stroke your massive ego. But I'm in Destin right now and won't be back in New York until Saturday night. Can we meet next Monday after school hours?

Thatch: Is Destin potentially giving your foundation a shitload of money? Because if it's not, get your ass on an earlier flight.

The thing is, he's right. I've been trying to get this foundation off the ground for years, and suddenly I'm acting like vacation is more important?

I glance out the windows, looking for Katy among the white sand of the beach, but she's nowhere to be found.

Me: You're right. I'll look at the airlines and let you know what I come up with. I just have to let my, well, roommate know about the change when she gets back from wherever she is this morning, but I doubt she'll be disappointed. She pretty much hates me.

Thatch: Ah, I see. You're mingling with all the college co-eds, you dirty dog. Hate fluffing your way through the spring breakers.

I roll my eyes on a laugh and send him a rebuttal. The last fucking thing I need in my life is to hang out with college girls. I'm about ten years too old for that. And, trust me, I got my fill of that when I was a wild college kid at NYU.

Me: I'm not mingling with college chicks. I'm staying in a condo in a mostly residential part of Destin with one of the other teachers from my school.

I decide to make myself a cup of coffee while I'm searching for flights. Surely a single cup of Joe isn't breaking the rules if I keep it black and avoid the use of Katy's sugar and creamer.

Thatch: You know, when Cassie was pregnant with Ace, she went through a bit of an early midlife crisis and decided we needed to go on spring break. We ended up in Panama City (not during actual spring break), and it was a fucking shitshow. She ordered strippers to our hotel room and forced me to pound tequila like I was twenty-one again.

If there's one thing about Thatch's wife Cassie, it's that she's probably the craziest woman I've ever met. She's outspoken and hilarious, and she has my eldest cousin by the balls. He would walk through fire for that woman. No question about it.

Me: Your pregnant wife ordered strippers to your hotel room?

Thatch: Magic Mark and Emma Bone.

I nearly choke on my coffee, but before I can even come up with a response to that, another text chimes through.

Thatch: Dude, it was terrifying. I didn't want any part of it, and Cass started to get jealous when Emma Bone was all up in my personal space and twerking her ass in my face. Thankfully, we stopped the erotic show before it got out of hand and just spent the night ordering takeout with the strippers and watching a movie. Honestly, I still have nightmares about that Panama trip.

Me: Holy shit, T. No wonder Ace is such a fucking handful.

Thatch: And he's our good kid. As you know, Gunnar is out of his mind.

He's not lying. Gunnar is quite spirited. His commentary on all things and willingness to dish the dirt on his parents never ceases to keep me laughing.

I lean my hip against the counter, but when I spot a box from The Donut Hole on the kitchen island, I can't stop myself from opening it and looking inside. Nestled inside the white cardboard are six donuts from the best damn donut shop in the country.

My mouth practically waters when I spot their famous maple donut topped with bacon. It might sound disgusting to put bacon on a donut, but it's quite literally one of the best things you'll ever taste.

My phone pings again, and I look to the screen while the smell of the donuts from the open box envelops me.

Thatch: What teacher is there with you? I'm struggling to understand why you're there with someone who hates you anyway.

Me: It's a long story. It's Katy Dayton.

My stomach growls, but I pull my own hand away as though it's not attached to my body. Katy's rules were explicitly clear.

But my stomach yells again as if to say, *Just do it. There're plenty of donuts here, and after you eat it, you can go get more to replace it before you head back to New York early.*

Before I can stop myself, I'm reaching down to lift the donut out of the box and taking a bite. The instant the sweet-and-salty combination hits my mouth, I swear my taste buds fucking break-dance on my tongue.

Goddamn, that's good.

Thatch: Oh shit. I think that's Gunnar's math teacher. He fucking loves her.

Me: She's a really good teacher.

Thatch: But she hates you.

Me: Pretty much.

Thatch: I like her already.

I snort and hold the donut between my teeth while I type out a response.

Me: Of course you do.

Thatch: You know, this is really giving me forced-proximity, enemies-to-lovers vibes...

Me: What the fuck are you talking about?

Thatch: Rom-coms, dumbass. This feels like a rom-com in the making.

Me: Big fan of rom-com movies, bro?

Thatch: Big fan of rom-com BOOKS. The movies can never compare.

Me: Sometimes, I really, truly struggle to understand you.

Thatch: Well, understand this. The meeting's Monday, 5 p.m. Don't change your flight.

I stand up straighter against the counter.

Me: What? But you said I needed to get my ass on a plane.

Thatch: That was before I knew the full situation.

Me: What situation? There's no situation.

Thatch: Oh, there's a situation, and it's a-brewing, baby.

I still don't really know what in the hell he's talking about, but that's not uncommon with Thatch. The best thing anyone can do when it comes to him is to avoid asking too many questions and just roll with the punches. At least now I get to have my meeting *and* my vacation.

I toss my phone on the counter and polish off the last bite in my fingers, just as I spot the still-open box on the counter. I didn't just eat one donut... I ate *two* donuts.

Ah fuck. And now I can't even soften the blow with the news of my departure.

Quickly, I make a concerted effort to clean up my donut mess so I can get my keys and head out to replace them pronto, but just as I'm setting my plate in the sink, the front door of the condo opens and Katy appears. She's clad in a white linen beach dress, and her hair is in loose waves on her shoulders.

She looks beautiful.

Unfortunately for me, while I'm staring at her, she's looking directly at the spot where the missing donuts should be.

"Are you eating my donuts?"

"No." *I already ate them.*

She stomps over to the kitchen island to look more closely at the inside of the donut box. It's easy access since I accidentally left the lid open too.

Her body stiffens and her shoulders rise toward her ears, and all I can do is brace.

Uh-oh...

Like a whip, her head snaps to me, and she narrows her eyes. "There are only four donuts here. I had six."

"What? Really? That's horrible," I comment, giving my best impression of shock and awe. "You think they screwed you over?"

"No, they didn't screw me over," she snaps. "*You* ate two of my flipping donuts." She stomps over to the sink and holds up a plate that unfortunately for me has a few pieces of leftover bacon on it. "And here's the proof."

Shit.

"So…I…might've eaten some of your donuts," I admit with a cringe. "But I swear, I was already planning on replacing them right now…" I hold up my keys as evidence. "And I only meant to eat one."

"First my wine, now my donuts." She lets out a deep sigh. "I was going to cut them all in half and share them with you, by the way, but looks like you took it upon yourself to take what you wanted. Now I don't even get a taste of two of the flavors."

Double shit.

"Katy, I am really sorry. I was texting with my cousin, and I was hungry and… Yeah… I guess I got a little out of control. In my defense, those donuts are like fucking crack," I say, offering my most apologetic, please-don't-be-mad-at-me smile that always works on my sister Lizzy.

But Katy lets out another deep sigh, lifts her hand up in the air and does something with her other hand behind it while glaring at me the entire time.

"What are you…?" I start to ask, but then I swear I see the tip of her middle finger peeking out above her hand. "Wait…are you flipping me off behind your hand?"

She ignores me completely and turns on her heel to grab a glazed donut from the box.

A whole ten seconds later, she's heading back for the front door.

"Where are you going?"

"To the beach," she responds and tosses her bag over her shoulder.

And then, with a slam of the front door, she's gone.

Nice work, bro. So much for getting on her good side…

Chapter Ten

Katy

Anger seeps out of my pores alongside my sweat as I try to settle into the beach chair I dragged like a corpse all the way from the supply closet, and sand sticks to every orifice of my body.

The Shadow Brothers trilogy is normally engaging enough to overcome almost anything, but for as much as my body is trying to purge my rage, the SPF seems to be keeping it locked in.

I can't believe that bastard ate my donuts!

I know being this angry over donuts might seem a tad dramatic, but it's the principle of the matter. I bought enough to share with Mack to be the bigger person, and still, he decided to bulldoze over me and take what he wanted before I got the chance.

I *hate* being bulldozed.

My father, bless his wild heart, is a bit of a bulldozer, and I spent most of my youth putting all of his whims and passions above what I wanted to do because of it. Hell, I still find myself doing that as an adult.

How about you not psychoanalyze yourself on vacation? I chastise myself. *Just move on from the donuts and the bulldozing and relax.*

I force my eyes back to the book. I've read this entire trilogy twice already, but it's hilarious and heartwarming and sexy and the exact mood I'm looking for on vacation. If I could focus on reading, I might actually get through the trilogy and be able to move on to Brooke Baker's latest release, *Accidental Attachment.* I'm sure there's a bookstore somewhere nearby where I could grab it.

But as I start reading where I left off yesterday, I find it nearly impossible to fall into a ghostly world. All I can think about is those dang donuts.

"Hey there, Katy Cat," a familiar voice summons from over my shoulder, his timing at an impeccable climax in the waves of my upset.

"I'm still mad at you," I mutter and move my eyes back to my book, even though I'm not reading a single word of it.

"And how long do you think you're going to be mad at me?"

I shrug one shoulder. "Days. Weeks. Months. Years? It could truly go any way at this point."

"*Years?* C'mon, Katy. Let me make it up to you. You name it, and I'll do it."

He circles my chair to stand in front of me, effectively blocking out the morning sun and casting me in shadow. I look up at him reluctantly, but his silhouette is dark against the brightness at his back.

Still, I can tell he's in baby-blue board shorts, his bare chest on display, with his paddleboard tucked under one arm. His hair is floppy and partially over his eyes, and just one day in the sun has deepened the tone of his olive-hued skin.

It's hard to make out his features with the sun at the angle it is, but realistically, that's probably what's making it possible for me to "look him in the eye" as I make the demand, "Find another place to stay this week."

A soft laugh escapes his lungs even though I'm not joking.

"How about I pick up breakfast tomorrow morning?" he offers, like it's a good alternative to me getting the rental to myself. "Anything you want and it's yours to devour."

"Meh. I like the 'you moving out of the condo' thing better."

"I know a great little diner that has the best blueberry pancakes you'll ever taste," he continues, completely ignoring my comment on purpose.

"I don't like blueberries." *At least, not ones laced with the disdain I'd feel sitting across the table from the Donut Stealer himself.*

Another laugh escapes his throat as he searches my eyes. "Why do I get the feeling that you're being difficult on purpose right now?"

My attention is already back on my book. "Probably because I am."

But my gaze's Mack reprieve only lasts so long. He squats down to meet me at eye level again, making it downright impossible to avoid him. "Katy, I'm really sorry for eating your donuts. Will you please forgive me?" He reaches out to gently pat my knee. "I promise I won't do it again, and for the rest of the week, I'll be a good boy and on my best behavior."

I snort at that, even rolling my eyes when he says *best behavior*. His idea and my idea of good behavior are two very different things.

But his big, lopsided smile is so close right now that I can make out the facets of green and brown and gold within his eyes, and I can even see that he has the tiniest hint of a scar above his right eyebrow. This argument needs to end. Pronto.

"How about you just go do your paddleboarding thing and leave me be?"

"Not until you forgive me first." His green eyes are persistent, practically begging me for mercy.

It all feels like…too much Mack for my equilibrium.

A huff jumps from my lungs, and before I know it, I'm saying the only thing I think will get him to not be so inside my personal space. "Fine. I forgive you."

"Yeah? You forgive me?"

I nod. *Anything not to have to stare so deeply into your stupid gorgeous eyes any longer.*

"Fantastic," he says through a growing smile. He pats my bare knee again with his big hand. "Now, I'm going to leave you be, and tonight, I'll handle getting dinner."

And then, he's back on his feet, walking toward the ocean with his paddleboard tucked beneath his arm.

Sheesh. Here, school, it doesn't matter. One way or another, I end up on the losing end of our battles.

How is it that Mack always manages to get what he wants?

"Excuse me? Do you think your friend is going to be coming back to the beach soon?" an excited voice asks from above me, breaking into my reading just as Killian Shadow is about to discover what killed him.

I know I've read this before, but that doesn't make the interruption any more acceptable.

"Hello?" one of the other college girls from yesterday adds when I don't answer her friend quickly enough.

I swear, tomorrow, I'm making a poster board sign to stick in the sand beside me that reads, *"Thanks for not talking to me while I'm reading."*

I look up from my book to find the whole hot-bikini-girl gang looming above me, their towels and cooler settled dangerously close to my current spot.

For the last hour, I've been gloriously Mack-less. He's been out in the sea, doing his paddleboard thing, and I've been chilling with my toes in the sand, falling into a world of humor and mystery. We were coexisting in the bubble of the beach without disturbing each other, and my earlier rage was actually starting to abate.

But here he is again, seating himself in my business, through a bunch of college girls who've been captivated by the idea of partaking in some of his *cock*tails.

"Your friend," the blonde repeats when I still haven't answered and nods toward the water. "Do you think he'll be coming back to the sand soon?"

I shake my head, eager to dispose of their presence. "He's not my friend."

"But you know him?"

"Yeah." I nod. *Getting to know every ounce of his annoying habits on a personal basis at this point.*

"Oh, okay. Well…" She pauses to glance out toward him again, and she digs her teeth into her bottom lip. "Do you happen to have his number?"

I find myself shaking my head, even though I do, in fact, have Mack's number programmed into my phone from when we were supposed to work on the fall carnival planning committee together last year. Communication is key in teamwork, and I believed that pretty fervently until it became obvious that the real key to teamwork with Mack Houston was getting him off the team.

"Well, I need a really big favor, and I'm hoping you can help me."

I tilt my head to the side, but she's already taking action. Before I know it, she's reaching down and picking up my cell phone from the top of my beach bag and handing it to me.

It's all I can do not to choke on my tongue.

"I need you to give him my name and number." She smiles like she isn't taking a leap to the fucking moon over my boundaries right now. "My name is Maddie," she continues as her eyes nod knowingly toward the phone that's now in my hands. "Just let me know when you're ready for my number."

I have a three-second vivid fantasy of jumping up from my chair and tackling her into the sand while I smash my phone over her head. But the reality of my pushover tendencies is hot on its heels, and before I know it, I'm typing in my passcode and pulling up a fresh page in my Notes app.

Holy hell, I'm my own worst enemy.

"You ready?" she asks, her voice painfully, gratingly excited.

"Yep." I nod.

She rattles off her digits, even punctuating the last four digits with her fingers twirling strands of her blond hair. It's like she's turning into a cat in heat just from the mere thought of Mack having her phone number.

"Okay, got it," I confirm and wiggle my phone in my hand as some psychotic show of good faith.

But she grabs the phone from my hands—without permission *again*—and double-checks that I've typed the number without any mistakes.

My mouth agape, she tosses my cell back to me and orders without shame, "Give it to him as soon as he's done, okay? We want to let him know our plans for tonight."

I smile through gritted teeth. "Mm-hmm."

"Thanks, babe. I appreciate it." She turns on her heel, she and her friends skipping back toward their setup mere meters away.

Beyond annoyed—and let's face it, it's mostly at myself—I jump up from my chair and toss both my phone and book into my beach bag.

My initial idea is to walk, but with the heat of the sun and my irritation working together, I feel like I'll absolutely expire if I don't do something to cool off, right this instant.

I *have* to get in the water.

Mack is still doing his paddleboarding thing, despite the physical exhaustion he must be feeling from doing it for so long, and it makes me realize why the man's body is so damn fit. I'm practically out of breath from my encounter with the Trollop-y Three and this short walk to the edge of the waves, and he's out there doing some *Amazing Race* type of crap.

The Gulf water feels warm on my toes but just cool enough that I can already feel relief from the Florida sun.

Gah, that feels good.

I generally prefer the pool over the ocean—since one has sharks and the other doesn't—but there's just something about the clear waters of the Gulf that make me feel okay to wade in the water. With the caveat of not going any deeper than my knees, of course.

When I can see my feet, I'm good. When I can't see my feet, *fuhgeddaboudit.*

I stare out toward the horizon, purposefully away from the muscly paddle-boarder, and walk deeper into the water.

And I just let my mind be still. I'm not thinking about lesson plans or laundry or my crazy parents or bills. I'm just…being.

I move back and forth with the flow of the water, and even to the left and right as the pull of the waves heading back out to the horizon sucks at my feet.

The toes of my left foot tap something sharp, and I startle, quickly adjusting all my weight to my right—and stepping directly onto something that feels like an honest-to-goodness knife.

The pain resonates like a real mothereffer, and a sharp screech involuntarily barrels out of my lungs. "Ayyeeeowww!" I groan and hastily fall back onto my butt into the wet, wave-swallowed sand behind me.

What was that?

I pull both my feet toward me in a cannonball tuck, leaving a trail of blood between my position now and the place where my right foot used to be.

Oh my God. The mere sight of it makes my stomach churn with nausea. Is there a gang of tiny Vikings in the water tasked with keeping pool girls like me relegated to the sand? Or am I just the unluckiest lady in the land?

Ugh. I *hate* the sight of blood, even and especially my own.

Immediately, I shut my eyes and try to breathe past the urge to vomit. *Just calm down. It's okay. Probably just a little scratch.*

I open my eyes again slowly, the tight skin of my slightly sunburned face pulling with the effort to force myself into the movement.

"Ah, no," I whisper to myself as the blood continues to pour out of my foot at a troubling pace.

Jerking my gaze away from the crimson wave and focusing instead on trying to find the culprit of this egregious act, I peer through the clear water intently. I expect to find a miniature gang of bikers or an all-out war between the Ocean Crips and Bloods, but the only thing I find is seashells.

I mean, seriously? A seashell did this? I can't even tell some cool story about how I survived this season's Sons of Anarchy: Ocean Edition?

Awkwardly, I try to lift my body to move myself entirely out of the water and get back to the stable haven of the dry white sand, but as I mentioned before, my fitness levels leave something to be desired. Without the use of my right foot, I end up looking like some kind of beached whale, scooting on her belly toward land.

I make it there, eventually, but the situation at hand doesn't improve like I'd hoped it would.

There's still *a lot* of blood coming from the arch of my right foot, and I'm still at a loss for how to stop it.

Katy Dayton, the teacher in me scolds. *This is* not *good.*

Chapter Eleven

Mack

Last time I saw Katy, she had her head turned up to the sun with the easy rock of Gulf waves swirling at her shins. Now, she's on her belly, half crawling, half scooting herself across the sand while small waves crash over her body.

Since only about three minutes have passed between the two—the time it took me to paddle around a cross-board current and reposition myself—I'd say it's a hell of a transition.

What is she doing?

I pause paddling and squint to try to see her better, and the first thing I notice is a dark liquid on both of her legs and in the surrounding sand.

Wait…is that blood?

Without wasting any more time since I'm pretty far away from the beach, I turn in her direction and paddle as hard as I can, still keeping a close eye on her while I do it without submarining myself and my board.

When she throws her head back, her breath escalating so hard that her chest actually heaves, a pit opens up in my stomach. Something is wrong. Really wrong.

Without hesitation, I push myself even harder, slicing my paddle through the water with firm strokes as I move back toward the beach. The muscles in my biceps and shoulders burn, but I ignore all their complaints and focus on getting to Katy as quick as I can.

The closer I get, the more I can make out her face and the more alarmed I feel. Instead of rosy, her skin is pale and ashen, and her blue eyes are wide with fear. Adrenaline dumps itself into my veins, and I find myself paddling even harder.

By the time I'm off my board and jogging toward her, she's lying flat with a hand over her eyes, her mouth turned up in a grimace. Blood empties from her right foot unimpeded.

"Katy? Are you okay?" I ask as I drop my paddle and board to the sand beside her.

She looks up, and her eyebrows pinch together in surprise at my presence. "I… Yeah…I'm fine."

"Interesting. That's not usually the adjective I use to describe myself when I'm hemorrhaging blood."

She swallows hard. "It's n-no big deal."

I squat down in front of her and gently reach out with my hand to steady her foot so I can take a look at it.

"Mack! It's fine. I'm fine," she tries to protest, pushing me away with her free hand, but I don't stop my assessment of the injury.

The arch of her right foot is gashed straight up the center, the wound gaping more than I'd like, and I can even see pieces of seashell inside it.

"Katy, this is pretty deep, babe."

She shuts her eyes. "I just need a Band-Aid."

"A Band-Aid?" A shocked laugh jumps from my throat at that. "That'd be like trying to put a human condom on a horse schlong. I hate to tell you this, but you need stitches."

"What?!" Her eyes pop back open immediately, aghast at my suggestion.

"I do not need stitches from stepping on a seashell, for Pete's sake! That's absurd. I just need to go back to the condo and clean it up a little. It'll be fine."

With a wide arm and an even bigger show, she stares me down as she attempts to climb to her feet and prove it to me. Unfortunately for her, she can't even make it past her knees without collapsing back to the sand.

"Katy, let me help," I plead as gently as possible. The last thing I want to do is piss all over her pride, but all the dignity in the world won't fix a laceration. "You need medical attention."

"Mack, I don't need help," she snaps back. "Not yours or anyone else's."

And that's when I decide to take action. I know from experience that Katy Dayton has the stamina to be difficult for just long enough to really harm herself. And I'll be damned if I'm going to let that happen.

With her bitching in my ear the whole time, I reach down and slide my arms under her body and lift her off the ground, until I'm securely cradling her to my chest.

"Mack! Put me down! Seriously! What are you doing?"

"I'm taking you to the ER."

"What? No! Oh my God, I don't need to go to a hospital!" she refutes and even slaps her hand against my chest. "I'm fine. It's fine."

I pause in the middle of the sand to stare deep into her eyes. "Katy, I know this is scary and I know you're in pain, but I need you to take a deep breath, okay? Just one big deep breath."

She nods, and I don't miss the way tears prick her eyes. Surprisingly, she even listens and forces one big inhale of oxygen in and out of her lungs.

"All I want to do is help you, okay?" I gently tap my forehead against hers. "That's it. I just want to make sure you're okay."

"Is it...is it that bad?" Her voice is barely a whisper.

"You definitely need stitches and probably an antibiotic, but it's going to be okay. I promise. Just a few stitches and you'll be good to go."

"Oh God," she whimpers. "I really, really hate blood and hospitals and needles. Especially, I don't know if I mentioned, the *needles*."

I smile at her nervous blather—something I don't think I've ever had the privilege of hearing from her—and promise her my best. "I'll be with you the entire time."

"You swear?" she asks. Seeing her this vulnerable makes my heart pound between the ribs in my chest.

"I swear," I affirm without hesitation. "I won't leave your side."

"Okay."

"Now, all I need you to do is not fight me as I try to carry you back to the condo," I say through a soft but knowing smile, "so we can get something to wrap your foot with. You think you can manage that?"

"It's not easy, but I'll try." Her voice is so small, but her sarcasm isn't missed.

"I appreciate the effort, babe," I answer with a quiet laugh as I lean down to grab her beach bag off the sand without setting her down and then book it toward the condo.

"What about everything else?" she asks, glancing over my shoulder, back toward the beach where her chair and my paddle and board still reside.

"We'll get it later."

"What if someone steals your paddleboard?"

"I'll buy a new one."

Her eyes meet mine for the briefest of moments, searching for something I can't discern, but eventually, she looks back toward the walking path.

"Thank you," she whispers in a voice that's so soft I almost miss it.

"Anytime, Katy," I tell her. "Now, let's focus on getting you to the emergency room, okay?"

She nods, and her bottom lip trembles. "Okay."

I don't know what it is about having Katy in my arms or the fragile look on her face, but it does something to me. Grabs ahold of something inside me.

All I see is *her*.

Chapter *Twelve*

Katy

With beeping machines, sterile walls, and the smell of bleach in the air, Destin Regional Medical Center is really taking some of the mystique out of Destin.

Nothing against this lovely facility and its staff, but I really, *really* do not want to be here and, as such, have spent the majority of the thirty minutes I've been here trying to think of a way to *Mission: Impossible* my way out.

Surely Tom Cruise would have procured a motorcycle and an AK-47 by now.

"Okay, Katy, I have something that will help take the edge off for you," my nurse Donna announces as she walks back into my room for the fourth time since we arrived. Donna is nice and all, but we don't really have the same priorities at the moment. She wants to hold me and my bleeding foot hostage, and I want to leave.

She holds up a syringe as she closes the distance between us. "Morphine will dull any kind of sharp pain you're having."

I grip the edge of the bed as I note just how big the syringe in Donna's hand is. I mean, it's *huge*. "I know you said morphine, but I also know you don't mean that torpedo needle in your hand. That would be ludicrous."

Donna smirks, all the time she spends on the job deadening her to my hysteria. "It's going in your IV, hun. You won't feel a thing."

"Are you sure I really need morphine? I mean, this hurts, but I—"

"I'm positive," Donna responds without a second thought or waiting for the end of my sentence. "Trust me, you need it."

Instantly, panic starts to set in. I've never had morphine—I barely even drink alcohol. Strong narcotics are the very last thing I want to dabble in. What if I get hooked like one of those people on that old *True Life* show and it ruins my whole life and I spend the rest of my days just trying to get a fast fix? *I'd lose my job! I'd lose everything!*

"I-I-I'll be better this time," I stutter as Donna approaches the tube in the crook of my arm they had to wrestle me to insert. "Tell Dr. Johnson he can come back in, and I'll sit still and let him look at my foot and do all the medical stuff he needs to do without getting violent. I'll be good this time, I promise."

Donna pauses with the syringe in the air right above my IV and looks to my right, where Mack sits in a chair beside me.

"Katy," Mack chimes in. "You need the morphine, babe."

"But I—"

"Take the morphine," he continues and reaches out to squeeze my hand. I think the gesture is nice until his grip strengthens, pinning that arm to the bed. I jerk and jolt as Donna attacks the other arm with the needle, but Mack keeps talking as if I'm not acting like something straight out of *The Shining*. "There's no reason for you to sit there in pain. Let Donna give you some morphine so you can relax. Hell, you might even be able to sleep through it."

"Almost got it," Donna mutters through gritted teeth, her voice clearly winded, but Mack talks right over her.

"Just take the morphine, Katy. It's no big deal. If I were the one in the bed, I'd definitely take it."

I search his face, trying to decide if he's being serious or just saying whatever he thinks he needs to say to get me to give in to the Pain Med Pusher standing next to me with a giant syringe in her hand. "You would?"

"Of course I would. Why wouldn't I?"

"Because you're, like, the OG adrenaline junkie," I snap back with narrowed eyes. "For your thirtieth birthday, you jumped out of a flipping plane…for fun. Not to mention, your daily workouts include going to a boxing gym. Also for fun, even though it leaves you bruised and limping half the time."

He searches my eyes for a long moment, and the hint of a smile starts to crest one corner of his mouth.

"What?" I question. "Why are you looking at me like that?"

"It's nothing. And yes, if I were in your shoes, I would take the morphine. So, how about you let Donna give you the pain juice so we can get this show on the road?"

"Done," Donna says, just as my shoulders leave my ears with the resignation of giving in.

"What?" I yelp, turning to Donna to find her already walking away and removing her gloves.

"The morphine. It's done."

The argumentative nervousness inside me wants to question her rapidly about the timing of consent, but the rest of me is too busy relaxing as the warmth of the good juice spreads across my body and into my limbs.

Oh boy. That's a little weird, but I definitely don't feel my foot so much anymore.

I don't feel my thoughts so well anymore either. Everything is spinning in a foggy alley of confusion, but Mack, much to normal Katy's chagrin, sits stalwart at my side.

"I think…" I pause midsentence when it feels like my mouth isn't connected to my face. I even reach up to feel my lips, verifying that they are, in fact, still connected to my jaw.

Dang, what's in this stuff?

Drugs, my mind tells me, and I giggle-snort.

"I think I like drugs."

"You feeling good, Katy Cat?" Mack asks, and I look over at him to note that he's still smiling that big, handsome, stupid smile of his.

"Don't call me that. We made a rule. No nicknames with cats or Katys."

"What did you say?"

"I said, *don't call me that.*"

Mack looks at me quizzically, and I start to question if being on morphine is supposed to feel like you're having a stroke.

Oh God, what if I am having a stroke? Maybe the whole seashell in my foot thing wasn't even a thing, it was a stroke thing.

Mack says something else, but I can't listen with how hard I'm having to concentrate on Domma as she does something with my tootsie footsie. I don't think they mess with feet during strokes, do they?

"Katy? Did you hear me?" Mack asks, and I just…I don't know…I decide I don't really feel like answering him.

I ignore him instead. He grabs my hand, but I lift it away with a jerk that nearly knocks poor Nurse Llama off my foot.

"Whoopsie woo!" I cry, clutching my arms to my chest and giggling.

Mack looks from me to the nurse, so I take the time to peruse the side of his face.

Goodness, his side profile is even handsome. It's kind of infuriating that the one person I really don't like, I find incredibly attractive. *Stupid, good-looking motherfucker.*

Instantly, I decide now is a really great time to give Mack Houston the middle finger. Discreetly, I lift my left hand and then proceed to hide my right hand behind it as I flip him the bird.

Ha. Fuck you, Mackie Mack!

He looks over at me, and his gaze flits from my eyes to my hand. "What are you doing?"

"Nothing."

He narrows his eyes, but he also smiles. "Are you flipping me off right now?"

"No." *Yes.*

"Hmm," he mutters. "Must be my mistake."

"Darn right." I shrug and casually put both of my hands in my lap, confident in my finger behind the hand concealment method. "Maybe you should get your eyes checked, bro."

"Bro?" he asks on a cackle.

"Yeah, *bro.*" I nod. "I mean, we are at the hospital. Surely someone can help you with your crappy vision."

Nurse Llama snickers from her spot at the foot of my bed, and she and Mack exchange some short conversation that I couldn't care less about. I close my eyes instead and think about how good it feels to take a little nappy nap.

"Okay, Katy. I got your foot all cleaned up and put a numbing cream on it. Dr. Johnson will be in shortly to put a few stitches in."

"Fan-fucking-tastic."

She smiles. Mack laughs.

And like a secret spy agent lady, I entertain myself by flipping Mack off behind my hand...*again.*

Suck on that, Mack Attack.

Chapter Thirteen

Mack

Katy stows her hands once more, having just attempted to hide her flipping of the bird behind a hand she put in the wrong place once again, and laughs her head off for the fifteenth time.

She's been the instigator of a riot, shouted complimentary things about my ass cheeks no fewer than a dozen times, and actually thrown down with a man who completed eleven years of schooling after high school alone just to have to deal with her morphine-drunk ass.

And for some insane reason, I've loved every minute of it.

I'll take the double-morphine-dose-needing, doctor-kicking, gluteus-maximus-loving version of Katy over the Mack-hating one any day.

"You're good at this, Doc. I can't feel a thing," Katy states, her eyes closed and a giant smile on her face.

Dr. Johnson isn't in the room anymore. He finished up with her sutures about ten minutes ago and already headed to his next patient's room.

Clearly, that second dose of morphine has her flying high into the sedative sky now.

"Dr. Johnson is all finished, Katy," Donna tries to explain to her for the tenth time. "You're all fixed up, and it won't be too much longer before you're discharged."

"Damn, that was quick," Katy says. "Super fucking quick."

I bite my lip to fight my laughter. See, the thing about Katy Dayton is that she never curses. But as it turns out, Katy Dayton on morphine curses *a lot*. If you asked anyone here at Destin Regional Medical Center, they'd tell you that fuck is her favorite word.

"Are you going to be with her for the next twenty-four hours?" Donna asks, and I nod.

"Yes. We're staying in the same condo all week."

"We weren't supposed to be!" Katy blurts out and starts cackling. "But we're stuck together like glue. I even saw his ass cheeks yesterday. His fucking ass cheeks, Domma Llama! Can you believe it?"

Obviously, Donna believes it. Partially, if not wholly, because this is the forty-seventh time she's hearing about it.

All I can do is shake my head on a laugh and look back at Donna again. "I assume she's not fit for solitude until the pain medication wears off completely."

"I am, too, fit for schlongs and 'tude!"

"You're fit for something, girl," Donna mutters good-naturedly. "Fit to be tied."

Katy's laugh is nearly identical to the hyenas in *The Lion King*.

Donna's smile is amused as she types a few notes into the computer near Katy's bedside, locks the screen, pushes the computer cart into the corner of the room, and heads for the door before looking back at me. "Just sit tight, and I'll get her discharged out of here in the next twenty minutes or so."

"Thank you," I murmur with a tip of my chin and a grateful smile.

"Thank you, Domma!" Katy shouts at the top of her lungs. "You're a fucking goddess!"

I can hear all of the other nurses' laughter from the hallway.

"Man, she's nice, isn't she?" Katy questions through a lazily adorable smile.

"She sure is."

"You know, Big Mack, it's too bad you're not that nice. Actually, you're kind of a dick most of the time."

I nearly choke on my own saliva. I guess we're moving on to cock talk now. "Excuse me?"

"You're a *dick*," she repeats, emphasizing the last word while miming a lewd jerking-off gesture to make sure I get it. "You purposely try to annoy me, your classroom is way too loud, and you also drink my wine and eat my donuts. Total Ricky Dicky move."

"I already promised I'll replace the wine and the donuts. And I am sorry about the noise. It's honestly poor planning that the school put a music room and a math room right next to each other, don't you think?"

"Whatever." She huffs out a sigh. "It doesn't matter anyway. You're gonna call thong-wearing Barbie and have a thrumble or whatever tonight anyway."

My eyebrows climb my forehead in confusion. "I'm going to what?"

"Thong Barbara," she states slowly, enunciating each syllable like she's talking to a child. "You gotta clean her tank or whatever. And don't worry, they don't care if you live behind a picket fence or not."

What in the absolute fuck is she talking about?

I'm about to ask some key questions to get to the bottom of it when Katy lurches for her bag that's across the room as the sound of her phone ringing inside echoes throughout the small space.

"I'll get it," I tell her and gently nudge for her to sit back before she falls out of the bed. "You're not supposed to get up yet."

"Jeez. You're *so* bossy," she complains before, thankfully, listening. "You'd think you owned this germ-bag of a hospital or something."

I pull the phone from the beach sack, and she immediately snatches it from my hands. I thought I might get a glance at the screen first just to see how badly she'd be embarrassing herself if I let her answer, but oh well. I guess the cat's out of the bag.

"Katy?" A deep, male voice bounces out of the receiver when she doesn't offer a verbal greeting upon pushing the screen to connect the call.

"Hey, Dad. I'm at the hospital," she responds but doesn't move the phone toward her ear, instead keeping it in her lap and even turning it facedown.

"*What?*" her dad questions, unable to hear her clearly.

"I said, *Hey, Dad. I'm at the hospital!*" she yells back, rather than putting the phone on speaker or lifting it to her ear or doing basically anything to make this phone call function.

I reach over and push the audio button to put it on speaker, and she smiles with a giggle as her dad asks for clarification.

"Did you say you're at the hospital? What the hell is going on?"

"Wow, I can hear him so much better," Katy remarks to me, rather than answering her father.

"Katybug, what's happening? Are you okay?"

I jerk my chin in an effort to urge her into answering the clearly antsy man, but she sighs the beleaguered breath of a woman put out. Before I know what's happening, she shoves her phone into my chest, declaring, "Here, you talk to him. I am so fucking tired right now. I swear, I could fall into a coma."

Oh Jesus. *She wants me to talk to her father?* I never do well with fathers.

"Katy?" I whisper. "I don't think this is a good idea. I mean—"

Her eyes are already falling closed.

"*Katy?*" her dad yells now, his panic imminent.

Shit. Am I really going to have a phone chat with her dad? Is this really what's happening right now?

Fuck, fuck, fuck.

On a deep inhale of oxygen, I lift the phone from my chest, and I about fall out of my chair when I realize that somehow during the time I switched the call to speaker, and now, Katy's managed to switch it to a *FaceTime call.*

That's right. I'm face-to-face with Katy's father. Right now. And his current expression feels a lot like he's a man who could kill me.

"Uh…hi," I greet while simultaneously panning the camera as far away from what looks like an unconscious Katy as possible. "I'm Mack Houston. I work with Katy at Calhoun, and I want to reassure you that she is doing fine, sir."

He's the opposite of what I'd expect from Type kAty's father. Instead of an uptight accountant or suit-wearing lawyer, a man with shaggy blond hair and bright-blue eyes in an Alice in Chains concert T-shirt stares back at me. I have no idea what he does for a living, but I swear, he was a rock star in a past life. "She's fine? Looks to me like she's in the fucking hospital, my man. Call me crazy, but those two things don't normally go together."

"Yes, sir. You're absolutely right. She's had some stitches and some medication for the pain…" I wince a little. "Hence, why you're talking to me, but she's completely taken care of and about to be discharged soon."

He narrows his eyes at me. "Stitches? What the fuck happened?"

Apparently, her father doesn't need morphine for fuck to be *his* favorite word.

"She cut her foot on a shell in the ocean and had to get a few stitches, but other than that, she's good."

"Damn," he comments and runs a hand through his hair. "Well, that's a shitty fucking thing to happen on your vacation."

For the first time since this crazy video chat started, his eyes start to feel a little less murderous. *Thank fuck for that.*

"For sure," I answer with a nod. "She wasn't too thrilled with the situation, sir."

He laughs like I'm a stand-up comedian giving my best lines, and I start to feel my shoulders settle away from my ears. "Not going to lie, Mack, I'm pretty fucking glad it was you handling Katy in the ER and not me. She's a bear when it comes to medical shit."

"Yes, sir," I agree with a smile. "She gave the staff here a run for their money,"

I admit, almost pridefully. "The doctor just barely missed getting his teeth kicked in when he was trying to suture her foot."

"That sounds like my Katy," he says, and I don't miss the affection in his voice. "She's as polite as a church mouse until blood and needles are involved. Then she turns into a heathen ready to brawl in a back alley."

I smirk. "You hit the nail on the head, sir."

"Enough with the sir," he retorts. "Sirs are for old men and uptight assholes. Just call me Kai."

"It's nice to meet you, Kai."

He smiles at that, but then his brow furrows as he searches my face. "So, wait…you guys are on vacation together? I thought she was going with her friend Anna."

I search my mind for Annas before finally settling on Ms. Anna Franklin, another teacher at Calhoun, who, come to think of it, I've seen hanging around Katy more than a time or two.

"Ah, yeah. We're not really on vacation *together*, so much as sharing space in a condo," I explain, forgoing the whole long story for a much simpler account of our circumstances. "I'm not sure about Anna's reasons, but she wasn't able to make it."

"Oh no." His amused smile consumes his entire face. "I bet my Katy was pissed about that. She isn't a fan of changes to her well-planned schedule."

I chuckle. Somehow I don't think telling Katy's father that he's just made the understatement of the century or that his daughter hates my fucking guts will help in his quest to feel secure in his daughter's care, so I keep my mouth shut.

"We're adjusting now," I say instead. "She wasn't expecting this injury either, but I can assure you, Kai, I'll make sure Katy has everything she needs."

"Good, good," he responds with a firm nod that shakes his shaggy hair. "You mind giving me your number, then? That way, I can get in touch with you if she's not answering her phone?"

"Of course," I answer, rattling off my number for him to take down. "Feel free to call or text me anytime."

"So, how bad is her foot?"

"Honestly?" I glance over at Katy to make sure she's still sleeping. "It was pretty bad," I tell him on a whisper. "She needed several stitches and will have to use crutches for the next week, but the doctor is confident it'll heal up nicely."

"Must've been one hell of a seashell."

"It was. Enough blood to make a good horror flick."

He grins. "Yep. A passed-out Katybug is starting to make a lot of sense."

"She'll be back to ordering me around in no time, Kai. I'll make sure of it."

Kai offers a soft but genuine smile as he considers me closely. "My girl can be anxious and standoffish and even give you a real hard time, but…once she lets you in, she's the best. There is no one like Katy. She has the biggest, most giving heart of anyone you'll ever meet." He chuckles lightly with a shrug. "And I should know. She's been giving and giving to me and her mom since the day she was born. Scariest day of our lives, finding out we were pregnant with her." He snorts. "She's been taking care of us ever since."

Realization of just how starkly different Katy's and my childhoods were hits me like a ton of bricks. I had the world handed to me. Katy had to hold the weight of it on her shoulders.

"It's hard to believe she's going to be thirty tomorrow," Kai adds in an almost tender voice, and his blue eyes turn nostalgic. "My baby girl is certainly all grown up these days. A full-fledged woman living her own life now."

Holy shit, Katy's birthday is tomorrow? I had no fucking clue, which makes me feel like an ass, considering how much Katy has ended up knowing about me. *But knowledge is power, and now I know.*

"Well, Mack, I guess I'll try to give her a call tomorrow and just remind my-self that I'll get to see her soon when we make the big trip up to New York in a few weeks," Kai continues. "Thanks for taking care of her. I'm going to update her mother Melissa on what's going on, and just FYI, you might receive a panicked call from her at some point this evening."

"Not a problem," I reassure with a quiet laugh. "I think if I can handle getting Katy's foot stitched up without her strangling me or the doctor, I can handle a call from her mom."

Kai cracks up at that. "You know, Mack, you seem like good people. I'm happy that Katy had your help today."

"I wouldn't have wanted to be anywhere else."

Kai offers a quick goodbye, and the call clicks dead a few seconds later.

And I'm left sitting there, in the hospital room with a sleeping Katy, wondering how this intensely honest feeling of being in the right place at the right time with the right woman came to be.

Chapter Fourteen

Monday, March 21st

Katy

The flesh of my cheek shakes as I wake, my eyes wincing at the strength of the Florida sun shining in through the windows of my bedroom.

It's morning, presumably, and my phone is officially vibrating with a call from directly beneath my face, but aside from those two obvious details, I'm at a complete loss for my current state of being.

After tapping the power button to reject Anna's call until my brain is functioning, I sit up in bed, slide the covers off my legs, and look down at my foot—which is absolutely screaming for attention.

Throbbing, nagging pain pulls at my wound, but the gauze is a fresh, clean white, having very obviously been tended to recently.

But as much as the care is apparent, the details of the whos and hows and whens aren't so much.

To be honest, the last thing I remember clearly happened yesterday—when Nurse Donna gave me the morphine bait and switch. I don't even drink more than a couple glasses of alcohol because I don't like feeling out of control, and after one day at the beach with Mack Houston, I'm missing an entire… well, sixteen hours, maybe? I don't even know what time it is.

Grabbing my phone from the bed, I check the time—nine a.m.—and am startled by the date at the top. It's officially March 21st. My thirtieth birthday.

What a way to start the next decade—wounded, confused, and willing to claw my foot off with my own hands if it doesn't stop hurting so bad.

I wonder what I was even like last night. And if I said anything embarrassing Mack Houston will almost definitely hold against me? Ugh.

I glance down at my phone again, as if it contains a portal to my answers. Sadly, I find none.

The home screen showcases several missed calls and text messages from my parents and Anna—two of her most recent feeling undeniably angry and coming in after I sent her call to voice mail—but the constant throbbing from my foot has made the decision to check in with them later a no-brainer. I know they're probably just wanting to wish me a happy birthday, but right now, I need food, coffee, and pain medicine. And not necessarily in that particular order.

I finagle my body around and put my good foot to the floor, before leaning over to the nightstand with my hand for some extra leverage. My pinkie brushes a piece of paper, stopping any and all progress immediately. When I pick it up for closer inspection, the jagged lines of Mack's handwriting give way to a personal note written just for me.

Katy,

Since you were pretty out of it last night, I figured I should remind you that you can't put weight on your foot. Use the crutches leaning right in front of you to get around.

And don't hesitate to call my cell if you need any help this morning.

-Mack

PS: I know you're probably rolling your eyes right now, but this is doctor's orders. You gotta follow them, babe.

I hate that he's right. I am, in fact, rolling my eyes at the mere idea of having to use crutches while I'm on vacation at the *beach*. One step in the sand and I'll be flat on my ass.

Despite my annoyance, I grab the crutches and put them to use standing from the bed and hobbling out of the bedroom.

The kitchen is my mission, and not so long ago, I would have laughed at myself for how pathetic that sounds. Anna and I had big plans to make this birthday one to remember. We were going to do a spa day and shopping, and I had even agreed to go dancing at a few Destin clubs.

Now, the closest I'm going to get to the spa is a cucumber in the fridge, and the club might as well be the moon.

I'm practically in full-on pity party mode as I finish the short, crutches-assisted walk down the hall, but when something bouncy smacks me on the top of my downturned head, I come to an abrupt stop and look up.

What the…?

Balloons and streamers in all colors of the rainbow cover what feels like every inch of the kitchen and living room. Even a giant "Happy Birthday" sign sits above the mantel.

Suddenly, I feel the need to blink incessantly. My eyeballs are doing their best to have a little rain shower.

"Happy birthday, Katy," Mack says softly, his board-short-covered hip hitched against the marble countertop beside the fridge.

"D-did you do all this?"

"I had to make sure you started your thirties off right." His smile is so damn genuine, it makes my heart pound like a kick drum inside my chest.

Mack did all of this? For me?

Boy oh boy, do I have the feeling I missed some things last night.

"How did you know it was my birthday?"

"Your dad."

My head jerks back in surprise. "My dad?"

"I had a nice FaceTime call with him yesterday while you were sleeping off the morphine."

"Oh my God."

Mack nods. Laughs a little. "You can't be mad because you're the one who handed me the phone when he called."

I cringe, hanging my head in my hands. I can only freaking imagine what else I did. "Oh. My. God. I just know I have reason to be mortified."

"Hey, don't be so hard on yourself." He flashes an amused wink in my direction. "Morphine tends to do that to people."

"Just…tell me. How far off the rails did I go?"

His non-response makes me groan.

"Oh no. I was a disaster, wasn't I?"

"Relax." Mack shakes his head on a soft chuckle. "Other than fighting half the ER staff, you weren't that bad."

"What?! Tell me you're joking!"

"You can have the truth, or you can have what you want, Katy Cat. But you can't have both."

"*Gah.*"

"Don't sweat it," he says with a shrug. "It'll be our little secret, okay? No one else will ever have to know you were *kung fu fighting*," he promises, singing the last three words like the giant goofball that he is.

It takes a strong roll of my eyes to bring my attention away from him and back to the condo and everything he's set up. The balloons and streamers are still there, hanging prominently throughout the kitchen and living room, the happy birthday sign still sits above the mantel, and upon this second look, I even see a bottle of wine and a box of donuts in a bow-strewn basket on the table.

This might be the sweetest thing anyone has ever done for me…

"Mack?"

"Yeah?"

"Thank you," I tell him frankly. It's what he deserves to hear. No games, no insults, no references to his shortcomings of days past. He stepped up for me in a way that I don't know if I could have stepped up for him, and he did it without guarantee of repayment. "For taking care of me yesterday…" I pause and wave my hand around the room. "And for all of this. You really didn't have to do any of it, but for some reason, you did. I can't tell you how much I appreciate it."

"I wanted to do it, Katy," he says, and his eyes feel so sincere it nearly takes my breath away. "I wanted to make sure you were okay yesterday, and despite the whole busted foot and crutches, I want to make sure you have a good birthday today. I'm sure this still isn't exactly what you had in mind—being that you're in the company of *moi* and all—but I hope it makes you feel just a little bit special."

I nod. It's all I can manage without giving away the gaggle of burgeoning tears in my throat.

"It's truly my pleasure," he responds, and a teasing, playful smile crests one side of his mouth. "Just like Chick-fil-A."

I snort at that.

He closes the distance between us and helps me sit down on one of the kitchen barstools, and then he grabs the box of donuts and bottle of wine from the table to bring them over to me.

Out of his back pocket, he pulls a box of birthday candles, and he sticks them one by one into the donuts of lore.

I couldn't swipe the smile off my face if I wanted to.

"Happy birthday, Katy," Mack whispers, taking a lighter to each of the candles until they're all blazing in front of me. "Make a wish, babe."

I meet his eyes for the briefest of moments and then lean closer as I rack my brain for a wish I want to come true.

Let the rest of the school year go well? Jeez, that's kind of lame.

Win the lottery? Those kinds of wishes never come true.

Let me know what it's like to kiss Mack Houston? Oh, what the—

But before I can take that last wish back or move on to a new one, a whoosh of air slides in from the condo's open balcony door, and *poof,* all the candles go out. Mack claps and cheers, and I just sit there wondering where in the hell that thought even came from.

Kiss Mack Houston?

Am I still high? I mean, seriously? How long does morphine stay in your body?

Girlfriend, the morphine is long gone, and with it, so is all that pent-up hate you had for Mack Houston.

Starting today, my vacation's got a whole new set of problems.

Chapter Fifteen

Katy

Piggyback-style, Mack carries me from the condo all the way down to the beach. "Crutches and sand are no-go," he said, right before he forced me to climb on his back and carried me out the front door.

This birthday, he insisted, was going to be a good one, bum foot or not.

And truth be told, at this point, I believe him. Between the donut cake, balloons and streamers, and the breakfast balcony chat that followed, I'm starting to learn there's more to my archnemesis than meets the eye.

And with as many muscles as he has, there's *a lot* of surface area to uncover.

I'm not surprised by the easy rhythm he said he's found with my father—the two of them even exchanging some messages this morning about my parents' plans to come to New York to spread my grandfather's ashes next month.

Is it super strange that Mack is now having text chats with my dad? Of course.

But Kai Dayton and Mack are both kids at heart. Easy to smile, hard to tame. My dad just never grew up after he had me, but Mack…well, he said himself that his parents and sister made him the center of their world.

I wouldn't know how to be the center of someone's world if I tried. My stubborn ass even tried to convince Mack that I didn't need to be carried down to the beach, as if my crutches wouldn't do a herkie-style split the minute they made contact with the grainy surface.

I shake my head to clear it of all these heavy thoughts and focus on the view. The sun is shining brightly in the sky, and the Gulf water is gloriously clear. It's just nearing noon, and the beach is already filled with kids playing in the sand and adults sitting beneath umbrella chairs.

As he steps off the small wooden path from the condo and into the sand, it hits me that he's currently sans paddleboard equipment. A memory from yesterday pops into my brain, one that distinctly recalls him leaving everything behind on the sand in order to get me to the emergency room.

"Where's your paddleboard stuff?" I ask, and he glances at me over his shoulder.

"Back at the condo."

"Phew. That's a relief," I admit and adjust my arms a little tighter around his neck. "I was afraid your stuff might've gotten stolen when that seashell assaulted me."

"I ran down and got it after we came back," he updates and squeezes my bare thighs playfully with both of his big hands. "You were otherwise indisposed from all the morphine."

"Ugh. Don't remind me."

His responding chuckle vibrates through his chest, and it makes the tips of my fingers tingle against his skin.

"Even though you suck at following them, I'm adding a rule to our boundaries list."

"Oh yeah? Tell me...what's another rule that's made to be broken?"

"We can never talk about morphine, or me on morphine, or bleeding feet again."

"You weren't that bad," he interjects and squeezes my thighs again. "You mostly just liked to use the f-word a lot and tell the nurse you saw my ass."

"*What?*" I release one hand to slap him on the shoulder. "I did not!"

"Look, I'd love to tell you more, but the rules say I can't talk about it."

I hate how well versed he is in sarcastic banter.

Oh, but the current smile on your face says otherwise, girlfriend…

I snub my brain's stupid thoughts and concentrate on the upcoming task at hand—paddleboarding. I'm no professional, but the more I think about it, the more skeptical I become. There's no way Mack's going to be able to keep my foot out of the water on that thing, no matter how good he thinks he is.

"Maybe we can just hang out on the beach since your paddleboard stuff is up at the condo anyway," I tell him. "No offense, but I don't think I'm going to have very much fun on that board, stressing about my foot."

"Don't worry, we're not paddleboarding."

"So, what? You just told me we were for your own amusement? Your sister must have had a field day growing up with you."

He laughs. "Well, she had it better than Satan's siblings, at least."

"Satan had siblings?"

He shrugs, his big smile falling just the slightest bit lopsided. "I have no idea. But I felt like if I was going to make you like me, I had to go big with the analogy."

"I don't dislike you," I protest, making his eyebrows shoot up to his hairline. "Anymore… I'm just confused about what we're doing."

He chuckles. "I didn't intentionally lie to you. Just changed my mind when I had a better idea. We're kayaking instead of boarding. That way, your foot is in no danger."

He doesn't waste any time adjusting my body from his back to his chest and gently setting me in the boat that, now that I know, was clearly our destination.

"How in the hell did you manage to get a kayak? You didn't even leave the condo this morning," I question as I look away from the sand and up into his eyes. I have to squint to see him through the sun's intense rays. For March, the weather's been unseasonably warm while we've been here.

"I called Fred."

"Who's Fred?"

"He's the rental guy," he says like I should totally know who Fred is. "You know, the guy with the booth who rents out kayaks and schedules parasailing and boat excursions…" He pauses to meet my eyes. "You really don't know Fred?"

"No." I shake my head. "I don't know Fred."

I swear, it's a true skill how Mack always seems to become friends with everyone, no matter where he goes. We've been in Destin for all of three days, and he's on a first-name basis with the kayak rental guy. Not to mention, when I started bitching about taking the prescribed Vicodin for pain this morning, he threatened to call Dr. Johnson because he has the man's cell programmed into his phone.

I don't have a lot of experience with physicians, but I'm pretty sure they avoid giving out their personal numbers to patients.

And don't forget he's been texting with your dad, too…

"Well, you're missing out. Fred is a cool dude." He continues rambling on about his beach buddy as he picks up one of the life vests that resides near my feet. "And he was nice enough to set up our kayak and everything." When he starts to put the life vest on me, I swiftly take it from his hands on a laugh.

"I can handle putting on my own life vest, Mack. I'm not completely useless."

He smirks. "Okay, Katy Ca—" He stops abruptly and finishes his sentence with, "Katy. *Just* Katy."

I direct a pointed scowl at him, but I also don't say anything and finish strapping the flotation device to my chest.

Once his life vest is on, he starts fiddling with my injured foot again. He covers the whole dang foot with another towel and a plastic bag he brought from the condo. Which, considering he wrapped my foot up in plastic be-fore we left, is starting to feel a little overboard.

"I think it's good," I say, slapping him away with soft hands. "As long as you don't flip the kayak over and send me catapulting into the water, my foot should be fine."

"You sure?" he asks, staring down at me from his perch on the sand. "Are you comfortable like that?"

"I'm good. Promise."

He searches my gaze for a long moment but, eventually, shrugs and proceeds to toss only one of the paddles into the kayak. "All right, Katy. Let's do this."

"Wait...I need the other paddle!" I exclaim, but his hands are already grip-ping the small rope knotted at the front as he carefully starts to pull me and the plastic banana boat into the water.

"No, you don't," he corrects. "You're the birthday girl. Your only job is to en-joy the ride."

I want to argue and tell him that I still have one good foot and two good arms, but Mack is a man on a mission, dragging the boat deeper into the water. Since it's the Gulf, there's not much action in terms of waves, but the first few feet in jostle the kayak from side to side, and I have to grip the edges to keep my balance.

"Hold on tight, Katy. Just a few more feet and it'll be calm again."

When the water hits his knees, he pauses his momentum to expertly hop into the front seat before I can question how in the hell he was going to get in the boat without tossing the whole thing upside down.

Pretty sure those rock-hard abs of his have something to do with that...

"Have you kayaked before?" I ask him as he starts to paddle us toward the horizon.

"Not since I was a kid."

"Well, color me impressed."

He chuckles and glances over his shoulder at me. "Let me guess, you thought I wasn't going to be able to get in without flipping you over?"

I snort. "Pretty much."

"Katy, you underestimate my skills," he says, and immediately, my mind reminds me of what Anna said about him… *"I'd bet my right tit he has a big cock and he's really good with his mouth…"*

Oh, for the love of everything, I cannot go there. Never ever *ever.*

I try to shake myself out of my randy thoughts and think about normal things like the way the sun bounces off the water. And how blue the sky looks. And how clear the water is. *And how delicious Mack's back muscles look when he's paddling.*

Instantly, the urge to slap myself across the face is strong.

"You okay back there?" he asks, and I nearly choke on my own tongue when I respond.

"Yeth… *Yes.* Of course. I'm good."

"So, you don't mind if I get us out a little farther?" he questions. "There's something I want to show you."

I peek over my shoulder and realize we're pretty far away from the coast already, and the people on the beach are still becoming smaller by the second. Mack's college girl fan club, specifically, is watching us intently, but I can't make out the expressions on their faces.

"Uh…like, how far are we talking?" I ask. "Because I prefer to visit Mexico by plane, you know. Plus, I don't even have my passport."

"Not too much farther," he says through a chortle and stops paddling to reach behind him and gently squeeze my leg. "I promise we'll be safe, okay? I won't let anything happen to you."

"Okay." I take one last look at his groupies and turn back toward him in front of me. "Truth be told, the open ocean might be safer for me anyway. I don't think the Barbie triplets are going to be too thrilled with me when I come back from riding shotgun in your kayak."

"The Barbie triplets?" he questions with a laugh. "What are you talking about?"

"Oh yeah. I forgot to tell you. I was supposed to give you their number yesterday, but then I kind of took a trip to Looptyville." I laugh lightly. "Seeing as I'm riding with you now, they probably think I withheld on purpose."

Mack snorts. "College girls?"

"Uh-huh," I mutter, wondering if the idea of younger women excites him. I absolutely loathe the fact that the thought of it makes me feel a little jealous.

"Huh," he huffs, paddling us farther with swift strokes. "And here I thought you were the only one pulling attention from the college crowd this week."

"Huh? What are you talking about?"

"Yesterday. Some college guys in the ocean couldn't stop talking about how you were 'fuck me' hot."

"Say what?" I practically chortle. "You are joking."

"Nope," he says confidently. "I heard it with my own two ears." My heart trills in my chest in the silence of his pause. "They're not wrong, by the way. Though I don't know that I'd use the same descriptors."

Mack Houston thinks I'm hot?

I don't know if it's the heat or the Vicodin I took this morning, but my heart feels all wonky inside my chest. Like it doesn't know if it wants to speed up or slow down.

I swallow hard against the weird sensation and make myself take a long, slow breath of air in through my nose and blow it out through my mouth.

"Almost there," Mack updates as he continues to move us skillfully through the water, conversation about the college co-eds long forgotten. Evidently, he's about as interested in those girls as I am.

We're *very* far out at this point, the coast feels like it's forever away, but the water is calm and there are no boats disturbing our path. Truthfully, it's almost serene being out here like this. Normally, my overthinking tendencies would have me on edge, but for some reason, I just feel calm. Relaxed, even.

Because you trust him.

"Okay," Mack says and rests his paddle in his lap. "We're here."

"Uh…" I look around and see nothing but water. "This is what you wanted to show me?"

"Not exactly." He grins at me over his shoulder and then pulls his cell phone out of the pocket of his board shorts. With a few taps to the screen, the opening beat of an all-too-familiar song starts to play loudly from the speakers.

"You brought me out here to listen to Donna Summer?"

He shakes his head and flashes a wink at me.

"Okay…?" I retort on an incredulous laugh. And I almost joke that this is how people end up on faded "Missing" posters, but I am rendered speechless when I spot a school of five or six dolphins swimming across the water not too far from our kayak.

"*That's* what I wanted to show you."

Their silver fins sparkle and shine beneath the sun as their bottlenoses slice through the water with ease. Seeing them this up close is better than any nature documentary I've ever seen.

Frankly, I'm floored. *Speechless.* And it takes a good ten seconds before I can even form words at the sight.

"Oh my God, Mack," I whisper, and my hand moves to cover my mouth of its own accord. "How did you know they would be out here?"

"I just happened to be playing a little music on my phone yesterday when I was paddleboarding, and it was like they could sense the vibrations or something. It's either that or they're huge Donna Summer fans."

The dolphins are a playful bunch as they swim around in the sea, occasionally jumping out of the water and diving back in. "This is incredible. They're so close," I murmur. "I honestly think I could reach out and touch one if I wanted to."

"I had a feeling you'd like this." Mack looks over his shoulder again, his gaze locking with mine. "Good surprise?"

"*Great* surprise." I tell him the truth. I even find myself reaching out to grip his shoulder with my hand. "I'll never forget this. Thank you."

He covers my hand with his own and gives it a gentle squeeze. "Happy birthday, Katy."

Despite my injured foot and the fact that Anna isn't here, it actually is a happy birthday.

Funnily enough, this right here, might be the best *birthday you've ever had, and it's all because of* him—*the man you used to tell yourself you hated.*

Chapter Sixteen

Mack

Katy's left leg pokes out from the blanket, her freshly tanned skin practically glowing from the extra few hours we spent out on the beach.

I'd only planned for us to be out there for an hour or two, long enough to show Katy my dolphin surprise, but when she got a second wind and wanted to lay out for a few hours, there wasn't a chance in hell I was going to say no.

I stare at her long leg a little too hard, and the dishes clank on the table as I try to clear our DoorDashed pizza dinner at the same time.

The loud noise is enough to make Katy's eyes jump to me, but I play it off with a sheepish smile and a wink. She's on the phone with her parents—has been for quite a few minutes now—and despite the small space and my new-found closeness with Kai and Melissa, I'm trying not to eavesdrop too much.

I know she thinks it's strange that I'm on a first-name, text-message basis with her dad, but it doesn't feel anything but normal to me. I'm a people person, and to me, the more I befriend, the better. Everyone has a unique story and perspective and something genuinely interesting to add to my life.

"Yes, Mom, I promise I'm taking care of myself," she says with her phone pressed to her ear. "The ER doctor is confident everything will heal up nicely and I'll be off crutches in a week."

I move to the sink to give her some space—and to make my pervy eyes face the other direction—and start washing up everything we've used so I can put it away. I've just put the last of the plates in the cabinet when Katy makes a simple declaration that makes my heart swell.

"Actually, it's been a pretty awesome birthday, despite the whole foot injury. A really great birthday, in fact. Probably the best I've had in a while."

I bring Katy a refill on her water and then head back to the kitchen to get out of her hair. I can still hear her talking, but I feel like maybe I'm at least giving her the illusion of privacy.

"Ha! Yeah, right," she answers through a snort. "There will be no bars or clubbing tonight. Just Vicodin to help with the pain, a hot shower, and bed… Shut up, Dad, I'm not lame. I'm tired, and the ER doctor told me I had to keep this foot elevated for at least forty-eight hours."

Without even thinking, I'm already grabbing a Vicodin from her pill bottle and carrying it over to her on the couch.

Her eyes meet mine, and she offers a thankful smile while also whispering, "I think I need two."

The fact that she's even willing to take a Vicodin tells me she's in some serious discomfort, so when she requests two—which is still within the prescribed limit—I don't hesitate to grab another one for her.

"Thank you," she mouths and downs both pills like a champ while I head back into the kitchen to finish cleaning up.

I wipe down the counters and spray down the sink and even tuck the leftovers away into the fridge. Luckily, just when I'm running out of things to do that'll keep me in the kitchen where I can hear the soothing lull of Katy's voice, my phone buzzes in my back jeans pocket with a text message.

Lizzy: Hey, kid. I need a favor. Tom has a work dinner on Friday, April 8, and we don't have anyone to watch Gracie. I'd just stay home, but Tom says if I don't go with him, his boss will end up kidnapping him and taking him on a six-day golf trip. I can't do six days by myself while Tom prisses around the golf course, Mack.

Thirty-one years old, and to my sister, I'm still "kid." I don't mind the nickname—she was practically a second mother to me, and I don't mind watching my adorable five-year-old niece Gracie either. It's never a chore to hang with her for the night, and to be honest, sometimes children understand me the best. Although, that doesn't mean I'll resist giving my dearest sister a hard time before I agree.

Me: Talk about booking out in advance. Did you want to schedule something for Christmas break also?

Lizzy: I know your little bachelor heart doesn't understand it yet, but this is how it goes when you're married with kids. So...can you avoid filling that day with one of your one-date bimbos to spend time with your favorite niece?

Me: Hey, sometimes, we go on two dates.

Lizzy: MACK.

I grin and type out a response.

Me: Yes, of course, I can make sure my schedule is cleared for Gracie.

Lizzy: That's a good uncle. :) We'll drop her off around seven.

I open up my calendar app to make a note in my phone. Lord knows I'm not going to fucking remember this when the time comes, but before I can enter the information, Katy's voice grabs my attention.

"Mack." She holds up a hand, her phone call ended and her crutches tucked under her arms. "Sorry to interrupt. I just wanted to let you know I'm gonna go in the shower."

I smirk, and she laughs with a roll of her eyes. "That's not an invitation. I just didn't want you to panic when you looked up and I wasn't there."

"I appreciate the consideration, but you can't take a shower," I tell her as I shove my phone back into my pocket. "Only baths."

"I'll keep my foot out of the water."

"*Katy.*" I stare at her. "You and I both know that's impossible. You have to take a bath. And even with a bath, you have to make sure your foot is wrapped up."

"But my bathroom doesn't have a bath. Just a walk-in shower."

I shrug. "Looks like you're going to have to take one in the hallway bathroom, then."

"Mack, how in the hell am I supposed to get in the bath like this?" she questions and pointedly glances down at her foot. "I'll fall on my ass."

"I'll help you."

Her eyes practically bug out of her face.

"Relax," I comment through a laugh. "We can manage it without me seeing you naked again."

I don't miss the way her cheeks flush a gorgeous shade of red.

"Not that I minded seeing you naked," I swiftly add because I can't stop myself from razzing her a little. "If you'd rather I did see you—"

"No! I definitely minded," she snaps back. I have to admit, now that her fiery side isn't laced with an overwhelming amount of loathing, I kind of like when she shows it to me. "So, if you're helping me, you can bet your butt I'm keeping myself covered with a towel the whole freaking time."

"Whatever makes you comfortable, babe."

She blows out an annoyed sigh, but to my surprise, she doesn't push any further. Instead, she offers a pointed roll of her eyes and starts heading down the hallway toward the bathroom.

"Is that my cue to follow you?" I question, trying my best not to sound like an excited asshole.

"Do I even have a choice?"

"Of course you do. If you don't want me in there, I could…I don't know. Call—"

She rolls her eyes. "Oh, come on."

A smile makes its way to my lips, and I don't try to hide it as I head down the hallway and into the bathroom where a now-grumpy Katy stands.

"Stop smiling like that."

"Like what?"

"Like you're…waiting on the show to start at Cirque du Soleil."

I dramatically tuck both of my lips inside my mouth and raise the white flag with two hands in the air. "I'm very serious right now because this is about to be a very serious bath, where nothing will go wrong and no one will see anyone naked."

"You're such a pain in the butt sometimes," she retorts as she plops her cute little ass unceremoniously down onto the closed toilet seat. When she tries to set her crutches against the sink and they start to fall forward, I catch them before they can crash into the wall.

But I definitely don't smile or say anything smart as I set them outside the bathroom and grab two towels from the hallway closet because, again, this is all *very* serious right now. I also grab the tape and plastic I left in there from this morning when I wrapped her foot to go kayaking.

"Okay, so how are we going to do this?" she asks once I start the bathwater for her.

"First, I'm going to wrap up your foot. Then, I'm going to shut my eyes and turn around while you get undressed."

Her mouth and eyes join forces to showcase a skeptical scowl. "And how am I supposed to get in the bath without you seeing me naked or falling on my ass?"

I hold up one of the towels. "You're going to cover the goods with this, and I'm going to be a complete gentleman and not look while I help you into the water."

She eyes the towel for a long moment, but eventually, she gives in and snags it from my outstretched hands. "If you sneak a peek, I swear, I will knock your head right off your body."

I bite the inside of my cheek to fight my laughter. "Understood."

Thankfully, not even ten minutes later, Katy's foot is wrapped and she's in the bath without any mishaps. The towel is still stretched over her body, and the only parts that are revealed include her lower legs and everything from the shoulders up.

"See?" I say with a smile. "That wasn't so bad, was it?"

She doesn't humor me with a response, instead eyeing me with a pointed look that says *just shut up already.*

But I don't take any of it personally. If anything, I'm entertained by her grouchy demeanor. Katy is the type of woman who is fiercely independent, and her current situation—requiring the help of someone else—doesn't sit fondly with her. This reaction is to be expected. And truthfully, I'm surprised there isn't more complaining on her end.

An idea hits me, and I take off running for the candles I saw in the kitchen cabinet.

"Mack, what are you doing?" Katy yells after me from her tiled-tub prison. "Where are you going?"

"I'll be right back!"

Katy is on edge upon my return, but I quickly light the surprise and shut off the main bathroom lights.

"What the hell, Mack? This isn't the Copacabana. I'm trying to get clean here."

"Oh, c'mon, don't act like you hate the candles," I counter as I sit beside the tub. "You and I both know this is every woman's chosen ambiance for a bath."

She doesn't say anything to that, and I know it's because Ms. Stubborn fucking loves the candlelight addition, in spite of her complaints.

I snag my phone from my jeans pocket and pull up my Spotify app to scroll through some of my playlists. "Any song requests?" I ask, glancing up at her as she rests her head back in the tub. Her eyes are closed, and the harsh lines of her expression from ten minutes ago are long gone.

"Surprise me," she says, making no moves to open her eyes or get washed up.

Obviously, the vibe is relaxation, so I do my best to accommodate. I find a random playlist I created years ago titled "Chill AF," and it feels pretty apt for the moment. Instantly, the opening beats of an Amy Winehouse song start to play, and Katy mumbles her approval.

"Love this song."

"You know, when I was in college, I was in a band, and we had a kick-ass cover for this song."

"For real?" Her eyes pop open at that. "What was your band called?"

I hesitate, and her smile grows. "Oh, this is going to be good, huh?"

I laugh and nod. "Armpit."

Several giggles jump from her lips. "Armpit? As in, the sweaty hollow of stanky BO?"

"Yep. I was the drummer." I smile. "We had groupies and everything."

"Mack with groupies? *Shocker*," she mutters, but her voice is teasing. "Can you still drum?"

"Of course I can." I quirk an eyebrow at her. "Music is my life."

"Prove it."

Without hesitation, I lean forward and proceed to drum to the beat of the current song on the edge of the tub and even start to include her lower thighs into the mix as my high hats.

I half expect her to push me away, but instead, she just giggles as she watches the impromptu show.

When the song switches over to "Ramble On" by Led Zeppelin, I don't stop delicately using the tub and her body as a drum. I add her calves and her shoulders and her arms into the mix, utilizing every visible part of her body as my own personal drum set.

Katy observes me, her eyes a little lazy now from the two Vicodin she took, but not so much that she's not fully aware of what a goof I am.

"It's like John Bonham is right here in the bathroom with me," she jokes.

"You know who John Bonham is?"

"Are you kidding me?" she retorts. "Kai Dayton is the biggest Led Zeppelin fan there is. When I was a kid, before every one of his motocross races, he listened to this very song."

"Smart man," I say and slowly bring my drumming solo on home with a few final taps to her thighs.

"Sometimes," she corrects, shutting her eyes again. "Most of the time, though, he's too wild for his own good."

The more I find out about Katy and her family dynamics, the more I understand why she is the way she is. Her childhood was the complete opposite of mine. Whereas I had two parents and an older sister who doted on my every need and, oftentimes, worried too much for my safety, Katy had two wild-child parents who forced her into a responsibility role most kids don't have to experience until they're actual adults.

The song switches over to an Arctic Monkeys tune from their *AM* album. When this song hit the radio back in the day, everyone loved it, and I still love it just as much as the first time I heard it.

"Man, I don't know if it's the Vicodin or the bath or the music or the candles or a combination of all of it, but I'm feeling really fucking good right now," she utters, her voice having taken on this breathy tone that incites a reaction from parts of myself I pointedly disregard.

Because with Katy using the f-word, I know for a fact that the Vicodin have kicked in.

It doesn't matter that she looks absolutely beautiful lying in the bath with her head back and her eyes half closed. She's vulnerable right now, and I can't take advantage of that.

Her full lips rest in this gorgeous pout, and her arms are lax at her sides. The towel is still on her body, although it's managed to migrate down from her shoulders in a way I'm trying to turn a blind eye to. The curves of her breasts are just barely visible now, and it's starting to wreak havoc on the memory I have of that first day in the condo when I walked in on her in the shower.

Don't go there, dude. We're trying to calm the libido—not rev it up.

In an effort to distract myself, I grab a washcloth from the cabinet below the sink and set it beside the body wash on the edge of the tub. As if to gesture, *now would be a really good time for you to get this bath moving along for my sanity…*

Thankfully, Katy takes both into her hands and begins to rub the soap into her arms and shoulders and legs. It's one hell of a sight, and I do everything I can not to notice how soft and smooth and perfect every inch of her visible skin looks.

This woman is a work of art. Leonardo da Vinci and Michelangelo would've sacrificed a hand to be able to paint the beauty that is her.

I turn around to face the door, both to give her privacy and to give myself a minute to calm down. I ponder the meaning of life and the curve of the earth and about seven million other things to keep my mind busy while the water sloshes behind me. It almost works, but the next words out of her mouth blow it all to hell.

"Can you get my back?" she asks, and I turn and take the washcloth from her hand without thinking.

As she sits up so I can reach her back, more of the towel starts to fall from her body, and she doesn't startle or stop its descent. She just lets it…*fall… slowly*…down her body until the wet material has completely pooled in the water above the apex of her thighs.

And it's like…she doesn't even care.

But this is Katy Dayton we're talking about here. She's got to care…right?

Instead of bringing attention to the situation and potentially embarrassing her, I concentrate on the task at hand.

I avert my gaze from her bared breasts and focus on the smooth skin of her back. But as I move the washcloth up and down in gentle circles, the tiniest hint of a moan leaves her lips, and it feels like it has the power to stop my heart.

"That feels so good," she purrs.

My voice officially on a vacation of its own, I keep washing her back while

Katy doesn't hide her enjoyment from the feel of my hands and the wash-cloth on her.

This is getting a little dangerous, bro…

The song switches over, and it's a remix of a song by BØRNS. It's called "Holy Ghost," and between the powerful opening that showcases a goose-bump-inducing violin concerto and the far-too-relatable lyrics, I feel like I've been punched square in the chest.

Without warning, Katy leans back into the water, and her hands are no longer lax at her sides. With her eyes staring into mine and her teeth digging into her bottom lip, she runs her fingertips ever so gently over her own skin. Over her shoulders and her arms and her belly.

Over her breasts and over the parts of her thighs that aren't currently covered by the towel.

I don't know what's come over her or what is even happening right now, but fuck me, this has to be the most erotic thing I've ever experienced, and my hands aren't even on her and I can't see between her legs.

It's all Katy. Her hands on herself and her eyes staring into mine the entire time.

Despite the part of me that is mesmerized by her, I fear the fallout of letting this go unchecked. In a shocking turn of events, I really *like* Katy Dayton. Respect her, even. I don't want some hormonal schoolboy moment when I'm caught up with her physical beauty to diminish the veneration I have for who I know she is on the inside.

"I think I should give you a minute," I manage to force through my lips as I stand from the side of the tub. But she's quick to stop my body's momentum with her hand, her grip on my wrist bordering on animalistic.

"Stay," she demands, and I forget to breathe.

Katy wants me to stay, in this bathroom, with her, while her hands continue to touch her body.

Fuck.

As her tongue sneaks out to lick across her lips, one of her hands slides beneath the towel. I can't see what it's doing, but I know that she's touching herself, *right there*, by the way the towel moves above her wrist.

Katy Dayton is touching herself. Right in front of me. And she's just watching me while she does it.

I'm pretty sure I'm dead.

I expect her to turn shy or embarrassed, but she doesn't. She's owning it. She's giving herself pleasure without remorse.

And fuck if that isn't the hottest thing I've ever seen.

The music continues, and I am powerless against the pull that is her. All I can do is sit there and watch her, my cock growing hard by the second beneath my jeans.

A little moan escapes her lips, and it takes everything inside me not to lean forward and swallow it down with my mouth pressed to hers.

Another moan comes shortly after that.

And more moans follow. Then, her lips part and her eyes fall closed and her thighs shake because she makes herself come, in the bath, right in front of me.

Holy fucking shit.

Burn me up and slather me with butter because I'm toast.

Chapter *Seventeen*

Tuesday, March 22nd

Katy

I wake up to the sounds of my phone ringing and vibrating on the night-stand. Half asleep and with a groan, I turn over on my side and reach for it without even looking at the screen.

"Hel-lo?"

Immediately, my best friend's voice is in my ear. "Oh *hello*, bitch. Are you purposely ignoring me?"

"What?" I scrub a hand down my face and try to force my eyes open.

"I've been texting you for two days now without a response! Yesterday, I called and texted you like a hundred times at least, trying to wish you a happy birthday, but you were MIA," Anna explains on a huff. "I'm pretty sure I left you five voice mails. One of which had a killer rendition of 'Like a Virgin,' by the way."

If Anna is one thing, it's Madonna's biggest fan. She's also *really* pissed at me. I can tell by the way every other breath is kind of growly.

"I...I'm sorry. It's been a busy two days, I guess."

"You sound weird. What's going on? Did I wake you up?"

"Yeah, actually, you did."

"Hold the fucking phone!" she shouts, and my eardrum pings in discomfort. "Are you telling me that Katy Dayton is still in bed after ten in the morning?"

What? There's no way it's after ten…

I pull the phone away from my ear to glance at the screen, and she is, in fact, correct. It's 10:12 in the morning, and my early-bird self is still in bed.

"Shoot," I mutter. "I didn't realize it was that late."

"Damn, girl. What have you been doing the past two days in Florida?" she questions on a laugh. "If you tell me there's some hot meathead lying butt-ass naked in bed with you right now, I will literally shit myself."

"You're gross. And absurd." I force myself to sit up in bed. "And sorry to disappoint, but it's only me, myself, and I."

"Lame-o!" she chastises on a laugh.

"I take it you're feeling better?"

"Getting there," she says. "But back to the important shit… You better tell me you did something exciting for your thirtieth birthday yesterday. If you say you read a book on the beach or ordered takeout and watched a movie in bed, I will be so disappointed in you."

I lean my head back on the headboard and shut my eyes. It takes me a minute to even remember the last time I spoke with Anna, but eventually, I realize I haven't talked to her since before my foot incident.

"Considering I had to go to the emergency room on Sunday because I sliced open my foot on a seashell, it's safe to say I wasn't out clubbing on my birthday."

"What the hell?" she exclaims. "Are you serious?"

"I have stitches in the bottom of my right foot, and I'm walking around with crutches to prove it."

"Oh my God, Katy! That's horrible."

"Tell me about it," I agree. "But good news is the doctor is confident everything will heal up nicely. Just need to use my stupid crutches for about a week."

"Tell me Mack is at least helping you out and making sure you have everything you need. Otherwise, you can bet your sweet ass he'll be my next call."

"Actually, he's the one who took me to the ER. And…" I pause, almost unsure if I should reveal this to her or not. She's like a raging bloodhound when she thinks there's the possibility of romance. "He's also the one who made sure I had a pretty awesome birthday yesterday, despite the bum foot."

"Wait a minute… You spent your birthday with Mack Houston?" she questions, and I can practically see the fur starting to coat her by the minute.

"You can stop sniffing for a trail to follow, Anna. Nothing wild happened."

I haven't even waded into the dating pool since my five-month relationship with a guy named Ricky a year and a half ago. It was all fun and games until I realized that Ricky had several other women in the water with us.

"Seriously, Katy, you're going to have to give me more than that. Otherwise, I'll be forced to believe that you ended the night doing the horizontal tango on his big dick."

"You are ridiculous," I insist. "It was all very platonic. He got me a donut cake, decorated the condo, and took me kayaking. We ended the night by eating pizza together," I tell her. "It was all really sweet…I guess?"

"You say that like you're skeptical or something…"

"I don't know," I answer while my thumb and index finger pick at some imaginary lint on the comforter over my lap. "I guess I never thought of Mack as a thoughtful kind of guy. But for the last two days, he has been."

He even ran a bath for me last night and—*oh my God!*

Unbidden and definitely unwelcome, a memory of last night fills my head.

Mack's eyes on me and the incessant throbbing that had developed between my thighs as he scrubbed my back with a washcloth.

The towel slipping off my breasts and me just letting it happen.

Touching myself.

Telling him to stay even when he tried to leave.

Making myself come.

Oh my God! I touched myself to a freaking orgasm…in front of him!

"Katy? Hello? You still there?" Anna asks impatiently, not privy to the absolute freak-out going on in my head.

"Y-yeah," I mutter past a thick tongue and dry throat.

"Did you hear anything I just said?"

"Um…" *I can't hear anything right now besides the words* come *and* masturbation *and* Mack *and* I'm an idiot.

"Oh, for fuck's sake," she mutters, her voice rising with irritation. "Mack is a *nice* guy. You may be having a hard time processing that because you're so deep in the quest to loathe him, but him being thoughtful with you really isn't all that farfetched."

"What do you mean?"

"*Katy.* He brings the ladies in the front office Starbucks every Friday and takes recess duty from Charlamaine every Wednesday so she can get home to meet her kids at the bus. He takes his cousin's son home when he needs him to, and even got Nurse Mona flowers on the anniversary of her mom's death. Everyone likes him because he's likable. Sure, it doesn't hurt that he's hot as fuck, but he's also really sweet and thoughtful and charming. Have you ever thought that maybe you're seeing a side of him that you just refused to let yourself get acquainted with within the walls of Calhoun?"

In a weird way, everything she's saying is making me feel worse about how far I took things last night. Because Mack actually being a nice guy gives all of these swirling feelings validation. And boy oh boy, does that make things complicated.

"No offense, Katy, but I feel like I'm talking to a wall right now," Anna says on a laugh. "I think you need to go drink some coffee. Wake up a little. And then you should call me back and tell me everything you've so selfishly kept from me about the last two days."

"There's not all that much to tell," I say in an attempt to feign nonchalance.

"Katy, honey, I've known you for way too long not to know when you're only giving me half-truths," she retorts. "Anyhoo, I'll be available when you want to call me and actually chat facts, okay? Love you!"

The line clicks dead, and I'm left wishing it would have killed me with it.

How in the h-e-double-hockey-sticks am I going to walk out of this bedroom and not burst into flames of embarrassment when I have to face my vacation roomie that I decided to give a masturbation peep show to less than twelve hours ago?

Chapter *Eighteen*

Thursday, March 24th

Mack

The red sauce bubbles as I stir through it with a wooden spoon, and the aroma of garlic bread emanates from the oven. The only thing I can see, however, is the image of Katy in the bathtub, touching herself while she looked at me.

It's been a couple days since that night, but I'd be a liar if I said I haven't had to take things into my own hands and make myself come a few times when the memory gets me too worked up.

It'd probably be more if I didn't think Katy would get skeptical about why I need to take so many fucking showers a day. As it is, I'm clean as a fucking whistle.

Katy's tits. And her thighs. And her hips. And the way her mouth parts when she comes. It's all I can see. Her body may as well be tattooed on the backs of my eyelids. I have her moans memorized, and thanks to the music we were listening to, I know the exact rhythm she likes to feel against her clit.

It's a mindfuck of epic proportions, and I don't know how I've managed to play it so cool in front of her for the past seventy-two hours.

The moment she finally came out of her bedroom at lunchtime on Tuesday, I knew she was in her feelings about the decision she'd made the night before.

She was nervous and awkward, so I made it my mission to be the definition of a cool cat about the whole thing.

I haven't brought it up. I haven't referenced it. I haven't even given her a look that I thought had the possibility of making her uncomfortable. It's as though, I, Mack Houston, am casually ignorant to what she let me watch that painfully glorious night, and as a result, she's finally started to relax around me again.

Though I do have a feeling that's why she's been so adamant to only take ibuprofen since Tuesday. Vicodin has too much power over her carefully calculated control.

But fuck, the things I'd sacrifice to be able to witness her like that again. I'd give organs if I thought it'd get me somewhere.

She's so fucking beautiful—more beautiful than I ever dreamed of—but she's so much more than that at the same time.

She's smart and funny, and when she's not busy hating me, she's the most intriguing woman I've ever met. When she lets herself, she can just go with the flow and live in the moment, even with her messed-up foot. Hell, the past three days, all we've done is hang out together. Eat meals together. Watch movies together. Even today, she sat on the beach for hours upon hours, entertaining herself with a book and a big bottle of lemonade as I paddle-boarded and swam and occasionally dropped my wet body down onto the towel next to her.

She didn't refer to me as a dog or an ass or an animal of any kind one time. I even caused sixteen large laughs, twenty giggles, and over one hundred smiles, for Pete's sake.

It was a surprisingly fantastic afternoon. One that's given me hope that I've officially gotten in her good graces *and* that I just might be able to overcome the challenge that is making Katy Dayton realize she should *like* me. *Because I sure as fuck like her.*

Hell, while Katy changed out of her wet bathing suit and washed the sand out of her hair in the sink, I ran to the market up the street and picked up a few supplies so I could make us dinner in another attempt to impress her.

Blinking frantically out of my haze as she shuffles into the kitchen on her crutches with a towel wrapped around her hair, I crack the door of the oven to take a look at the garlic bread and shut off the burner to the pasta.

"You're cooking dinner?" She freezes when she sees the spread on the stove, and her eyes come to mine. "I thought we were going to order pizza again?"

"Just call me Betty Crocker, babe." I sheathe my hands with the oven mitts on the counter and waggle my eyebrows with a grin before pulling the bread from the oven and setting it on the waiting hot pads on the corner.

Katy laughs, and the line of her quirky, cute smile makes my chest throb. *God, how have I managed to pretend my crush on her wasn't this big for so long?* The truth is, I think I've always had a little thing for the teacher next door.

"Wow. Thank you," she remarks, her voice a soft caress. "I can't deny that my stomach is happy to see a home-cooked meal after doing takeout the last few nights."

"I hope you like spaghetti."

"Are you kidding? I love it. I would marry it if a union with food were legal."

"Is a union with food *illegal*? Or is it just the kind of thing no one's actually tried?"

"One-way ticket to federal prison, I think."

I laugh. "Most likely."

Quickly and efficiently, I drop the pasta into the colander to drain it and then mix it back in the saucepan to bring it together. It smells of tomatoes and basil and oregano, and my stomach growls audibly in response.

"I'll get the plates, silverware, and hot sauce," Katy offers, pulling the towel off her head and folding it precisely on the counter. She runs her fingers through her long, still-damp locks a few times, and I silently wonder how one woman can be so naturally gorgeous.

I almost tell her to sit down and let me handle all the stuff she's doing, but since she's become a bit of an expert at navigating on her crutches, I let her have her needed independence.

"Hot sauce?" I question, scrunching up my eyebrows. "On spaghetti?"

"You don't put hot sauce on your spaghetti?"

"Uh, *no.*" A soft chuckle vibrates through my chest. "I'm afraid not."

"Man, you're seriously missing out. Hot sauce goes on *everything,* and it does it beautifully," she insists, hugging the red-orange bottle to her chest. "I'm honestly sad that it's taken me until today to notice the bottle of Frank's in the pantry. You can bet your butt I would've been using it all week."

"You put hot sauce on *everything?*" I question. "Surely you're exaggerating."

"*Everything,*" she emphasizes. "Spaghetti, pizza, steak, French fries—you name it, and I'll put it on it. But hey, it's okay if you have a less-sophisticated palate. I won't judge."

"Is that your way of calling me a food Neanderthal?"

"Definitely not," she disagrees. "If I were going to make a caveman-style reference to your personality, you'd know it in no uncertain terms."

"Good to hear."

She grabs the plates from the cabinet and a couple of forks from the drawer and takes them over to the small kitchen table to set our spots before placing the bottle of Frank's Hot Sauce right in the center, like it's a floral centerpiece or something.

"I think we're just about ready to eat," I announce as I put the spaghetti into a dish and the garlic bread into a basket.

I follow in her footsteps toward the table, and when I get to my spot, she smiles up at me from her seat. A brilliant, megawatt kind of smile that makes my heart do weird, flip-floppy things inside my chest.

"This smells delicious," she says as I scoop a helping of spaghetti onto her plate. "Thanks again for doing this, Mack."

"It was my pleasure, Katy Cat."

"*Ugh.*" She groans, but then, a soft, almost-whisperlike giggle escapes her throat. "When are you going to stop with that awful nickname?"

"I wish I could say soon, but…" I waggle my brows. "It's more like never."

"Well…I guess that only leaves me with one choice," she answers, and I quirk a questioning brow in her direction.

"And what's that?"

"Kick you out of this condo for good."

I laugh. "Good luck trying with that bum foot."

"I could use the left one."

"But then what would you stand on?"

"Fine. I guess I'll have to utilize Plan B, then."

"I hope Plan B doesn't involve torture."

"Just the metaphorical kind. I'm going to come up with an equally awful nickname for you." She winks at me. "Tit for tat, you know?"

"I give you free rein to do your worst, *Katy Cat*," I answer playfully and sit down in the chair across from hers.

"Okay," she responds, and a mischievous grin crests the corners of her mouth as she picks up her fork from the table. "Shall we dig in, *Mack-N-Cheese?*"

"Mack-N-Cheese?" I bark out a laugh. "That's your worst?"

"Oh, don't worry, I'm just getting started, *Big Mack*."

"Already been done, babe."

She eyes me curiously.

"You utilized that one in the ER."

"Oh God, I really don't want to talk about all the things I said and did when I was high on morphine."

Instantly, I think, *she probably doesn't want to talk about what Vicodin and a hot bath make her say and do either.* But I definitely keep it to myself.

"Next time I have an emergency, they're going to have to sedate me,

Mack-aroni," she adds and then giggles again. A real, girlish peal of laughter that leaves her pretty little lips like a song and urges a smile to damn near lift my cheeks to my ears.

"So, are all my nicknames going to be food-based?"

"I'm not sure yet, but it's highly likely, Mack-aroon."

I can't not laugh at the last one.

Damn, this woman, she sure is something.

Once you peel away her prim-and-proper and always-professional layers, her center is soft and gooey and fucking fun. *And sexy as hell when she really lets herself go.*

🍎

Katy twirls her fork on her empty plate, and I smile at the simplicity of her fidget. It took us an hour and a half and two microwave heat-ups to get through our plates between conversation, and I don't know that I've ever had a more interesting night.

We've certainly come a long way from the first day we found ourselves in this condo together. Her smiles come easily, and her laughter rings off in waves of chest-seizing melodies. I take a quick swig of the beer I picked up at the market earlier and pause for her reaction to my explanation of my family dynamic.

"Wait a minute… So you're only a few years older than me, but your parents could basically be my parents' parents?"

I laugh. "Well…if I followed that sentence correctly, then I think yes. They had me fifteen years after they had my sister, Lizzy. Unexpectedly."

"Wow."

"It was great, honestly. I never knew a time when I didn't have someone interested in what I was doing. My family is supportive in a way that made me want to be supportive of other kids who maybe didn't get such a lucky draw."

"The reason you became a teacher."

I nod. "What about you? What sent you down this path?"

She shrugs. "I've always been driven to help people. To set them up for success. My parents had me at sixteen, and a lot of people turned their backs on them. They had a couple of teachers, though, who made it their mission to make sure the three of us had a chance. They tutored them for free to complete their GEDs and even helped set them up with first jobs that could accommodate a kid."

"That's incredible." I smile. I can't help it. Stories like Katy's are the kind I live for. It also makes me a little sad that it's taken us this long to actually get to know each other like this.

"It was what they needed to make it," she says with an agreeing nod. "And they worked hard. I can't thank my parents enough for the life they gave me. But out of the three of us, I've always been the old soul."

"And I'm the good-time guy," I add with a teasing grin. "No wonder you can't stand me."

"I never said I couldn't stand you."

I chuckle. "Maybe not out loud, but…c'mon, Katy Cat, everyone at Calhoun knows you're not my biggest fan."

"No… I mean…" Her cheeks turn a gorgeous shade of pink as she trips over her words. "You're just…"

"What? Horrible?"

"N-no. I…" She stammers for a moment, and a guilty grin covers her mouth. "I was going to say you're somewhat of a thorn in my side at work. But, hey. The more I think about it, you're right. It's probably the school's fault for putting our classrooms where they did."

"You don't have to try to make me feel better."

"No, really," she answers, and her voice rings out with raw honesty. "Most of my issues are noise-related, and well, I guess you are a music teacher. It's never going to be quiet. I just wish you weren't right next door. I mean, you have to understand that teaching math to elementary kids with a live concert echoing inside my classroom isn't exactly easy."

Damn, I guess I never really thought about it like that.

"And I'd be a real jerk if I didn't admit that you've surprised me on this unexpected vacation," she says, but her voice is quieter than before. "Besides stealing my wine and donuts, you've been really great to me. Who knows, if it weren't for you, I might've let myself bleed out on the beach."

Inside, I'm fist-pumping the air at her words, but on the outside, I keep my shit together.

"I'm glad I was there," I tell her and mean every word. "And when it comes to work, maybe I can petition the school board to start a foreign classroom exchange program," I joke, making her laugh outright. She's beautiful always, but cackling like a hyena? Her infectious joy just about makes my heart stop.

"Sounds like a plan," she eventually says once she catches her breath. "I'll apply for one in the east wing."

"Only problem then is that I wouldn't see you every day."

Her eyes lock with mine. "Yeah, and?"

The truth is too close to the tip of my tongue to hold it back.

"And then I'd have to miss you."

Even when she's stalking into my classroom, flashing the stink eye and ready to read me the riot act over volume level, I'm still happy to see her.

Fuck. I'm *always* happy to see her. And this vacation with her hasn't done anything but magnify that.

Chapter Nineteen

Katy

Setting my plate in the sink, I take a deep breath and try to get my head right.

My body buzzes, and my stomach turns over on itself with an unexpected wave of emotions. Mack Houston would *miss me* if he didn't see me?

My brain reels as I try to make sense of the reality I've known for the last five years teaching at Calhoun versus the experience of this vacation. Even though it started off as rocky and included a trip to the ER, I've had fun with him. The most fun I've had in a really long time, if I'm honest.

Is Anna right? Has Mack been likable this whole time, and I've just been the neurotic pain in the ass preventing myself from seeing it?

The me who's spent so many years teaching beside him thinks it's impossible, but the me who's experienced him taking care of me and making sure I had a good birthday and is currently stuffed full of homemade spaghetti and garlic bread, compliments of him, thinks differently.

I turn from the sink and lean my hips into it, conscious of just how fast my head is spinning and the very real danger that I might not stay up without the assistance.

Just face the facts, girlfriend. You don't hate Mack Houston. You like *him. A lot.*

My head feels like a minefield, trying to wrap itself around this past week. I mean, has Mack really grown on me that much? *Yes, he certainly has.*

When I almost jump out of my skin when his arm brushes mine as he sets his dishes in the sink, I redirect my thoughts to simple things like cleaning up.

"Do you want me to help with the dishes?" I ask, even though I'm pretty sure they'll all end up broken if I try to handle them right now.

"No way, Katy Cat. I've got it covered."

I nod, grabbing my crutches and scooting away from the sink to put some space between us but carefully keeping the support of the counter.

Still, I don't know what the hell to do with myself. I shift my weight from side to side and chew at my cheek to no relief. My body feels like a live wire, zapping and surging with the conflict-waging war inside.

I started this week thinking Mack Houston was the one man I hated, but now it feels like the world is topsy-turvy and I've been wrong about him the whole time. Despite the wine and donut fiasco, he's been sweet to me. He's been thoughtful and kind, and he's never hesitated to help me out when I needed him.

That, combined with the fact that I've always secretly considered him one of the most attractive men I've ever seen, is not proving to be an easy thing to comprehend.

It was a lot easier when I thought he was just an uber-hot jerk.

How am I supposed to move forward with the realization that he's actually an uber-hot, super-fun, unbelievably considerate guy?

My eyes find their way to where Mack stands at the sink. His hair hangs over his forehead in the sexiest way, and his biceps flex as he moves dishes from the sink and into the dishwasher. His jawline is strong like a male runway model, and his lips even look soft and full from his side profile.

I'd be an idiot if I weren't willing to admit that Mack Houston is a stone-cold fox. It's why any woman who ends up in his vicinity has to pick her jaw up off the floor. It's why every female coworker at Calhoun giggles and blushes when he flashes a smile or wink in her direction. It's why those college chicks wanted me to give him their number.

And it's why you couldn't take your eyes off him when you were touching yourself in the bath...

Just the mere thought of that night has my skin vibrating with a thousand different emotions. A part of me is completely embarrassed, but there's another part that's turned on by the visuals I have from it.

Maybe you should just kiss him and see what happens...

Or maybe I should just go to bed before I do something crazy.

Yeah. That's probably exactly what I should do.

"I guess I'm going to head to bed, then," I say quietly, but my words just urge a pit of disappointment to fill my stomach.

Mack nods, smiles, and then jumps from his spot at the sink, holding up a finger. "Oh, wait! Just one thing I almost forgot." He runs into the pantry mysteriously, and I can't help but watch his firm ass as he goes.

There's that ass you've been secretly gawking at all damn week.

He digs around in there, I can tell by the sound, and when he pops back out, he's holding up a book—a very *specific* book. *Accidental Attachment* by Brooke Baker. The one I was telling him just this morning that I wanted to find a bookstore for. As he emerges, he hoists it up to show it to me, and my heart trips over itself like a clumsy kid over their shoelace.

"I ran out before, while you were cleaning up from the beach. I'm pretty sure it's the one you were talking about, but you should double-check it just to be sure. I'll go back if it's not right."

I blink and stare down at the book in his hands. "You got me the book I was talking about this morning?"

"Of course. I saw a bookstore right by the market where I picked up the groceries, and I know you finished the trilogy today. I couldn't not get it for you."

Overcome by the entirely unexpected gesture, I cross the room with the help of one of my crutches, press up onto the toes of my left foot, and before I can stop myself or second-guess it, I put my lips to his cheek. His skin smells of salt and sea and cleanliness at the same time. It's confusing, sure—but it's also unbelievably arousing.

Pulling away, I give my head a quick shake to clear it. "Thank you."

"You're welcome." He smiles simply, and his eyes stare down at me, searching my gaze with his own.

The space feels charged, and I'm frozen in place, unable to remove myself from his presence. Mack's eyes are a bright, grassy green, and I can't look away from them while it feels like my whole body throbs.

Just like that night in the bathtub, I'm powerless against it. But this time, I do it with a completely clear head.

Because if I'm honest with myself…I don't want to run away from it.

His hypnotic eyes explore mine, and my eyes flit down to his lips. They're full and pink and look downright kissable. Like, if I pressed my mouth to his, I'd experience some kind of kiss euphoria that only fantasies are made of.

Mack is the metal and I'm the magnet, and the only thing I can do is step closer. Move closer. To him.

I've already spent too much time trying to avoid him. And I just…can't anymore.

For once in my life, I need to give in to what I'm feeling without overthinking or second-guessing, and his plush pink lips look like the perfect place to start.

So do it. Kiss him.

Before I know it, I'm using his shoulder to brace myself as I stand up on the tippy-toes of my left foot again, but this time, instead of his cheek, I push the flesh of my lips against his mouth. I barely notice the resounding crash my crutch makes when it hits the hardwood floor behind me.

His sharp intake of air and his strong hands gripping my waist and pulling me closer to him are all I can feel. It's the only motivation I need to lose every last vestige of control.

Sexual tension snaps and lightning of attraction strikes, and I swear to all that's holy, the whole world explodes.

I can no longer deny my truth.

I want Mack Houston. And I want him *bad*.

Chapter Twenty

Mack

I lift Katy off the ground, and she wraps her legs around my hips. Her hands run the length of my jaw, and if it weren't for the pounding, thrumming, war-drum-style heart in my chest, I might think I'm dead.

Jesus Christ, she's really kissing me. She's kissing me and I'm kissing her, and her ass is in my hands right this very moment.

She tastes like spaghetti and garlic bread in the most amazingly not off-putting way, and I have the sudden and irrational need to absorb her body with my own.

It's like all of my fantasies have come true, and I don't know how to fucking cope with it.

Is this really happening? I need something to tell me this is really happening.

She moans when I sweep my tongue across hers, and a jolt of arousal makes my dick come to life in my pants. She's tiny, and with this rush of adrenaline, I feel like I could throw her right through the ceiling.

I don't want to, of course—in fact, I want to hold on to her as tightly as possible—but if I did, I could.

"Mack," Katy breathes, pulling her lips away from mine just long enough to let an anticipatory shiver run down the length of my spine. There's a nervous air to her tone, and a shred of panic makes my fingertips dig into the flesh of her ass a little tighter.

"Are you okay? Do you want to stop?"

Katy smiles, leans forward to take my mouth with hers once more, and then pulls away gently. Her eyes swirl with a promise of a thrill. I thought the bathtub was the most erotic moment I'd ever experienced, but I swear, I'll never know a look as seductive as this one. "No, I don't want to stop."

Thank God.

"Take me to bed, Mack."

My feet are moving before my brain can even process it.

Carrying and kissing simultaneously, I head toward my bedroom and gently lay her back in the center of the bed. She looks dainty and beautiful in the middle of the expansive space, and I can only think of one good thing that would make her fit better. *Me.*

Climbing up quickly, I seal my mouth to hers again and groan in satisfaction when she lifts her hips up to meet mine, grinding to emphasize the contact. She licks her lips on a reflex, and because of our proximity, catches mine with the tip of her tongue.

"Fuuuck," I moan, digging a hand into her hair and taking her mouth deeply. But something makes me pause, a tiny thought that reminds me of her injury. "Shit, your foot," I say and start to pull away, but she just wraps her arms around my neck and pulls me back to her mouth.

"It's fine," she breathes, her warm breath brushing against my lips.

And then she kisses me hard, even greedier than before, and a moan jumps from my lungs and into her mouth as she rolls me onto my back, peeling her tank top over her head and revealing perfectly perky breasts in a see-through lace bra. In one exquisite motion, the bra's gone too, and I have to take a deep breath to calm myself as she shifts herself on my already-hard cock temptingly.

Our movements become frantic as she paws ferociously at my shirt, and I quickly lean up to rid myself of the fabric with a curl of my abdominal muscles. It knocks her off-balance briefly, but she uses it as an opportunity to yank her pajama shorts off, and I know without a shadow of a doubt that this has to be divine intervention from a higher power.

"Katy…you're so fucking beautiful."

She blushes, tilting the apple of her cheek toward her shoulder in a brief display of shyness. It's beautiful, just like everything she does, but I'll be a monkey's uncle before I let insecurity slip in and derail this beyond-perfect moment. I reach up and cup that side of her face with my hand, bringing her back toward me until our mouths meet once again.

She pulls at the button of my jeans, dislodging it easily enough so that I can reach down to my hips and shove. My hard dick pops free like a jack-in-the-box.

Trust me, there's absolutely no question whether or not I'm enjoying the moment, but there's something that I simply have to do. Something I haven't stopped thinking about since I saw her touch herself in the bath.

Gently, I move her to her back again and slide my body down hers, kissing every bare inch of her body as I go. First, her neck, then her shoulders, then her breasts and her belly, and I don't stop until my mouth is hovering right between her thighs.

Her pussy is gloriously bare in front of me, and I lick my lips at the sight.

"I've been thinking about this," I tell her and let my tongue sneak out to take one tiny lick against her core. "Ever since you let me watch you come in the bathtub, I've been thinking about what you taste like."

She whimpers, and I take another lick, this time letting myself savor her sweet and tangy taste. Her hips jolt forward, and her hands find their way into my hair.

"Fuck, you don't disappoint," I whisper against her already-wet pussy. "I've never tasted anything as fucking sweet as you."

She moans, and I can no longer hold myself back from pressing my mouth against her and eating at her pussy in all the ways I've fantasized about doing.

I lick every inch of her.

I slide my tongue inside her.

And I suck at her clit, loving the feel of her swelling inside my mouth and the way she only grows wetter against my tongue.

Her thighs shake and her fingers grip the strands of my hair tightly as more moans start to fall from her lips. She's close. *So close.* And my dick grows rock hard over the thought of knowing what she feels like when she comes against my tongue.

"Mack, not like this," she whimpers, and I look up to meet her eyes. "Your cock," she says, but she doesn't give me any room to refute. "I need your cock inside me."

She shifts her body away from mine, moving down the bed until she's straddling my hips. Her blue eyes are wild and heated in the most erotic way as she takes my bare cock, places it at her opening, and slides me inside her.

Katy Dayton is riding my dick.

Her head falls back and her breasts push out, and the most delicious, deep, breathy moan escapes her lungs. "Mack. *God.* I feel so full," she pants as she moves herself up and down on my cock.

She feels so fucking tight around me, and it makes stars dance behind my eyes. I have to shake my head several times to stop myself from coming in a blazing glory of shock.

I flip her onto her back, keeping my cock pressed to the hilt the whole time. Katy whimpers and moans, and I don't think I've ever seen or heard anything more beautiful than her in this moment.

"More," she begs. "More. *Please.*"

"Such a greedy girl," I tell her, gripping her thighs and driving my cock inside her. "I fucking love it."

She turns impatient and starts lifting her hips to meet mine.

"That's a good girl. Take your pleasure. I want to know what your pussy feels like wrapped around my cock when you come."

She moans and angels sing and violins play, and my brain overworks itself into a frenzy trying to catch a single thought and hold on to it.

But I can't hold on to anything but her. I can't do anything but feel her, touch her, kiss her, push my cock inside her.

I don't stop until I see her mouth part and her eyes fall closed and hear those glorious moans I've heard before.

I don't stop until I push myself to the hilt and come inside her.

Chapter Twenty-One

Friday, March 25th

Katy

A soft, suction-induced bruise mottles the skin behind my ear, and the insides of my thighs ache with the tenderness of reawakened muscles.

My hair screams of sex, and my lips are flushed and raw from heavy contact.

Every part of me is vivid in a way it hasn't been in years, and I can feel the intricacies of every inch of skin.

I look undeniably sexy—and the sex was indisputably good—but still, a deep seed of panic and overthinking grows in the pit of my stomach.

Mack Houston is naked in the bed you just left, and you didn't use a fucking condom.

My grip intensifies on the rim of the bathroom sink, and I pull from the bottom of my lungs, searching for my breath.

Just relax. Just breathe. And remember that you're on birth control.

I wish I could text Anna and tell her about my current debacle, but my phone is somewhere in the living room with my crutches, not to mention she'd have to go through several phases of "I knew it!" and "I told you so!" and I just don't have the bandwidth to handle that.

But I do wish I had an outlet—somewhere to turn to get outside of my own brain for just a few seconds at least. Something to work through my thoughts with before facing Mack again. Something to challenge the part of me that questions everything so damn much.

I like what we did together—quite frankly, I liked it a lot. But vacation sex and real-life relationships are two completely different things, and like it or not, Mack Houston is my Calhoun Elementary School neighbor.

Will I spend my days thinking about what his penis looks like? Or when we're back in our normal environment, will I start to resent him for making me like him?

If I had the strength, I'd kick my own ass for complicating things so—

Thump, thump, thump, a tap on the door sounds, interrupting my thoughts and completely throwing me off my schedule of freaking out.

"Katy?"

My entire body freezes at the sound of his voice, my still-naked body practically yelling into the void of the small bathroom.

"Katy?" His voice gets closer, making it clear that he's leaned in close to the door to help me hear him. "You in here?"

"Y-yeah." I force myself to answer, even though I'd rather just disappear into thin air, never to be heard from again.

"You okay?"

Nope. Definitely not. "Mm-hmm. Just freshening up a bit."

I roll my eyes at how stupid that sounds, but I don't know what else I expected myself to say. All my toiletries and clothes and basically anything I'd need to do anything are down the hall in my bedroom—where a woman with logical thinking would have spent the night last night so she wouldn't have to feel this way this morning.

Silence stretches itself in the air, and I don't know how much time passes before his voice fills my ears again. "Well, I've got your crutches. I'll leave them by the door, okay?"

"Yepperooski," I practically cheer before dropping my head into my hands and mouthing myself the riot act.

His footsteps retreat, and I turn back to look at the wanton woman in the mirror.

To the Katy Dayton I know so well, she's practically unrecognizable.

Right at this moment, I just can't decide if that's a good or a bad thing.

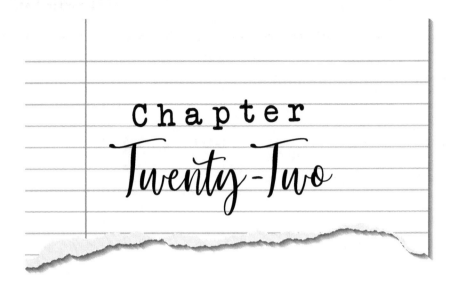

Chapter Twenty-Two

Saturday, March 26th

Mack

Today is departure day from Destin. Big Mack and Katy Cat's spring break vacation has officially come to an end.

I'd usually get up and head to the beach to get in some final ocean time since my flight's not until one o'clock, but after seeing how yesterday went, I rearranged my morning entirely. I stayed in my room until nine, hoping to give Katy a little time to reach some sort of equilibrium, and then came out ready to reengage her on all the reasons she decided to initiate sex with me in the first place.

But it takes no more than a quick look around upon leaving my room to figure out that Katy has already left the condo.

Her bedroom is empty, her suitcase is gone, and it appears she spent a good part of her morning making sure all the last-day cleaning tasks that are listed on the condo's agreement were completed.

I don't know how she managed it all with crutches, but the kitchen is pristine, the living room has been vacuumed, and even the trash has been taken out.

I had planned on doing all that myself after we talked while she read on the beach or relaxed on the couch or whatever else she wanted, but just like yesterday, it seems avoiding me is Katy's number one to-do list item.

It doesn't take a genius to figure out why. Less than thirty-six hours ago, we had hot, perfect, mind-blowing sex that I know we both enjoyed.

But I have to imagine going from hating someone with the passion of a thousand suns to banging them with your coworker's wrestling glory days looking on is a lot for a control-freak-minded person to handle.

The lack of a condom probably isn't helping the situation either, but I know from getting the Vicodin she was taking out of her purse for her that she's also on birth control.

Obviously, I wasn't thinking about that in the moment of the sex, but I definitely thought about it afterward when I realized how careless I'd been with protection. It's certainly not my MO.

Still, I understand it's a hugely personal thing, regardless.

I check the kitchen one last time for a note explaining that she's left to have another breakfast with her mysterious Destin friend named Shelly Shore—the ridiculous and most likely untrue excuse she gave me yesterday to avoid me—but when I don't find anything but the welcome booklet and a lone bag of coffee in the fridge, I resolve myself to the fact that she's gone.

Poof. Just Houdinied herself right out of our shared vacation and back to reality.

I consider taking one last paddle and grabbing lunch with Fred again before I leave, like I did yesterday in Katy's absence, but something about the view from this empty condo doesn't make the beach seem appealing anymore.

Time to head to the airport and take a one-way flight back to real life.

It only takes me twenty minutes to get to the airport rental car drop-off, and another ten minutes to sign some paperwork, pay my final bill, and head to the entrance doors of Destin's airport.

The place is sardine-sized, compared to airports like JFK, but I guess there's a beauty in that. It's easy to find the TSA Security checkpoint, and I can even spot my gate on the other side of it through the protective glass.

Once I check my paddleboard with my airline, I roll my carry-on suitcase toward the small line that's formed within the TSA stanchions, but I only make it halfway toward the line because I spot the early-morning Houdini herself.

Katy sits on a bench near an airline check-in area with her head in her hands and her elbows resting on the top of her rolling suitcase. Her crutches lean against the empty spot beside her.

She's distraught, and it doesn't even occur to me to evade her like she's been dodging me.

"Katy?" I ask when my approach alone isn't enough to get her attention.

Slowly, she lifts her head from her hands and meets my eyes. "Uh…hi."

"What's going on?"

"My flight got canceled." She blows out a frustrated breath. "And right now, the next flight they can get me on is Monday morning. Though, they told me I could stay on standby for the next forty-eight hours, but I'd just have to make sure I'm at the airport."

Oh shit.

"Why did your flight get canceled?"

She shrugs. "Staffing shortage or something."

"And you're just going to sit here? For God knows how many hours and hope they get you on an earlier flight?"

"I don't really have any other choice. I can't drive with my foot, so a rental is out."

"What time was your flight today?"

"Eleven," she says. "I take it yours is still good?"

I nod. "Supposed to take off on time at one."

"That's good. At least one of us is going to make it back to New York on time."

"Are you on standby for my flight?"

"No." She shakes her head. "My first standby flight isn't until 3:15."

Fucking hell. It'd be one thing if that takeoff were guaranteed, but on standby, she could be here for hours upon hours.

"Do you want me to—"

"You should probably start heading to your gate." She nods toward the security checkpoint line that is filled with people waiting in several layers of stanchions, dismissing me before I can finish. "I heard the TSA line has been taking an extra thirty minutes." She looks sad and defeated, and I'd do nearly anything to change that, but she's made it pretty clear at this point that I should be on my way.

I force a smile full of more shit than sugar. "Good luck with standby. I hope you get on a flight soon."

She offers a small wave goodbye, her way of telling me she's done chatting, and all I can do is turn and head toward the TSA checkpoint.

But just before I enter the stanchions, I end up switching paths entirely.

I'm sure Katy Dayton has a plan she can live with. But goddammit, I have a better one, and I'm not taking no for an answer.

Chapter
Twenty-Three

Katy

Eighteen hours and forty-four minutes. That's how long the drive back to New York with Mack will take. And technically, since we're already three hours in, there're only fifteen hours and forty-four minutes to go.

Mack pulls the rental SUV into a gas station located just outside Montgomery, Alabama, and brings us to a stop beside an open pump, and I ask myself for the seventeenth time since we left Destin Airport how I ended up here.

The only answer I can come up with is...by force.

Don't get me wrong, Mack canceling his flight that was in good standing just to drive my pathetic butt back is chivalrous in a way I didn't know still existed. I'd checked the rest of the flights for the day, and every single one had a full seat map and a list of standby customers ten deep. I wasn't getting on a flight today, barring a miracle, and Mack Houston saved the day.

Still, that doesn't mean that I wouldn't have chosen to keep avoiding him and the giant sex-shaped elephant in the room if I'd been in complete control of the situation.

"I highly recommend you use this stop for a bathroom break and to load up on snacks because I'm going to try to keep us on the road until we're outside of Atlanta," he says as he puts the car in park and cuts the engine.

"And how far is that?"

"Four hours." He winks and hops out of the driver's seat. He shuts the door, but the driver's side window is still open. "We need to get nine hours of driving in before we stop for the night. Otherwise, we won't get back to New York on time."

"So…we're stopping somewhere for the night? Like at a hotel?"

"Yep." He leans into the driver's side window. "I didn't get enough sleep to drive us eighteen hours straight through."

The mere idea of sleeping in the same hotel room with the man I had sex with two nights ago is a little more than I'm prepared for, but…it's not like I have a choice or any reason at all to bother him with my complaints.

He gave up his nonstop, quick flight to take on the task of an eighteen-hour road trip just so I didn't get stranded in Destin.

If I'm going to bitch, it's going to be to myself, in a dramatic inner monologue of cinematic proportions.

"You okay with that plan?" he asks when I don't offer any kind of verbal response to his update.

"Of course. Sounds good."

Mack turns toward the pump and starts the process of filling up the tank, and I decide to heed his advice and head into the gas station to pee and grab some snacks.

Thankfully, the restroom is clean and easy to navigate on crutches and doesn't even give off the scary movie vibes that most gas station bathrooms do. No stark, neon lighting that keeps flickering ominously or brown stains on the worn-down tile floor that make you wonder who got murdered.

In no time at all, my bladder is emptied, my hands are washed, and I'm browsing the food and drinks sections inside the station. Potato chips, Twinkies, M&M's, Reese's Cups, the snack selection is a little too on point for someone who's failed Weight Watchers twice in her adult life.

Man, I sure could crush a pack of Hostess snack cakes right about now.

I glance toward the front of the gas station and see Mack is already at the checkout counter and realize I need to get a move on it. I grab a coffee, an orange, heart-healthy trail mix, and a turkey sandwich quickly and make my way to the front just as he's heading out the door.

By the time I crutch my way back to the SUV with my bag of well-balanced sustenance in tow, Mack is grabbing his receipt from the pump and getting into the driver's seat.

"All set?" he asks, and I toss my crutches in the back seat.

"Yep." I nod and hop on my left foot to get into the passenger side. "And next stop for gas, I'm paying."

"I'll think about it," he replies with a little smirk and starts the engine.

"I'm serious, Mack. There's no way I can let you pay for everything. We need to split the costs, at the very least." When he doesn't say anything to that, I add, "You're already doing me a super huge favor. You don't need to go full gallantry, okay? I'll accept no showings of you falling on your sword again. The fact that you were willing to give up your flight and drive me back to New York is more than enough. Truthfully, it's too much."

"So..." He glances at me out of his periphery as he brings the SUV back onto the highway. "What you're saying is that I'm basically your knight in shining armor?"

I snort at that. "Watch yourself, Houston, your youngest-child syndrome is showing."

He laughs at that. "What is that supposed to mean?"

"It means that you thrive off constant compliments and positive reinforcement."

His eyes dance with humor. "If that's me, then what do you thrive off, Ms. Only Child?"

"Bourbon and poor choices," I answer sarcastically, doing my best to make my voice sound like Gerard Butler.

"Is that...a line from *London Has Fallen*?"

I shrug. "I love Mike Banning."

"Maybe your life hasn't been as controlled as I thought. I never would have figured you for a bloody movie kind of gal. What's going on in that psyche of yours?"

"Do you moonlight as a therapist?" I tease. "Because I don't remember scheduling a session."

"Okay, Katy Cat." Mack grins at me out of his periphery. "My analysis is stopping now. How about you pass me my bag of snacks from the back seat, instead?"

"What's your poison?" I ask him as I set the bag in my lap.

"Remind me of my options."

"Uh..." I pause and open the bag, rummaging through his loot. "Reese's Cups, Cheetos, Twinkies, Twizzlers..." I look over at him when I realize he went with all the delicious junk food choices my inner child is pissed at me for not getting. "Good grief, Big Mack, this is diabetes in a bag."

Mack waggles his brows at me. "I'm a growing boy, Katy. I need my nutrients."

"Ha! Get real! There is nothing nutritious about what's inside here."

"It's a road trip, babe," he rebuts incredulously. "You're not supposed to get healthy shit. You're supposed to get everything that's neon."

"Well, you definitely accomplished that."

"What'd you get?" he questions and nods toward my bag that rests on the top of the dashboard.

"I went for normal stuff."

"And what does normal stuff entail?" he questions, and before I know it, he's snagging my bag and pulling it into his lap.

"Hey!" I exclaim and snatch it right back from him. "Eyes on the road, buddy!"

"Fine," he says, chuckling. "Then you tell me what you got."

"Why does it matter?"

"Because I let you see mine. Now you have to show me yours."

Everything in my body is fighting against coming alive for the sexual connotation in his words. It's like Pavlov's freaking vagina over here at the authoritarian trill in his tone. I manage to clear my throat of saliva enough to list off my haul. "Turkey sandwich, trail mix, and an orange."

"I don't know whether I should laugh or cry for you."

"What? Why?" I retort as I turn to look at him and nudge his shoulder accordingly. "There's nothing wrong with my snacks."

"Katy," Mack responds with wide eyes. "You got an orange. At a gas station. I didn't even know gas stations sold fruit. I honestly thought that was illegal."

"There was a giant bowl of them near the counter, and there's no Big Bear on our tail, so I'd say I'm within the confines of the law."

"Go figure. I guess I missed them when I was grabbing my king-sized Twinkies," he answers through a soft chortle. "Which, if you don't mind, hand me those sugary snack cakes. I have a feeling they're going to be just the ticket."

I grab his Twinkies from the bag, even opening the plastic to make it easier for him to eat while driving. They smell like a freaking dream, and when some of the whipped cream filling gets on my fingers, I'm very tempted to lick it off.

I discreetly lift my finger to my lips and swipe that sugary whipped cream filling off with my tongue.

Sweet Jesus. I forgot how good Twinkies are.

In the name of consumptive solidarity, I open up my turkey sandwich and take a big taste. The first bite is lackluster at best—the meat is rubbery, the lettuce is wilted, and the wheat bread is one day away from being stale.

It takes a strong effort to swallow the bite down, and I have to wash the aftertaste away with a healthy sip from my coffee to really complete the painful cycle.

Note to self: gas station lunch meat is a no-go.

Mack, on the other hand, is over there enjoying his Twinkies so much, he's practically moaning with each bite.

I stare down at my pathetic turkey sandwich with disdain. When it doesn't turn into a sweet, cream-filled treat, I wrap it back up and shove it back in the bag. The last thing I need is to get sick off bad lunch meat from a gas station during a long road trip. Poisoned meat poops would really up the ante on our already awkward status.

"Fuck, these are good," Mack says through another moan, and I can't stop myself from looking over at him as he takes another big bite.

I kind of hate how good those Twinkies look right now. And he has *four* of the heavenly bastards. Who in the heck needs four Twinkies at one time?

Plus, he still has a whole bunch of other delicious snacks to eat.

And all you have is an orange and trail mix that doesn't even have the M&M's in it.

"Are you really going to eat all four of those Twinkies?" I chastise, and he looks over at me briefly.

"I was planning on it," he says without remorse. "Why? You want one?"

"No." I shake my head, but I swear on all that's holy, it's moving itself up and down. "Of course not."

"You sure you don't want one? Your head's going the wrong direction."

"I'm good."

"Oh, c'mon, Katy," he says, and his smile is nearly too big for this SUV. "It's okay to admit that you have snack envy right now. I get it. And I do applaud you for trying to go the healthy route, but it's okay to have regrets."

"I don't have regrets."

He takes one of the Twinkies out of the package and waves it in front of my face. "You sure you don't want this? I mean, I'm willing to share with you."

There's a part of me that wants to tell him off, but I fear if I did that, he'd remove the possibility of a Twinkie. And let's be real...I want one real bad.

"You would really share with me?"

"Of course," he says. "I'll share all of my snacks with you."

I reach eagerly for the Twinkie when he pulls it back just slightly, glancing between me and the road. "There's just one condition on the offer."

"Of course there's a condition. Why didn't I expect as much?"

"It's really easy, I swear. You just have to answer one question, and the answer has to be honest."

"That's it?"

He nods. "That's it."

"Okay, what's the question?"

"Oh. Yeah. That's the one other thing. You can't know the question until you promise you'll answer honestly."

I roll my eyes. "That sounds like two conditions."

"Take it or leave it, Katy Cat." He laughs and takes another bite of his Twinkie. "*Mmm-mm-mmm.* I have to say, these might be the best Twinkies I've ever had."

I don't humor him with a response. Instead, I cross my arms over my chest and look out the window, watching the trees and highway road signs pass by at a quick pace.

"Just FYI," Mack adds. "I'd decide soon because I'm already diving into Twinkie number two."

I glance over at him once more, and he's not lying. The man is already halfway through the second Twinkie in that package. Soon enough, he'll be diving into Twinkie number three.

You better move it or lose it, sister.

"Okay, fine!" I exclaim. "I agree."

"And you're going to answer the question honestly?"

"Yes."

"Promise?"

"*Yes, Mack.*" I groan. "I agreed, didn't I?"

"Fantastic," he says and hands me the package with two snack cakes left inside. "Consider yourself two Twinkies richer."

Oh boy. I grin like a child who just convinced her parents to buy her a Barbie after they said no. And I certainly don't hesitate to take a big bite out of one of the snack cakes. The instant the soft vanilla cake hits my tongue, a small sound of delight escapes my lungs. And that sound is echoed when the whipped cream filling follows.

"Good?"

"Hell yes."

Mack glances at me briefly, and when I raise my eyebrows in impatience, he dives right in. "Why did you freak out after we had sex?"

My cheeks heat to a balmy one thousand degrees, and the cinch of his trap tightens around my ankle. I don't know how I didn't see this coming, but this is what you'd call cornered and then some. "*That's* your question?"

He nods. "I would have asked sooner, but you've kind of been avoiding me since the moment we finished." He shrugs. "So, what better time than now?"

I am shocked. *Floored.* This is the last place I thought his question would go. I mean, seriously? Is he really asking me that right now?

"I haven't been avoiding you."

"You basically ghosted me."

"I did not ghost you."

"Change your gender and your name, and you could be a Shadow Brother."

What can I even say to that?

You could tell him that he's right...

"Listen," he adds, and his voice is so soft, so tender, it takes me by surprise. "I'm not judging you. And I'm not upset. I just want you to know that I enjoyed that night. Really fucking enjoyed it. So much so, I was hoping for a repeat. I want to make sure I didn't do anything or say anything that would give you reason to avoid me, you know?"

"You wanted a repeat?"

"Hell yes." He reaches out and gently squeezes my thigh. "Lots of repeats. As many repeats as I can get, actually. That night with you was incredible, Katy. You were incredible. I didn't hurt you, did I? Scare you somehow? Because if I did, you need to—"

"You didn't hurt or scare me, Mack," I whisper quickly, unable to let him go even another second thinking he might have done something wrong. "I promise."

My fingers fiddle with the edges of the Twinkie package in my lap. "I got a little freaked out because we work together," I eventually find the strength to push out. "But I enjoyed that night too. So much I scared *myself.*"

Mack squeezes my thigh again. But he doesn't say anything else. Doesn't ask me any more questions. Instead, he hands me his cell phone once he's pulled up his Spotify app. "Every road trip needs a soundtrack," he states. "It's already hooked up to the Bluetooth. Just need you to play DJ."

The change in subject is an unbelievable relief, and I'm eternally grateful. I blow out the breath I'm holding and curl one corner of my mouth into a smile.

"Mr. Music Man is putting me in charge of our road trip playlist?"

"I trust you, babe."

Yeah. Scary thing is, I'm starting to trust him too.

Chapter
Twenty-Four

Katy

At a little after eleven in the evening, Mack pulled us into our final stop in Raleigh, North Carolina. We finished the day with almost ten hours of driving, and he booked us a room at a Marriott that was just off one of the highway exits.

He's still refusing to let me pay for anything, but there's no way I'm going to let that slide. If he keeps this up the whole way back to New York, I'll just sneak a check into his mailbox at school.

I grab my toiletry bag from the sink and run a brush through my wet hair.

I don't know what it is about being in a car all day, but it always makes me feel like I need a shower. Which is crazy because it's not like I was doing anything besides sitting there, playing music, and eating half of Mack's junk food snacks.

Of course, I didn't get to take a full shower because of my foot, but I did manage to wash off my body and my hair via the sink. Not the most ideal scenario, but it's the best I can manage.

Once I toss on a pair of pajama shorts and a tank top, I finish my nightly routine of brushing my teeth and washing my face.

When I hobble out of the bathroom on my crutches, Mack is perched on the only bed in the room, watching television. He requested two queen-sized beds, but a room with a king-sized bed was all they had available.

I still have no idea what the sleeping arrangements are going to be, but I'm electing not to think about it. Beggars can't be choosers and all that.

Though, beggars certainly were begging the other night when you told him to take you to bed.

"Feel better?" Mack asks, pulling me from my thoughts, and I force a smile to my lips.

"A lot better." I toss my toiletry bag on the chair that holds all the stuff I brought in from the car. "Bathroom's all yours," I add, and he doesn't hesitate to jump off the bed.

"Fantastic."

It doesn't take long before I hear the shower water switch on, and my mind decides to remind me that there's a completely naked Mack Houston inside this hotel room with me. Visuals of his tight ass and firm pecs fill my head, and I force myself to sit on the edge of the bed and grab the remote and find something to watch on TV.

I flip through what feels like a hundred channels, but I can't stop thinking about all the things I definitely shouldn't be thinking about.

Mack's handsome smile.

And Mack's contagious laugh.

And Mack's flexing biceps.

And Mack's really big peni—

Immediately, I grab one crutch, totter off the bed, and try to busy myself with organizing my overnight things by the chair. But sadly, everything is already organized because I'm far too type A and despise clutter and chaos.

The water shuts off, and for some insane reason, I quickly hobble back over to the bed, climb inside, and pull the covers over my entire body and head at a record-breaking pace.

Oh yeah, hiding under the covers is really going to make this better.

My heart thrums wildly inside my chest, while my mind won't stop thinking about what it felt like to have sex with the man inside that bathroom. It's crazy and irrational, but hell's bells, it's all-consuming, and a throb starts to make itself known between my thighs.

My breath comes out in warm pants, and it starts to make the air underneath the covers feel stifling. It's not long before I have to throw the sheet and comforter back off my body as the sounds of the bathroom sink turning on fill my ears.

When the sink shuts off and the bathroom door opens, I pretend that I'm watching whatever is on the television. But truthfully, I have no clue what's playing. It could be a movie. It could be a TV show. It could be a freaking infomercial. It could be anything, and even though my eyes appear fixated on the screen, they are surreptitiously stealing glances of Mack as he walks back into the main area of the hotel room.

His bare chest is on display, and a towel situated across his waist is the only thing that's keeping him from being completely naked right now.

Heaven help me.

He grabs a pair of boxer briefs out of the duffel bag he brought inside and slides them on under his towel. And I try to act like I don't know what's happening, even though I very much know exactly what's happening. I know every detail of what's happening.

I'm a sick, sick woman.

Mack shuts off the lights, leaving only the light from the television on inside the room, and climbs into bed beside me. "Whatcha watching?" he asks as he fluffs a pillow up behind his shoulders.

"Uh…" I pause, still completely clueless about what's on the television.

Thankfully, Mack is able to put two and two together. "*Friends* reruns," he says and flashes a grin at me. "Nice."

"Yeah," I respond through a weird laugh that doesn't sound like my own. "Gotta love Chandler Bing."

Mack looks over at me again, and the light of the television bounces off his handsome face. But when his eyes lock with mine, his expression turns from a relaxed smile to a furrowed brow. "You okay?"

"What?"

"Are you okay?" he asks again, and something inside me just…shifts.

It's like I can't keep pretending that he's not affecting me. I can't keep thinking about the other night and not want to experience it again.

Technically, you're still on vacation. Why not have a little fun before it officially comes to an end tomorrow?

"I want a repeat." The words fall from my lips, and I'm powerless to stop them.

His mouth turns down at the corners. "A repeat?"

I don't know why or how, but in that moment, with Mack only in a pair of boxer briefs, stretched out across the bed, it's like some sex-crazed demon possesses my body.

And this bitch is wild in ways that I never knew I could be. She wants to have sex with Mack Houston one last time before this spring break vacation ends, and she wants to do it right now.

"I want you to fuck me," I say, and for the first time in my life, I witness what a speechless Mack looks like.

"I-I…what?" He trips over his own words, and there's just something about the fact that I have that kind of power over him that emboldens me further.

I move my body over his, straddling his hips and pressing the throbbing spot between my thighs against his length. He's already rock hard, and it goes straight to my head.

"Please," I beg, and for some insane reason, I don't feel an ounce of shame in it. I just feel…greedy and horny and like this is exactly what I need to survive. I reach down and grab his hands, sliding them under my tank top until they're covering my breasts. "Please, Mack."

"Fuck, Katy," he whispers and expertly pinches at my nipples in a way that only makes me throb more. "What are you doing to me, babe?"

"I could ask you the same question," I whisper, and he moves his hands to my hips, gripping them tightly, and he grinds himself against me.

"Fuck," he mutters again through a raspy groan. "I love it when you're like this."

I lean down and take his mouth in a kiss. But it's not an easing into things kind of kiss. *No way.* I kiss him hard, tugging at his bottom lip with my teeth and sliding my tongue into his mouth to dance with his.

His breath becomes a moan, and I inhale it hungrily.

"Katy," he says against my lips, his hands gripping my ass. "I want you. Right now. But I don't have a condom. And...well...we didn't use one the other night, but..."

"I'm on the pill," I whisper back, still kissing him. "And I'm clean. Promise."

"So am I."

"Then, fuck me. Now."

He surprises the hell out of me by taking control. He flips me to my back and tugs my panties and sleep shorts down my legs with ravenous hands. His mouth is on my skin then, kissing and licking and sucking a path up my inner thighs, and he doesn't stop until he's right where I need him most.

His breath is warm against my aching skin, and my back arches when his tongue sneaks out and licks a path across my wet center.

I moan and grip at the sheets with my hands, and he doesn't let up. Instead, he licks and sucks at my clit, even sliding his tongue deep inside me.

His hands are all over my body as he eats at me. Grabbing at my hips and my breasts and my ass. He's everywhere, all at once, but it still doesn't feel like enough.

"Inside me," I pant. "I need you inside me."

"Ah, ah, babe. Not yet." He continues to eat at me. "Be a good girl and come on my tongue first, then I'll give you my cock."

His words push me right over the edge, and I come hard while he laps up my juices like I'm the most delicious thing he's ever tasted.

My orgasm feels like it twists through every part of my body, and I'm barely aware that he's flipping me over to my belly and adjusting me so I'm propped up on my elbows and knees.

He runs his big hands the length of my back, and he doesn't stop until they're firmly gripping my ass. "You look so good like this. Splayed out just for me."

And then he pushes my thighs farther apart, kneels behind me, and slowly slides his thick cock inside me.

Inch-by-inch, he fills me up, and with each thrust, he makes my breasts rub against the comforter in the most deliciously arousing way. It feels so erotic, so forbidden, that my pussy clenches tight around him.

"You're always such a good girl the way you take my big cock. Makes me so fucking proud of you," Mack says, and his voice is so raspy, so thick with need, it's nearly my undoing. "And you always feel so fucking good. So tight. So warm. So perfect. It's like your pussy was made just for me."

Holy hell.

He starts up a mind-blowing rhythm, driving his cock in and out of me with deep, heavy strokes. And I don't think I've ever felt anything better than this right now.

I don't know how long we stay like that, how long he fucks me until I can't see straight, but I know that when Mack buries himself to the hilt and comes, I go right over the edge once again.

So far, the man's batting a thousand.

Chapter
Twenty-Five

Sunday, March 27th

Mack

"I want you to fuck me," Katy begs from her normally prim-and-proper mouth.

My cock strains to get close to her, and I search for the neuron in my brain that knows how to follow her command. But my limbs won't move, and my tongue is tied, and Katy goes from looking hot and ready and wild to hurt in an instant.

I fight to get close to her, struggling to tell her I want her, but everything is rebelling against me.

Suddenly, I'm falling into a black hole with no end, and it's only when a gasp jolts me all the way awake that I realize I wasn't in the first place.

"Shit," I whisper, craning my neck to see Katy still sleeping in the hotel beside me, blissfully unaware of my fucked-up dream.

I scrub at my eyes and shake my head to clear it. This version of things might not have been reality, but last night was.

Katy begged me to fuck her, and I swear to God, it was the hottest thing I've ever heard in my life.

Truth be told, last night was even better than the first time. Katy was un-inhibited, and she didn't hold back at all. She gave in to the moment and let herself feel everything.

I don't know if I've ever seen her look so fucking beautiful.

The morning sun has started to rise, just barely giving sunlight through the hotel curtains, and it's like my internal clock made damn sure I woke up before Katy. A brief analysis of my little morning dream where the thing I wanted most was completely unattainable suggests I'm just a teensy bit gun-shy about her sneaking out on me again.

Her gorgeous body is still completely bare, only a sliver of the sheet and comforter covering her. Her long lashes fan across her cheeks, and her pouty lips are lax with sleep.

I reach out and gently slide a piece of her hair out of her face and tuck it behind her ear. The movement makes her startle slightly, enough that her eyes begin to open.

She blinks past the drowsiness until her still-sleepy gaze locks with mine.

"Morning," I greet softly and reach out again to rub my thumb down her cheek.

"Morning," she whispers back, and it's impossible to miss the hesitancy in her voice. It's like she's still recounting last night's events while her mind is trying to figure out how to react.

This is where waking up before her and getting my bearings gives me an advantage. The first time we had sex, she woke up before me, and it gave her too much time to overthink and freak out without giving me the benefit of a counter defense.

I refuse to let that happen again.

"We're going to have to get moving soon if we want to fit in another round of hot sex before we get on the road."

"Excuse me?" Her eyes go wide, but a laugh also jumps from her lungs.

"What? You don't want to have hot sex with me, Katy?" I tease and pull her body tight against mine. "Because I sure as hell feel like that would be the perfect start to our day. Very nutritional, in fact. And I know how much you love for things to be well-balanced."

She giggles, but when she feels that my cock is already hard against her hip, she surprises the hell out of me by reaching down and wrapping her hand around my length.

"Is this for me?" she asks, fluttering her eyelashes in this adorable fucking way.

"Happy birthday, babe."

"My birthday is over," she says, but she also starts to slowly stroke her hand up and down.

"Then, happy birthday to me."

"Your birthday isn't for another two months."

"You know when my birthday is?"

"Pretty sure everyone at Calhoun knows when your birthday is, Mack. You treat it like it's a national holiday."

"Well, the world is certainly lucky to have me." I grin at that, but I also moan when she starts to rub her index finger across the tip of my dick. "But do you know what I want right now?"

She tilts her head to the side. "What's that?"

I run my index finger across her forehead. "You."

"Really?" she asks, her face crooked up curiously. I nod, and she shrugs. "Well, I want to know what you taste like."

"I-is that right?" I question while practically choking on my own tongue.

She smirks. "I wonder how we'll decide who wins."

I put up both hands immediately, rolling onto my back in defeat. "Oh, you win. You win anytime you want."

She nods. Licks her lips. And proceeds to slide her body down mine until her mouth is mere inches away from my throbbing cock.

Fuck me.

"Who are you, and what have you done with Katy?" I say with a laugh, and she just grins up at me.

"Maybe you don't know me as well as you think you do."

Or maybe you're finally letting go and doing what you feel, I think to myself.

"I can be wild sometimes," she whispers and then licks her tongue down my length. "I can be a lot of things, actually."

I nod. Katy Dayton is *definitely* all the things and then some. I've always thought so—

She moves her lips and tongue down my length, sucking me toward the back of her throat, and it feels so fucking good that I can't think about anything else.

Katy Dayton is sucking my cock.

Holy fucking shit.

I've always had endurance in this arena, but there's just something about seeing her pretty little mouth wrapped around me that is almost too much to handle. It takes everything inside me not to come right on the spot.

Eventually, though, when I almost can't take it anymore, I lift her back up my body and adjust her thighs so they're straddling my hips.

"Ride me."

I don't have to tell her twice.

With her hands gripping my shoulders, she rides me like a pretty little rodeo queen, her hips gyrating and thrusting on top of me as she moves herself up and down my length. Her breasts bounce with each of her movements, and I reach up to grip them in my big hands.

A moan falls from her lips, and her eyes become hooded.

"That's a good girl," I tell her through a clenched jaw and grip her hips when her head falls back. "Don't stop, babe. Keep going. Make yourself come on my cock."

I'm hanging on by a thread at this point. My dick is pulsing so hard with the urge to come that I have to grit my teeth to keep myself contained.

And when I feel her squeeze me tight in rhythmic waves and her body vibrate with her climax, I come so hard I almost pass the fuck out.

"I normally start my day with coffee," Katy whispers in a breathless voice, her head resting on my chest and her body still entwined with mine. "But I guess this is a pretty good way to start the day too."

"You guess?" I question through a chuckle and tickle at her ribs.

She giggles and squirms with a shrug and a wink and, eventually, disentangles her body from mine and uses one of her crutches to get off the bed. "Come on, Mr. Dirty Talker. We better get on the road."

"Mr. Dirty Talker?" I question and lean up on my elbows.

"Bingo, buddy. It's your thing." She laughs again, but she also flashes a little wink at me. "But don't worry, I didn't mind."

Didn't mind? As in past tense?

Why don't I like the sound of that?

Chapter
Twenty-Six

Mack

"You really didn't have to drop me off first," Katy says as I pull the rental SUV to a stop in front of her apartment building. "I would've been fine taking the subway back after you returned the rental."

"It's no big thing. I'll drop this off at JFK, grab my paddleboard from baggage—assuming it made it—and take the subway home. I'll be at my apartment by eleven at the latest."

"Are you sure?" she questions, and I answer by cutting the engine, popping the trunk, and hopping out of the driver's side door.

Katy feels like she's putting me out by having me drop off the rental car by myself, but after twelve hours on the road, she really needs to get settled, rest her foot, and get ready for the day tomorrow without the extra activity.

I'm used to next to no sleep, and I've got the stark advantage of being fully ambulatory.

I make quick work of her luggage, and she meets me on the sidewalk, using one of her crutches to help keep the weight off her injured foot.

"Why do you keep using only one crutch? Pretty sure you're still supposed to be using two," I comment, and she shrugs me off.

"It's fine, Mack. I'm barely even putting weight on my foot."

She reaches for the handle of the bag in my hand, but I pull it back, adjust her purse on my shoulder, and take her loose crutch into my other hand. I head for the front door of her building, looking back to check on her, only to find she hasn't moved a step.

"What are you doing?" she asks, staring at the luggage in my arms.

"I'm helping you inside."

"I can get it," she snaps back. "Trust me, you've already done way too much for me."

"Woman, I swear, you need to just let people help you sometimes," I say through a teasing smile. "You're not putting me out. I want to help you, okay?"

"Fine," she grumbles. "But you're only helping me to the elevator."

I ignore that comment and jog ahead of her so I can hold open the door to her building. Thankfully, she doesn't hassle me about that and moves toward the elevator.

I follow her lead, and when the cart arrives, I don't hesitate to step right inside with her, all her belongings still in tow.

"*Mack,*" she chastises, and I just grin.

"You know, the more aggravation you give me about helping you, the more time I'm going to be parked illegally. It'd be a real bitch to have that rental get towed."

She huffs out a breath and hits the button to her floor.

Seven flights up, and the elevator dings its arrival. Katy hobbles out on one crutch, and I follow her the short walk to her apartment door.

She reaches into the purse that's hanging on my shoulder to get her keys and unlocks her door without much issue.

I step into her apartment but stop in the entryway and set down her belongings.

"So...uh...thank you," she says, turning back toward me and tossing her keys down onto the table by the door.

"You gotta stop thanking me," I tell her with a smile. "I'm always happy to help."

"So…" She pauses and glances down at the floor. "This was…an interesting vacation." Her eyes are on their way back to mine, I can tell, but they're moving really fucking slowly.

"Definitely unexpected."

"And tomorrow…we're back to work."

I smile down at her. "That we are."

"Back to being…*coworkers*."

I furrow my brow. "What are you trying to say?"

"I don't know." She shrugs. "I guess…I'm just saying that while what happened in Florida and stuff was fun, it can't happen again, you know? We work together."

Ah, I see. So, when she was speaking in the past tense at the hotel this morning, *this* is what she meant.

I almost want to laugh at how predictable this situation is. This *is* Katy Dayton we're talking about here. She overthinks and overanalyzes, and she likes to have everything planned out to a T.

She likes to know what to expect. In all situations.

And I am…well, the opposite of all those things.

"Don't you agree?" she asks, her gaze carefully searching mine. "This has to be just a fling, Mack. Just something fun that happened when we were on vacation."

I could give her a hard time here. Really press her for why she's going this route.

But that's not how you handle a woman like Katy.

You can't push her. You have to let her ease into shit. Otherwise, she'll run like she did after the first night we had sex. Hell, even that morning after the glorious bath time experience, she looked like a prisoner searching for an escape route until I managed to put her at ease by acting casual and not bringing it up.

So, I do exactly what I know I need to do right now to not push her over the edge. I just offer a smile and shrug. "Yeah, okay. Whatever you say, babe."

She starts to open her mouth, but I cut her off by leaning forward and pressing a chaste kiss to her lips. "Get some rest. I'll see you tomorrow...*coworker*."

But as I head out of her apartment and toward the elevator, I'm certain of one thing—*Katy Dayton is a hell of a lot more than a coworker, and I plan to keep it that way.*

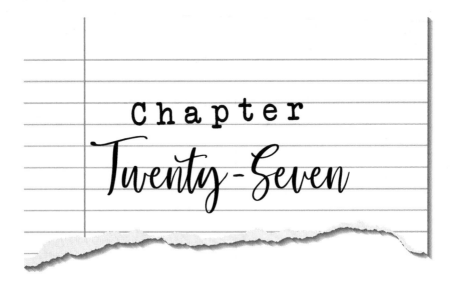

Chapter Twenty-Seven

Thursday, March 31st

Katy

"Bye, everyone. Make good choices and enjoy your day," I announce as my second period heads out of my classroom in a single-file line.

They wave and offer cute little smiles on their faces as they follow the lead of Alma's teaching assistant, Olivia, and I walk back to my desk—*without* crutches—until the last student has left my room. As of Tuesday afternoon, my stitches have been removed, and I've been cleared to be full-weight-bearing on my foot. *Thank everything.*

It's still a little tender, but being able to walk on it is a heck of a lot better than trying to navigate crutches in a building full of elementary students. Their awareness of their own two feet and propensity for clumsiness made Monday quite the crapshoot when I was still tottering around here on those stupid stilts.

Thursdays, my third period is normally my free period, and I use that time for catching up on emails and grading papers and prepping lesson plans. Sometimes, I'll even stroll over to the teachers' lounge to gab for a few minutes with Anna, but since I've been avoiding her scrutiny on the whole Mack situation, my classroom is the place to be. But today, I have a legitimate excuse—a parent-teacher meeting with Seth Brown's mom, Sammy Baker.

I love Seth. He's one of my most adorable students and has an incredibly bright mind. But he's also one of my most difficult and disruptive second graders.

The other children often follow his lead—or at the very least, fall into his distraction—and the last few days since we've come back from spring break have been some of the worst of the semester. I know everyone's still getting back into their routines, but the longer I let Seth go without consequence, the further he'll take his shenanigans.

The last thing I want is for any of my students to get behind or fall through the cracks—especially when they have as much potential as Seth Brown does.

While I wait for Sammy to arrive, I pull my cell phone out of the top drawer of my desk and check the screen for notifications. There's a message from a certain somebody who's been texting me ever since we returned from Destin on Sunday night, and I shouldn't be surprised—he's been full contact since the moment we got back. And yet, I still am.

Maybe it's unfair of me, given how great he was all week long in Florida, but when it comes to Mack Houston, I'm always waiting for the bottom to fall out.

Mack: Let's meet for dinner tonight so we can start preparing for Career Day. I know the perfect spot. 7:30 work for you?

I almost want to laugh at the abrupt change of tone in this message. I even find myself scrolling through all of his previous texts from this week to compare.

Mack: I'm new at this "we're just coworkers" business, so I just want to make sure I understand. Am I allowed to tell you that you're beautiful? Because you are. And when I think about dirty stuff, like how delicious your pussy tastes when you come on my tongue...should I keep that to myself?

That text came in on Sunday night, after he'd dropped me off at my apartment. And even though I blushed like a teenage schoolgirl and had some seriously dirty visuals pop up inside my mind, I chose not to engage.

Mack: You look stunning in pink, Ms. Dayton. Coworkers can say that, right?

That was Monday's gem that referred to the silk blouse I wore.

Mack: Happy Tuesday, to my beautiful coworker Katy Dayton. I hope you have a wonderful day, babe. And I hope I don't spend too much time thinking "repeats."

That message greeted me bright and early on Tuesday morning.

Mack: I know you're reading all these texts. And I'm just wondering when my beautiful, amazing, sexy coworker is finally going to respond… 😉

And that one came in last night. Obviously, I did *not* respond.

Although, I haven't completely ignored him. At school, I've been nice and friendly, but I've also had to flash more than a few pointed glares in his direction whenever his smiles have gotten a little too inappropriate or his hands have managed to discreetly brush against my arms or hip or back whenever we're in the same room together.

The man is persistent with a capital P.

But this sudden shift in tactics is quite amusing. He's seemingly dropped the flirtatious route and is trying to keep things all business by acting interested in doing planning for the Career Day Principal Dana assigned us to organize together.

I'm not sure I'm buying it. My gut tells me this is his way of trying to coax me into more *fun* with him.

The kind of fun that you're still fantasizing about…

No matter how tempting Mack Houston might be, I know I have to stay strong in my decision to keep whatever happened during spring break in the past.

Sure, our impromptu vacation definitely changed my view of him, but Mack isn't the kind of guy you date or get into a relationship with. He's the guy who has half the females in the city on speed-dial in his phone.

Still, given the nature of this message, and my ever-consistent call to professionalism, leaving him hanging on Career-Day-related planning isn't going to help either of us.

I glance at the clock and see that Sammy Baker is running a few minutes behind, and while I wait, I decide to finally give him one text message response.

Me: *I can't do dinner. How about a thirty-minute meeting in my classroom after school today?*

Frankly, I've already started the Career Day planning myself. The flyers I printed up this morning—that are currently sitting on my desk—are proof of that. But I won't snub Mack out of his role entirely. At least, not unless it's wholly necessary.

I half expect Mack to respond right away, no doubt with something witty, but to my surprise, no message comes in.

I wonder briefly if this is some other kind of tactic—reverse psychology of some sort—but I don't get the time to stew on it before Sammy Baker finally walks in, her eyes a little wide and her hair just slightly out of place.

"I am so sorry," she says by way of greeting as she hurries into my classroom and plops her purse down onto one of the empty student desks. "I had a late delivery at the restaurant."

"It's no problem." I stand, shake her hand, and then hold up a finger as I run to the closet in my room to grab an adult-size chair. She smiles gratefully as I carry it toward her. "I thought this might be a little more comfortable to sit in."

"Thank you. I really hope I haven't messed up your schedule by being ten minutes late."

Normally, I might feel a little annoyed at her tardiness, but as I've gotten to know this year, Sammy is an awesome, working, single mom of two boys who's just trying to juggle all the things.

I'm not in that place in my life right now—but I might be someday. And I hope people will have compassion for me.

"I have a free period right now, so there's nothing to apologize for."

"Okay, good," she says through an audible sigh of relief. "Now, I'm guessing you didn't want me to come in because Seth is your most well-behaved student, and you want to give him an award."

A laugh jumps from my throat. "No, not exactly."

Her face crumples in resignation. "What has he done this time?"

"Well, this week has been a little…hectic with Seth," I tell her honestly. "Monday, he brought in a whoopee cushion."

"Oh God," Sammy says on a sigh that almost makes me laugh.

"Tuesday, he…well, he farted the National Anthem while everyone else was trying to do their subtraction worksheet. And on Wednesday, he pretty impressively told a Nate Bargatze joke about his wife being the 'man of the house.'" I shrug. "I recognized it since I'd just watched that special. But as you might suspect, he was supposed to be doing math-related work at the board when he started his stand-up routine."

Her sigh is so loud it could be heard In China, and her cheeks are flushed a brilliant crimson.

"Ms. Baker, I really—" I start to continue, but she cuts me off.

"Please, call me Sammy. I mean, at this rate, we should basically be the best of friends with how many parent-teacher meetings you've had to schedule with me this year."

"Don't sweat this, Sammy. The purpose of this meeting isn't to chastise the job you're doing or even suggest that Seth is in some way 'bad.' I definitely don't think that, and I know you're a really good mom," I explain and mean every word. "My biggest priority is making sure he doesn't get behind. I know he's smart. And I know he is capable of a lot. But I'm struggling with consistently keeping him on track in the classroom. Some weeks, he does great. But other weeks, we're really focused on being disruptive."

"He is a smart kid. He really is." Her normally pretty smile turns sad. "But as you know, there have been a lot of changes in Seth's life in the last couple of years. I have a feeling his disruptive behavior coincides with phone calls with his father. Unfortunately, his dad isn't the most present at the current moment, only calls to check in occasionally, and I think Seth is having a hard time with that." She pauses for a second, adding, "Though, the Nate Bargatze thing is definitely on me. I just watched that special too."

"That makes sense," I agree, thankful for the insight. "And I'm really sorry you're going through all of this. Divorces are hard, and when you have kids involved, I can imagine they're even harder."

"Oh, you have no idea," she says through a snort. "Some days, I feel like a mom at the playground who is trying to keep her fifty-five kids from running out in the street. It's been rough, but I do feel like we're really finding our way in New York."

"I'm glad to hear that."

"You're too nice for your own good. I honestly feel like I'm indebted to you because of all the hassle my son has given you this year," she says through a soft sigh.

"You are not indebted to me," I refute. "This is part of being a teacher, Sammy."

She nods, but her mouth is still turned down at the corners.

"Plus, for as inconvenient as it is sometimes, Seth is immensely entertaining. I wouldn't be surprised if he finds a career in show business."

She starts to open her mouth, but when her eyes flit to a spot on my desk, she pauses for a long second before saying, "Not to change the subject entirely, but do you like that author?"

I glance down and see that she's spotted my current lunch reading material, *Accidental Attachment*. "Brooke Baker? Oh my goodness, I *love* her. She's one of my favorite authors. Have you ever read any of her stuff?"

"I've read all of her stuff. Funny thing..." Sammy smiles in a way that I can't quite discern. "I actually know her...pretty well."

I stare at her in disbelief. "You know Brooke Baker?"

"She's my sister."

"Are you serious?" My mouth parts in shock, and my palms just find their way to my desk with an audible slap. "Brooke Baker is your sister?"

"I know it's crazy, but yeah, she is."

"How cool is that!" I say, and a big smile consumes my face. "Well, you should tell her one of her biggest fans is Seth's teacher. I swear, The Shadow Brothers trilogy is the best thing I've ever read."

Sammy grins. "I'll definitely tell her."

My phone vibrates on the top of my desk with a text notification, and I almost ignore it until I see the word "emergency" in the message.

"I'm so sorry, but I need to check this really quick."

"Of course."

Mack: Big emergency related to Career Day. Can you meet me in the auditorium after school? 4:00 p.m.?

What the heck? Did something happen to the auditorium?

While I'd love to ask him a thousand questions about what is going on, I refuse to be rude and send a quick *Yes* back before setting my phone down on my desk again.

"So sorry about that, Sammy. Now, where were we…"

"What is this Career Day?" she asks and points to the stack of flyers on my desk.

"Oh, it's just a day for the students where we invite some people in the community to come in and talk about their careers. I'm in charge of planning it with another teacher."

"If you don't mind my asking, who's coming in to talk?"

I cringe and laugh at the same time. "I'm still working on that part."

"Well, I'd love to help you out with this," she says, and her mouth morphs into a proud smile. "I have two people who would be great for this."

"Really?"

She nods. "A writer and an anesthesiologist."

"Wait… Are you saying your sister would come in and speak?" I can hear my own volume rising exponentially.

"It's for sure happening on April twenty-second?" Sammy asks, pointing to the flyer.

I nod. *Not that Mack knows that's the date I chose yet.*

"I'll double-check the date with her, but I know she'd love to. Though, I should note that she has a medical condition that involves a service dog. That's not a problem, is it?"

Not only would I get to meet Brooke Baker, but I'd also have two speakers lined up? This is the best damn news I've heard all week.

"Of course not!" I'm nodding like I'm an actual bobblehead toy you get at a baseball game. "I honestly think that would be a great learning lesson for our students."

"And the anesthesiologist specializes in pediatrics. So, he's great with kids, and I'm sure he'll know just what to talk about to keep them entertained."

"That's perfect," I respond, and I find myself leaning forward to hug her. "Seriously. Thank you. You have no idea how much you're helping me out, Sammy."

She hugs me back, but she also laughs. "Oh, trust me, with all of the trouble Seth has caused this year, I am the one who owes you."

Chapter Twenty-Eight

Mack

The hallways are empty and quiet as I walk from the front office to the auditorium. It's a quarter till four, and pretty much everyone has left the building for the day. There may be a few cleaning staff left in the classrooms, but by and large, the school is abandoned.

A perfect situation, if you ask me, for my little "emergency meeting" with Katy.

I haven't had any one-on-one time with Katy since I dropped her off at her apartment on Sunday night, and despite my attempts to dispatch a meetup via text, I still don't know when this unfortunate stretch is going to come to a natural end.

So, instead, I'm ending it myself with a little white lie about an emergency with Career Day. As if that could even be a thing?

My in-person flirting has been more successful than my texts, as her scowls have been half-assed at best, and on more than a few occasions, I've even gotten secret smiles and laughs out of her.

It's a far cry from the way things used to be, back when she hated my fucking guts, and it's only emboldened me further in my pursuit of her.

I step through the doors of the auditorium and note there's only one light on beside the stage. The room looks massive when it's this dark, and my footsteps echo off the walls as I make my way up the tiled center aisle and find a seat near the front.

I pull my phone out of my back pocket to check the time. The screen show-cases 3:55 p.m., along with a few missed text notifications. With five min-utes to spare until Katy is supposed to meet me here, I decide to open up my inbox and tap the first unread message.

Kai: A good buddy of mine owns a motocross track about forty minutes out-side the city. Even has two bikes we can borrow. Want to put your money where your cocky mouth is, City Boy, and have a little race when I'm in New York at the end of April?

Yes, I'm still text buddies with Katy's dad. Two days ago, we had a banter-filled back-and-forth about motocross racing, and I might've told him I could take him.

Me: Bring it, Old Man. Name the time and place, and I'll be there.

Frankly, my motocross experience is minimal at best, and I'm ninety-nine percent sure Kai will kick my ass. The man is a retired professional, for fuck's sake.

But I've never been one to back down from a challenge.

Kai: HA. I knew I liked you, kid.

I tap the screen into the next missed message in my inbox and find a text from my big motherfucker of a cousin.

Thatch: Investor meeting. Next Friday at 4 p.m. My Manhattan office.

Me: I'll be there.

Thatch: Your ass better be. I've already had to reschedule this fucker twice.

Me: Technically, I was ready and able to be there for both meetings. The first time, you told me to stay in Florida because of something you read in a book. Monday, you didn't even give me a reason.

Thatch: If this is how you're going to try to schmooze the investors, things aren't going to end well.

Me: You're right. I appreciate the opportunity. It doesn't matter why the first two meetings didn't happen. I'll be at this one.

Thatch: Just FYI, if you try to cancel on me last minute, I'll sic my wife on you. I've never seen her actually castrate anyone, but she sure does love to talk about it.

Me: Like I said, I'LL BE THERE.

Thatch: Great. How did all that forced proximity go, by the way?

I start to text him back with as few details as possible, but the sounds of the auditorium doors swinging open and then swiftly slamming shut with a crashing *bang!* take priority.

Katy's walking down the aisle, squinting into the mostly dark room as she tries to locate me, and I shove my phone back into my pocket.

"Mack?" she whisper-yells. "Are you in here?"

"I am, but you don't need to whisper," I answer through a laugh and stand to my feet. "Pretty sure we're the only people left in the building."

It's hard to see in the shadows, but I swear she rolls her pretty little eyes as she closes the distance between us.

Thankfully, the light is better as she gets closer. I would have hated to have missed the way her toned legs look beneath the little floral dress that fits her body in the most delicious way. It's this soft lace material that only showcases a hint of her curves, but the memory of their every detail is vivid enough in my mind to paint a much more extensive picture.

Fuck, she's beautiful.

"What's the big emergency?" she asks impatiently, looking around like something's going to jump out and bite her.

"Follow me." I grab her hand and lead her up the stairs of the auditorium stage and don't stop walking until we're hidden behind the massive red velvet curtains located stage left.

"Mack, what are you doing? What's going on?"

I grin down at her. "Just making sure we have some privacy."

"Privacy?" She crosses her arms over her chest. "What are you talking about?"

"I know we're just coworkers now, but I feel compelled to tell you that I've missed you." I step a little closer, ensuring that our chests are mere inches from each other. "A fucking lot, actually."

"Huh?" Her nose scrunches up in the cutest way, and her blue eyes scrutinize mine. "What is happening right now?"

"Katy," I whisper her name and reach out to run my index finger down her cheek. I even stop to brush a piece of her hair behind her ear. "This just-coworkers thing doesn't feel right, you know?"

In a matter of seconds, I watch her face go from puzzled to outraged. "*This* is the emergency?"

I shrug. "My need to see you was urgent."

"You said it was about Career Day!"

"Did I?" I question and punctuate it with a dramatic tilt of my head. "Are you sure?"

"Mack Houston!" She smacks at my chest, but she doesn't step away from me. "Do not tell me you brought me here to flirt with me."

"What can I say, babe? Sometimes, desperate times call for desperate measures."

"Desperate?" she repeats through a snort. "What do you have to be desperate about?"

"Isn't it obvious?" I retort and take one step closer to her, this time making sure our chests are pressed against each other. Carefully, I wrap my arms around her waist and pull her even tighter to me.

She doesn't pull back. If anything, she willingly moves forward.

Hell yes.

"I haven't stopped thinking about you, Katy," I say as I just barely brush my lips against hers.

"Y-you haven't?" Her voice is a mere whisper. And her breasts move against my chest as I feel her take a big inhale of air and slowly let it escape her lungs.

I shake my head, and my lips brush hers again.

"You are so much trouble," she chastises, but I don't miss the way her gaze flits from my eyes to my mouth and back to my eyes again.

"You know, I could say the same thing about you," I counter. "I don't think it's healthy for me to be so obsessed with having more fun with you."

She searches my eyes, and I decide now is the time to go big or go home.

"Isn't it obvious, Katy Cat?" I brush my index finger down her cheek, savoring the soft skin beneath my fingertip. "You drive me fucking wild."

"I do?"

I nod again, and this time, I move both of my hands to her cheeks, cupping them tenderly as I lock our gazes together. "I'm going to kiss you now."

She stares back at me, her gaze flitting between my eyes and my mouth again, and I give her five seconds to decline before I make my next move.

Five.

Four.

Three.

Two.

One.

My lips to hers, I take her mouth in a gentle but carefully coaxing kiss. She tastes like the fruity gum I often smell her chewing in the teachers' lounge, and it feels like a victory that I can finally know the flavor is strawberry.

And when I feel a moan vibrate from her chest, all bets are off. My kiss turns hungry, and I slide my tongue past her lips to mingle with hers.

Her body melts against mine, and it's my undoing. I grip her ass in my hands, and I lift her up until she wraps her legs around my waist. Without thought, I move us toward the nearest wall and press her back to it.

Her lips turn demanding, kissing and sucking at my mouth in passionate waves. She grips my shoulders, and then she moves her hands to my hair, tugging at the strands in desperation.

And her hips, *her fucking hips*, they gyrate and wiggle against mine until my cock grows hard as stone beneath my khaki slacks.

I slide my hands under her dress and her panties to grip the bare flesh of her perfect ass, and that only makes her grind harder against me.

Our moans mingle and dance, and I don't know how long we stay like that, but fuck, I'm so close to losing it completely and tearing her panties off her body that I don't know how I manage to contain myself.

Beneath her straitlaced exterior, Katy Dayton is a sexpot. I've experienced this on more than a few occasions, and it's done nothing for my sanity. If anything, it's only made me want her more. Seeing her let herself go feels like a secret honor that I want to keep for myself.

There's only a sliver of rational thought left inside my head, and I know if I don't focus on it, try to hold on to it tightly, I could end up pushing us in a direction that could make Katy leave this auditorium with regret.

And regret is the last thing I want her to have when it comes to us.

I want her to crave. To need. To want.

"We have to stop, babe," I murmur against her mouth. "I don't want to stop. But we need to stop."

"I know," she says, but her lips and hips still move against me.

Fuck. Fuck. Fuck.

I am practically drunk off her, almost three sheets to the damn wind, but somehow, someway, I dig deep and find the last ounce of willpower in my body.

I coax her mouth to slow down, easing our kisses from greedy to soft. I slide my hands out from under her dress, and once I ease her to her feet, I find a way to gently disconnect us entirely.

Her hand goes to her lips, touching the swollen flesh with wide, surprised eyes. "What in the hell was that, Mack?"

"An emergency."

She scowls at me, but she also laughs. *Thank fuck.*

"Let me come over to your place tonight," I request. "So we can finish what we started."

She searches my eyes for a long moment and then surprises the hell out of me by saying, "No," with a mischievous smile on her face as she does it. It's a contradiction, but it feels like a good contradiction.

"No?"

"No," she repeats and stands on her tippy-toes to press a kiss to my mouth. "See you tomorrow, Mack," she says as she turns on her heel, even offering a little wave goodbye over her shoulder as she walks down the steps.

And just like that, she leaves me standing there on the auditorium stage with a hard cock and a dropped jaw.

That final move of hers feels like some kind of game she's playing with me, and hell if I'm not more than a little intrigued to see where the chips fall next.

Chapter
Twenty-Nine

Saturday, April 2nd

Katy

At a little before five in the evening, I step through the doors of The Diner. It's a hip little restaurant in SoHo where I'm meeting Anna for dinner.

Since I'm ten minutes early and I just got a text from her letting me know she's running ten minutes late—both typical for us—I grab a booth by the window and order an iced tea while I wait.

As I squeeze a lemon into my drink the friendly waiter by the name of Susie just brought, my phone pings with a text notification. I pull it out of my purse, half expecting it to be Anna saying she's running another five minutes late, but I'm pleasantly surprised when I see it's from my crazy father.

Daddio: Do you know where my insurance card is?

This, right here, is typical of my relationship with my parents. Even hundreds of miles away from them, I still have to help them keep their life organized.

Me: In the file cabinet in Mom's craft room.

Daddio: Are you sure? Mom said it wasn't in there.

Me: Who do you trust more to keep track of documents? Me or Mom?

Daddio: Good point. By the way, how's your foot, Katybug? Still connected, I hope.

Me: I went to the doctor Tuesday, had my stitches removed, and now, I no longer need crutches. Pretty much back to my normal activities.

Daddio: Glad to hear you're running full steam again. Did you still manage to enjoy the rest of your trip with Mack Attack?

Mack Attack? My dad is on a nickname basis with him?

Me: I didn't go on the trip with Mack, Dad. We just ended up being stuck in the same rental together.

Daddio: But you had fun?

Oh yeah, you definitely had some serious fun with Mack Attack *in Destin.*

And during your road trip back to New York.

And don't forget about yesterday afternoon in the auditorium…

I scoff at myself and send a response that doesn't involve revealing my sex life to my father.

Me: Yep. I had fun. Well, as much fun as you can have in Destin when you can't actually swim in the ocean.

Daddio: When we come into the city at the end of the month with Gran, I've made some motocross plans with Mack Attack. You wanna join in on the fun?

What?

Me: What do you mean, you made plans with Mack?

Daddio: We're gonna motocross it up, Katybug.

Have I entered an alternate universe? Not only are they nickname buddies, but my dad has plans with Mack, too?

Me: When did you and Mack even talk about this?

Daddio: A few days ago. I texted him.

"Sorry, I'm late," Anna's voice pulls my attention from my phone, and I look up to find her hurrying into the booth seat across from mine. "I'd love to say that it was because of traffic, but you know it's just who I am. I didn't even leave my apartment until I was supposed to be here."

I laugh at that and slide my phone back into my purse. "No worries. I already ordered you a Diet Coke."

"You're a goddess," she says and takes a sip of it.

A few moments later, our server Susie stops at our table, and we order our meals—a turkey club with fries for Anna and a grilled chicken sandwich with a salad for me.

As Susie heads for the kitchen, Anna places her elbows on the table and rests her chin on top of her hands as she fixes her gaze on my face. "Okay, Ms. Avoidance. It's time for you to spill the details about your Destin trip. Don't think I haven't noticed how you've been getting into school with just enough time to make it to your classroom and spending your free period doing *work,* of all things." She rolls her eyes.

"I haven't been avoiding you," I fib while offering my most innocent face.

"Uh-huh, *suuuure* you haven't," she derides. "Spill it, sister. What happened in Destin?"

"Spill what?" I volley back. "I went to Destin. Got stuck with Mack as a roomie. And ended up slicing my foot open on a seashell. That's it."

"Ah, ah, ah." She waves her index finger at me. "If that were the case, I'd have seen you more than once this week. Plus, I can tell by the way you look."

Instinctively, I paw at my hair, and she smiles. I scowl. "I don't look any different."

"Sure, you do. You have the sex glow." She waves her hand in front of my face theatrically like it's some kind of proof.

"What?" I exclaim on a laugh, my cheeks suddenly feeling *very* warm. I smack her hand away and sit back in my seat.

"Come on. Don't play coy. I'm not afraid to hear about a little anal play."

"Anna!"

"*Katy*," Anna challenges back. "Tell me now, or I'm going to keep shouting every embarrassing thing I can think of."

My eyes narrow, and she proves her muster immediately. "Double penetration! Nipple pinching! Puss—"

"Okay, okay, chill. I'll tell you."

I mean, this is my best friend, and the best friends' rulebook adamantly states that you tell each other everything. I might as well get it over with.

"Things *did* happen in Florida. And on the way back from Florida. And they might've happened two days ago in the auditorium, but that's *all* that will happen."

"Holy shit, I knew it!" She reaches out with her index finger and pokes me in the shoulder. "I knew all that sexual tension would eventually come to a climax!"

"What sexual tension?"

"The two of you have been in enemies-to-lovers foreplay since the moment you met," she answers. "Hell, it even made me horny sometimes just watching you guys interact in the teachers' lounge."

"You are off your rocker! I hated him."

She laughs like a damn hyena. "Well, you sure as hell don't hate him now. I'm just disappointed I wasn't there to see the shift of the tide."

"You're sad you weren't there to watch us have sex?"

"So, it was full-on sex then, huh?" She waggles her eyebrow. "How many times?"

"Too many times," I admit on a groan.

"And…" She pauses and leans closer to me, even dropping her voice to a whisper. "Were my predictions correct?"

Good with his mouth and a big cock.

All I can do is close my eyes and nod.

"Hell yes!" Anna whoops in delight. "I knew that man was good in bed. It's written all over his handsome face. Gah! I am so happy for you! After the bullshit Ricky put you through, you deserve to have some good sex."

"No need to get all crazy about it," I say by way of trying to calm her randy ass down. "It was just a vacation fling. It's not going to be a regular thing."

"Why the hell not?"

"Because this is Mack Houston we're talking about. For starters, he's my co-worker, and he's the last guy you get in a relationship with."

"Who said anything about commitment?" Anna retorts. "I'm not saying to marry the guy. I'm saying to have some damn fun."

"But I work with him…"

"Great. Easy access. Just don't bang him during school hours, and you're all set."

I cringe over the fact that I almost did that two days ago in the damn auditorium.

"Wait…" She pauses, narrowing her pretty brown eyes at me. "Don't tell me you actually did the dirty in—"

"No," I cut her off before she can say it out loud. "It did not get that far."

Anna squeals. "Holy hell, my best friend is finally letting her little floozy out. I flipping love it."

"You're a terrible influence, you know that? You shouldn't be condoning this type of behavior."

"But see, that's exactly why you're friends with me. You need me to encourage you to shake up your Marie Kondo life so you can give in to being a little bad sometimes."

I wish I could say that I think she's completely nuts, but there's a part of me that wonders if Anna is right. Would it really be wrong to have a little more fun with Mack?

Just a *little* more temporary fun?

When I look across the table, Anna is nodding at me. "Yes, Katy. Whatever you're thinking right now, *yes*."

"You don't even know what I'm thinking," I snap. "I could be plotting someone's murder, and you're just sitting there and encouraging it."

She eyes me knowingly. "The only murder you're plotting is of your vagina, and it'll be from Mack Houston's massively huge cock."

"Oh my God." I groan and drop my head into my hands. "I think I need to ignore you for a few minutes. You're making me question my sanity."

"Okay, that's perfect because I need to run to the bathroom before our food gets here," she says and reaches out to squeeze my shoulder. "You can ignore me while I'm gone."

When I glance up at her, she offers a wink at me before hopping up from the booth.

A moment later, she disappears inside the bathroom, and my phone pings with another notification. I check the screen to find another text from my dad.

But instead of opening it, I find myself scrolling to a different chat.

I even find myself typing out a message.

You can come over tonight.

And then, I hit send. God help me.

I'm sweaty, naked, and lying in my bed while my lungs try to regain their equilibrium. Every nerve ending in my body feels like it's been given a Valium.

"I think you riding me might be my favorite position, Katy Cat." Mack's raspy, slightly breathless voice fills my ears, and I turn on my side to take in the view of his gloriously naked body stretched out across my mattress.

Okay, so don't judge me, but I guess I'm taking Anna's advice.

And after two orgasms in the matter of an hour, that advice is looking to be pretty dang fantastic.

"Is it too early to suggest a round three?" he asks as he reaches out to brush a piece of my hair behind my ear.

"You're a lunatic." A snort escapes my nose. "And my body needs fluids and sustenance before I can do anything."

"Okay," he agrees with his signature sexy smile. "Food first, then sex."

I shove at his shoulder and start to hop off the bed, but he's too quick and yanks me back down into his arms.

"What the hell?" I say around a few giggles, but Mack just squeezes me tighter to his chest.

"You always feel so soft, Katy Cat. I couldn't resist."

"And I see you're still holding strong with that nickname, huh?"

"I can't help myself. You'll always be Katy Cat to me." His smile is big and brilliant, and for some crazy reason, it makes me smile too.

I almost tell him about the nickname my father uses for him, but for some reason, that conversation feels wrong to have at this moment while I'm still naked, in his arms, and fresh off orgasms from his skillful mouth and penis.

"You can't help yourself from doing a lot of things," I tease him instead.

"Like what?"

"Pretending there's a Career Day emergency to get me to the auditorium."

"It worked, though." He waggles his brows at me. "And your little game when you left the auditorium worked too."

"What little game?" I question, and my nose scrunches up of its own accord.

"You know the game, babe," he says and reaches up to tap the tip of my nose. "The sole purpose was to make me want more. And well, obviously, it worked."

So, I *might've* toyed with him a little before I left him standing on the auditorium stage. I don't know why I did it, but it just came naturally. It also felt like he deserved it for purposely getting me so riled up at school.

"I don't know what you're talking about," I lie and pointedly change the subject. "And speaking of Career Day, I am officially assigning you the task of getting another speaker for the event. It's April twenty-second, by the way."

"April twenty-second? Who decided that?"

"Me."

"I should've figured as much." He laughs. "But I guess I'll just be thankful you're actually letting me help you with something."

"Pretty sure Principal Dana didn't give me a choice."

"When it comes to you, I'll take whatever I can get." Mack presses a hard kiss to my mouth. "Now, how about some food?" he adds and smacks a playful hand to my ass. "I think a pizza delivery sounds like perfection."

"Only if it's Marco's."

"Babe, count me in. Marco's is my favorite."

"Mine too."

"See?" he retorts as I get off the bed and snag a T-shirt from my closet. "We have more in common than you think, Katy Cat."

Oh boy. I certainly hope that's not the case. *Yeah, but that's only because you might find yourself getting a little too attached to his version of fun.*

Chapter Thirty

Friday, April 8th

Mack

As I walk into the massive office building that my cousin runs his billion-dollar empire from, my phone vibrates in my back pocket. I pull it out to check the screen, but disappointment sets in when I see it's not who I was hoping it would be.

Sarah Starbucks 59th Street: Hey, stud. You got any plans tonight?

If I'm honest, I only sort of remember who this Sarah is—pretty sure I met her five or so months ago—and her message isn't the least bit enticing to me.

Now, if the sender were someone by the name of Katy Dayton, I'd be all fucking in.

Besides flirtatious text messages and stealing quick kisses in her empty classroom, I haven't had any alone time with her since last weekend at her apartment. I'm hoping desperately to remedy that soon.

I don't bother with a response to Sarah-whoever and slide my phone back into my pocket.

Aside from Katy, I don't want to talk to anyone right now.

I'm nervous as hell, wearing a suit I bought two nights ago, and so out of my element you can't even find me on the periodic table.

"Hi," I say to the security guard at the fancy marble reception desk. "I'm here for a four o'clock meeting with Thatcher Kelly."

He smiles benevolently—he obviously knows what a big deal my cousin is.

"Take this pass and head on up to the twenty-fourth floor. Kelly Financial will be down the hall to the left, and you can check in with the receptionist there. I'll let them know you're on your way up."

With a grateful nod, I head to the shiny, gold-doored elevators and take a quick ride up to the twenty-fourth floor.

Once I step out, I make my way down the marble hallway and walk through the see-through glass door that says **Kelly Financial** on the front in gold letters.

His assistant greets me with a smile. "Mack Houston?"

"That's me."

"They're already waiting for you in his office," she says and points toward the closed door behind her. "You can head on back."

"Thank you."

"It's about damn time!" Thatch booms before the door to his office can even shut behind me. Technically, I'm on time, but I know in these deals that on time is actually late, and I should have been here fifteen minutes ago.

"Sorry I'm running behind. I had dismissal duty, and one kid's dad was late picking him up," I apologize and note that all four men in the room, including Thatch, are dressed in suits and ties that I'm willing to bet they didn't buy off the rack like I did mine.

"No worries," Thatch dismisses before introducing me to the room. "Mack, this is Kline Brooks, the man who runs the TapNext empire. This is Wes Lancaster, the asshole owner of the Mavericks. And last and certainly least is Caplin Hawkins, corporate lawyer to the rich bastards of this city."

All three men roll their eyes at Thatch's colorful introductions, but I'm so in awe of the amount of business savvy in this room, I don't even laugh.

"Nice to meet you." I shake hands with all three men. "I really appreciate your taking this meeting with me."

"If I'm honest," Caplin chimes in with a smile, "we didn't have a choice."

I grin at that. "I have to admit, this might be the one time I'm thankful for my cousin's mulish tendencies."

Kline laughs, Wes nods, and Caplin crosses his arms over his chest.

Thatch just smiles like a man who loves any and all attention thrown his way. "I know how to get shit done. That's why you're all friends with me."

"Well, that, and the fact that we can't seem to get you to go away," Wes jabs and I laugh.

Just a few simple barbs and I'm already feeling more at ease. "Thatch, I have to say, I like your friends more than I like you already."

He chuckles at that in good humor, clapping a hand at my back, and gestures for us all to move to the large conference table inside his massive office. "Let's take a seat, boys, and dive into the meat and potatoes. I need to make sure I'm out of here by five or Cassie will guillotine my dick."

My cousin's wife is one awesome but crazy chick, so it's not a stretch to believe him.

I hurry up and grab the packets I created from my backpack and hand them out. "This is the actual business plan of how Music in Motion will be run, as well as the monthly and yearly goals, and how investments and future donations will be handled. Cash flow isn't exactly the goal here, as with other nonprofits, but the more strategic we are with the funding, the more music programs we'll be able to save."

"Are you sure you guys are related?" Wes questions. "I don't think I've ever seen Thatch this prepared for anything in his life."

Thatch scoffs. "Says the fucker who trusts me to invest his billions."

Kline and Cap are quiet, reading through the information in front of them meticulously. Nothing like casually looking on as a few billionaires evaluate your dream project.

Talk about a puckered asshole.

I've spent the last two years preparing for this, but knowing this is the moment—where it either fails or succeeds, period—makes it feel like I haven't prepared at all.

"This is really good," Kline remarks after some of the longest silent minutes of my life. "It's thought-out and reasonable in its goals. Not to mention, it's a noble cause. When are you hoping to get the foundation up and running?"

"Once I get the investments I need, I think I can get everything up and running within six to eight months."

"Ballsy timeline, but I like a man who knows how to step up to a challenge." Cap nods. "You're a music teacher, correct?"

"I am."

"Will you be quitting that job to run the foundation?"

"No." I shake my head adamantly. "That's the last thing I want to do. I know myself well enough to know I belong in the classroom, and someone else, with a whole lot more business experience, belongs at the helm of Music in Motion. It's my dream to be able to keep music alive, and in order to do that, I shouldn't be in charge," I admit with a laugh.

Wes searches my face but eventually nods. "I'm actually glad to hear that. A lot of people start foundations in the name of filling their own pockets."

"True that," Cap agrees.

"I'm not looking to fill my pockets. I don't want to draw a paycheck or anything. I have a passion for what I do for a living, for the support I got in pursuing music growing up, and this foundation is a way to make sure the kids in our city can experience the music education they deserve. I honestly think it's vital in childhood development and growth. Music allows kids to express themselves in ways that they normally can't. It also cultivates imagination and creativity."

Thatch smiles at me like a proud father. "You're a better man than most, Mackie. Proud of you. Proud of what you're trying to do here."

We chat for another ten or so minutes, each guy in the room asking me any questions that come to mind. And even though no one openly agrees to invest, I do feel like this meeting has things heading in the right direction.

The vibe is good. It's lighthearted. It's relaxed. And I sure as shit hope it means all four of their deep pockets will be opening for my foundation soon.

"Mack, do you mind making sure Gunnar gets home from school Monday?" Thatch asks as the conversation starts to drift away from Music in Motion. It's the perfect opening for my news, and I don't waste the opportunity.

"Yeah, of course," I agree. "It's the least I can do to repay you for agreeing to speak at Career Day on the twenty-second."

"Excuse me?"

"Did I forget to tell you?" I ask innocently. "Sorry about that."

Kline, Cap, and Wes all snicker to themselves, glancing between one another when Thatch's hackles rise.

"Cute plan, Mack, trying to trap me into something I didn't agree to, but it's not going to work."

"It's no big thing. You just come in and speak to the students about your career. They might ask some questions for a few minutes. I just thought you'd be a good addition to a crowd of people with regular jobs." I shrug. "I mean, you're a billionaire, you know?"

Thatch's eyes narrow. "Are you buttering me up?"

"It's ten minutes tops where you get to command a room, T. You won't even have to prepare, you know? You're such a natural leader."

Kline snorts as Cap whispers, "Oh, he's good."

"I really did mean to ask you about it. I've just been so busy lately with work and the foundation and helping you and Cass out with Gunnar whenever you ask me..."

"You're such an ass," Thatch comments through a groan.

Both Cap and Wes start laughing.

Kline smiles like the Cheshire cat.

"Wow. That's real good of you, Thatch," Cap comments with a big-ass smile. "Speaking at your son's school. What a great dad."

"Yeah," Thatch mutters. "Anything for the kids."

I grin. "My thoughts exactly."

"Speaking of your school, how's the pretty little math teacher you shacked up with for the week?" the dick fires back shamelessly.

"What pretty teacher?" Cap asks, his eyes far too intrigued.

"My man Mack here spent the whole week in Destin with his coworker Ms. Katy Dayton. My son Gunnar loves her, by the way. Says she's the prettiest teacher in the whole school."

"You guys dating?" Kline asks.

You fucking wish you were dating.

"No." I shake my head. "We ended up double-booking the same rental and had to stay there together for the week."

"No shit?" Wes questions on a laugh. "Talk about a coincidence."

"Right?" Thatch chimes in. "Some real forced-proximity kind of vibes, huh?"

"Man, I love a good forced-proximity romance," Cap agrees, and Wes's groan is loud enough to bounce off the walls of the office.

"Oh, here we go. Soon you dicks will be trying to start that fucking book club up again."

"Book club?" I question, and Wes shakes his head as if to say, *don't ask.*

"A while back, Cap made us start a romance book club to woo his now-wife," Kline explains on a sigh.

"Worst few months of my life," Wes adds.

"Tell me this, Mack…" Cap's attention moves back to me. "Did all this forced proximity include one bed?"

When I don't offer anything but a groan, it only urges them on further.

"Oh shit! I think there was one bed!" Thatch singsongs.

Cap nods excitedly. "Hell yeah, there was. Were you a naughty, naughty boy?"

"Just tell me one thing… Did you fall in love with her yet?" Thatch pries, and I roll my eyes. His light up with unbridled joy.

"You did, didn't you? Fuck me, they always fucking fall, fellas."

"Don't you need to head out, cuz? It's almost five. Surely you want to avoid the dick-lynching."

"I think someone's avoiding," Cap teases, and Thatch's laugh is practically a bellow.

"Fluffing right, son. Mack is definitely avoiding."

"Guys, leave him alone," Kline chimes in. And I almost think he has my back, but then he adds, "Just make sure you invite us to the wedding, okay?"

Fucking hell.

All four men erupt into more laughter, and everything inside me sizzles. Maybe if I were further along in my pursuit of Katy, this razzing wouldn't bother me so much, but I'll be damned if I can even pin the woman down, let alone be talking about a wedding. I run a frustrated hand through my hair.

"How did this meeting go from investing to weddings?" I question on an incredulous laugh.

"Welcome to the insanity," Wes answers with a knowing smile. "Shit always seems to go that way with this bunch. Just be happy you didn't have to suffer through their book club."

"Speaking of book club," Cap voices and puts both of his elbows on the table. "I think we're going to have to start up another one on behalf of me taking a dive into the published-author pool." He smiles proudly. "I'm in the process of publishing a children's book with Max Monroe."

"What the fluff?" Thatch questions, and his face is surprisingly irritated.

"You know Max Monroe, don't you?" Cap asks Thatch, his intention to piss him off unmistakable.

"Of course I fluffing know them. They wrote a book about me and Cass long before they wrote one about you, asshole."

"Technically speaking, I was the first," Kline chimes in, surprising me.

"What do you mean, you're publishing a children's book?" Thatch questions, barreling right over everyone else in the room.

"Just what it sounds like, dude. I'm speaking English," Cap retorts.

"T, you're awfully pissed over this. What's the deal?" Kline asks, his eyes curious as he glances back and forth between the two men.

Thatch doesn't hesitate to explain his anger. "Because no less than two weeks ago, I told this motherfluffer that I wanted to write a kids book with Philmore in it. Got the idea after I read *Accidental Attachment* and went down a Brooke Baker rabbit hole and found out she has a service dog."

"Who is Brooke Baker?" Even Wes is confused now, but he doesn't get any explanation because Cap's next response turns up the volume on Thatch's anger.

"What can I say, T?" Cap shrugs. "You saying you wanted to write a kids book made me think that I should publish that book I wrote for Ruby—with a few enhancements, of course."

"You're such a dick, dude!"

"How am I a dick? I already wrote my book. Why wouldn't I publish it?"

"So, uh, now is probably a good time to leave the room," Kline whispers toward me while Thatch and Cap rise from the table in some sort of standoff. "These two will be at for a while."

"I'm going to make sure my book gets published first, you fucker!" Thatch bellows.

"Ha! Challenge accepted, my man!" Cap cackles. "As you know mine is already written and has a release date scheduled!"

"What? When?"

"Like I'd tell you that!"

"Yeah, they'll definitely be at it for a while," Kline adds and nods toward the door. "Save yourself while you can."

"What about you guys?" I question, glancing between him and Wes.

"We gotta referee," he says through an audible sigh. "Make sure these two idiots don't try to kill each other over fucking children's books."

Wes overhears Kline's remark and grins at me. "We'll definitely be in touch soon, Mack," he says over the continued arguing between Thatch and Cap. "I can promise you that."

Kline nods in agreement, and I take them both at their word, grabbing my shit and heading out of Thatch's office before I end up in the crossfire.

By the time I'm in the elevator and heading toward the front lobby, I find myself laughing at the absurdity of this whole debacle.

Honestly, none of it should surprise me. Thatch is notorious for being a loose cannon, and even moonlights as a tattoo artist, which I'm pretty sure is a first in the world of billionaires.

Thoughts of my razzing fresh in my mind, I take out my phone and text my supposed—according to the moguls upstairs—future bride.

Me: I miss your sexy ass.

She sends me back an eye-roll emoji. I smile.

Me: When can I see you again?

Katy: I might be free tonight…

I know Katy Dayton well enough to know that she doesn't mince words. She can be stubborn, fierce, and tell it like it is when she wants to. And this coy and playful response of hers has me downright reeling in excitement.

Me: You might or you are?

Katy: It depends on what the plans are.

She doesn't give a shit what I have planned. I just have to set the hook.

Me: Come over to my place around 7. I'll feed you dinner and eat your perfect pussy.

Katy: I guess I can fit you in.

Fan-fucking-tastic.

I don't waste any time sending her my address.

This will be the first time I have Katy over to my place, and I'll be damned if it's going to be anything less than orgasmic.

Chapter
Thirty-One

Katy

I'm on the subway, and I don't have any underwear on.

This is certainly a first for me. It's not every day your beaver can feel the breeze of the tram doors opening and shutting.

I have never, in all my thirty years, done something as wanton and daring as this for a man.

My eyes move across the aisle, where a woman in a gray business pantsuit and white silk blouse sits. She's currently reading something on her phone, and I glance down at my current attire—a khaki trench coat and a pair of nude patent leather heels.

A little thrill runs through my chest when I think about what Mack will do when he realizes I've come over to his place with nothing on underneath my coat.

Oh boy.

Even though I've seen him every day at school, teased and flirted and secretly kissed him when no one was around, it's been a week since he came over to my apartment. Courtesy of him, that night *and* the next morning included a lot of sex and a lot of orgasms, but I've done nothing but crave them ever since.

I'd be a big fat liar if I said I wasn't ready for more of his brand of fun.

Or maybe it's our brand of fun?

Whatever it is, I guess I can officially say I've thrown caution to the wind and I'm just enjoying it. Temporarily, of course.

The subway jostles from side to side as it slows for its next stop, and my bare nipples rub against the material of my coat. The odd sensation causes the teeniest throb between my thighs, and the logical, not-impulsive-at-all side of myself is scandalized by my current behavior.

But I refuse to feel any shame for my actions.

I decided to give in to some fleeting fun with Mack, and that's exactly what I'm doing. There's nothing wrong with this…*right?*

Right.

Brakes squeak to a stop, and I gingerly stand up from my seat, making sure my coat keeps all my tits and bits covered as I walk off the tram and head up the subway steps. Thankfully, Mack's place is only a two-block walk from this stop.

A soft breeze threatens to open the bottom of my coat, and I quickly run my hands down the edges to prevent that from happening. It's one thing to be willing to be naked underneath your jacket in the name of turning a man on, but it's another thing to flash your hoohah at your fellow New Yorkers as you make your way to his place.

Not to mention the wrenches a public indecency charge would throw into my career as an elementary teacher.

Thankfully, no vag or nip slips occur, and I finish the short walk to Mack's building in under ten minutes. It's a nice complex with a doorman and a front desk, and once I check in with the security guard in the lobby and get the okay, I head to the elevators.

Just as I'm stepping into an available cart, my phone pings from my purse with a notification. Simultaneously, I pull it out and hit the button for Mack's floor.

A quick glance to the screen and I see a message from my best friend.

Anna: Want to go out tonight? Grab a drink? I feel like the fibers of my couch are fused to my ass at this point. I need to see the world again.

Me: I'd love to, but I have plans.

Anna: Staying in your apartment and grading papers doesn't count.

Me: Yes, it does. But tonight, I have actual plans. I'm not at home.

Anna: If you tell me you're with Mack, I will be so proud of you. Hell, I might have to send you a fucking Edible Arrangement or some shit to celebrate you finally realizing you should always take my advice.

An I-told-you-the-dick-was-big Edible Arrangement? That might be a new category for them.

The elevator dings its arrival to Mack's floor, and I send Anna one last text message, purposely choosing not to hold back the truth.

Me: Don't send the Edible Arrangement until tomorrow afternoon. I don't plan on going home tonight, and I don't want the fruit to go bad.

Anna: Oh my God. You two are officially enemies turned best-frenemies-that-are-fucking! It's a whole situationship. I LOVE EVERYTHING ABOUT IT.

As I step out of the elevator, my phone pings again, then two more times, but I shove it into my purse on a laugh. Clearly, Anna is losing her shit, but I have more important matters to attend to.

Hot sex with Mack for as long as the two of us can handle.

My heels tap against the hardwood floor in a sexy way I've only heard in movies, and I feel emboldened as I walk down the small hallway toward his apartment. I've never been this kind of woman—the kind of woman who takes what she wants and doesn't apologize for it—but maybe now I am.

I come to a stop in front of his door and give myself a moment to take a cleansing breath before I lift my hand to knock three times against the wood.

Mack opens it a few moments later, and he looks so damn sexy in his white

T-shirt, jeans, and bare feet that I put my money where my horny mouth is and unbutton my jacket before we even say hello.

"Hey, Katy Cat. I tried to text you—" he starts to greet, but I cut him off by flinging open my coat so he can see what lies beneath.

"I hope I'm not overdressed," I whisper in my most seductive voice, and his eyes go so wide, I fear they might pop right out of the sockets.

"Shit," he yelps, slamming the door closed behind him and shoving me back so he can step into the hallway with me. It's definitely not the reaction I expected, but I don't even have any time to think about it.

"Uncle Mackie, I want pizza!" a tiny child's voice calls through the now-closed door.

"Gracie, what have I told you about being so bossy?" a louder, more adult voice responds from somewhere in his apartment, and it's my turn for my eyes to bug out of my dang head.

"Who's there, Uncle Mackie?" The little voice is closer now.

"Shit," Mack says again, slamming my coat closed and wrapping his strong arms around me just as the door cracks open behind him.

"Y-you're not alone?" I stutter, his full-on bear hold so tight, I can't even move my arms.

He leans his head back ever so slightly to meet my eyes and whispers, "I tried to text you. I forgot I agreed to watch my niece tonight until they just showed up five minutes ago."

"Who is it, Uncle Mackie?" the little voice asks from right behind him now. Fairly certain I'm covered, I shove Mack back enough to get a look at the source—the absolute cutest little girl I've ever seen. She has brown pigtails and big brown eyes, and she's staring at us with the curiosity of that monkey George.

"Gracie, this is my friend Katy," Mack says without stepping fully out from in between us. "Can you go back into the living room for a second? We'll be in in just a minute."

"Why?"

Mack's chuckle vibrates through his chest. "Because I have to tell Katy a secret."

"But I love secrets!" Her eyes meet mine. "And I'm really good at keeping them, Katy! Promise!"

Oh my God.

"Gracie?" someone calls from behind her, but it's not long before they're standing right beside the little girl. "*Oh,*" the very pretty woman I'm deducing is Lizzy says after one look at my heels and coat. It's clichéd enough that she recognizes the situation for what it is. "Hello…"

Oh my God.

Mack's sister totally knows I'm naked right now, and we've never even met before.

Could this *be* any more awkward? Chandler Bing would think not.

My heart is pounding wildly in my chest right now, and I'm certain my cheeks are the shade of Taylor Swift's red lipstick.

"So…Katy…" Mack sighs in defeat. "This is my sister, Lizzy."

"Hi…" I pause, clear my throat, and try to ignore the fact that the only thing preventing his sister and niece from seeing my boobs and beaver is a very thin layer of untied material. "It's…uh…nice to meet you."

"And it's *really* nice to meet you." Her responding smile is nothing but tickled and amused. "I've never had the pleasure of meeting one of Mack's female friends. I have to say this has truly made my day."

"Lizzy," Mack interjects, his body still facing away from his sister and niece. "Do you mind taking Gracie into the living room for a moment?" His voice has taken on an edge of irritation. "I need to tell Katy something important."

"Oh, riiiight," Lizzy agrees with a smile. "Something important. Got it."

"But I want to know the secret!" Gracie objects, and Lizzy just moves her back into the apartment on a laugh.

"It's not the kind of secret kids can know, honey."

"Ugh! I want to be an adult so bad!"

Once the coast is clear, Mack steps away enough to give me free mobility, and I hurriedly button myself back up.

"So...this was unexpected," he says, and I let out a groan.

"Ya think?" I snap back.

"If I'd known what I was walking into, I probably wouldn't have left my apartment..." I pause and drop my voice to a harsh whisper. *"Without any freaking clothes on."*

He waggles his brows at me and leans forward to whisper, "But fuck do you look hot, babe."

"Shut up," I retort on a half laugh, half sigh. "Now is not the time."

He grins at me. "Would now be a good time for me to grab you some sweatpants and a sweatshirt?"

"I think now would be a good time for me to go home."

"What? Why?" he questions. "Stay. Hang out with me and Gracie tonight."

"Mack." I scowl at him. "You can't be serious? I'm lucky I didn't flash your family like some kind of deranged pervert, but your sister knows exactly what this getup means. She doesn't want some floozy staying here and watching her daughter with you."

"You're not a floozy or a deranged pervert. At least, not outside of the confines of the bed."

"You are seriously not right in the head."

"Just stay," he pleads and steps forward to place his hands on my face. "I've missed you, Katy. I want to see you."

Goodness, when he says it like that, it's almost too much for me to deny.

"But your niece is here..."

"She'd love for you to stay and hang with us tonight."

"*Mack.*"

"*Katy.*"

"Uncle Mackie!" Gracie yells at the top of her lungs through the door. "Will you ask Katy if I can know the secret, and *oh!* Ask her if she wants to eat pizza with us!"

"What do you say, Katy?" Mack eyes me with a big, knowing smile. "Are you really going to be able to let down that little girl in my apartment? I can tell she's already excited that you're here."

I huff out a sigh, knowing full well I can't *not* give in to his request. His niece Gracie's cute little face has made that impossible. "How do you always manage to get what you want?"

Mack's smile consumes his face as he leans forward to whisper into my ear. "If you're a good girl and eat all your dinner, I promise I'll make sure later tonight, after Gracie gets picked up, I'm going to be a good boy and eat all of my dessert."

Well, *hell.* That's quite the promise, huh?

Looks like you're going to get what you want too.

Mack's sweatshirt and sweatpants might dwarf my body, but they're certainly an improvement over what I showed up in ten minutes ago. Obviously, I still feel awkward and on edge—*I mean, who wouldn't?*—but I've made my bed, and now I'm going to woman up and lie in it.

Gracie comes running up to me and grabs my hand. "C'mon, Katy! We need to decide on pizza!"

Mack grins at me from across the kitchen, where he stands chatting with his sister Lizzy and a man I can only assume is Gracie's father.

Gracie guides me toward the group of adults and points to a takeout menu that sits on the kitchen island. "You gotta choose your toppings! I like peppers, but that doesn't mean you have to get 'em. Uncle Mackie doesn't care if we each get our own pizza!"

"You like *pepperoni*," Lizzy corrects with a soft smile. "Not peppers."

"That's what I said," Gracie counters with a tiny hand to her hip. This little girl can't be a day over five, but she has the attitude of a teenager. It's the cutest thing I've ever seen—especially since I can give her back to her parents if the 'tude gets too strong.

"I actually like that topping too," I tell her, and she does a little happy dance.

"Yay! We want pepperamies, Uncle Mackie!"

"You got it, Gracie Lou," he says with a smile and pointer finger to her nose. She pulls down a fist of victory and takes off for the living room. In her wake, Mack does the official introductions. "Katy, this is my brother-in-law Tom and my sister Lizzy, whom you…sort of already met."

Tom's smile is neutral and friendly, but Lizzy's smile is all-knowing. *Oh, we met each other, all right.*

"It's nice to meet you both." I try to smile rather than cringe. "I probably would've worn something else if I'd known I was meeting Mack's family. When he invited me over, I swear I had no idea you'd be here."

Lizzy grins at that.

Gracie, despite being in the living room, is a little girl who hears everything. "But I liked your dress!" she exclaims. "I think you should go put it back on, Katy!"

Hahahaha…help me.

"Uh…that's so sweet, Gracie," I manage to push out through a dry throat. "But I think these sweatpants are going to make it a lot easier to eat pizza and play some games tonight."

"Oh! Games are a good idea!" Gracie exclaims with a big ole grin. "I'm gonna find us some games to play right now!"

She takes off, running for a closet in Mack's living room where I assume cards or board games or a combination of both reside.

"So…how do you two know each other?" Lizzy asks, and Mack is the first to answer.

"We work together."

And for some reason, I can't resist chiming in with, "And I mostly tolerate him," with a teasing smile that makes Lizzy laugh.

"That sounds about right," she says and looks between the two of us. She starts to open her mouth, but Tom wraps his arm around her shoulders and pulls her close to his side.

"We better get going, Liz. Dinner and the opening speech start at eight."

"Yeah, Liz, you better get going," Mack agrees with a smirk. "Don't want to miss the big work dinner, you know?"

"We'll talk later, bro." She eyes him with a pointed stare that I don't quite understand but doesn't offer any explanation. "It was really nice meeting you, Katy," she says, meeting my eyes. "To be honest, I'm relieved there's an actual adult in my brother's apartment tonight."

"Hey, now!" Mack refutes, but I offer Lizzy a little wink.

"Don't worry. I'll keep him from getting any crazy ideas."

Both Tom and Lizzy laugh, and Mack responds by wrapping his arm around my back and discreetly pinching my ass.

He also leans down and whispers, "I might have to spank you later for that" into my ear while Tom and Lizzy tell Gracie goodbye.

It started with a reverse walk of shame, but maybe tonight won't end so badly after all?

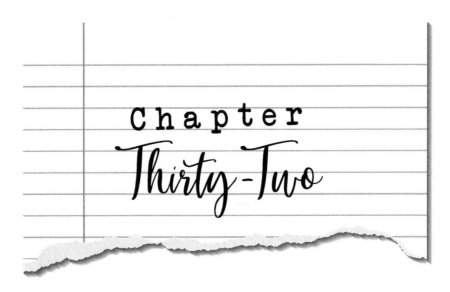

Chapter
Thirty-Two

Mack

"Do you know how to braid hair?" Gracie asks as she takes it upon herself to plop down into Katy's lap.

The sofa feels warm and comfortable after sitting on the floor for our fifth game of UNO—the last of a twenty-game stretch featuring every damn game in this apartment—my hamstrings are sore from our kitchen dance party, and my stomach gurgles from all the pizza and ice cream sundaes.

I don't know how Katy has the energy to entertain anything else at all from the cute little cheater, but somehow, she does.

"Do you want one braid or two braids?" Katy asks and gently tugs on the ends of Gracie's pigtails.

"I want one big braid," my niece demands. Katy doesn't waste any time undoing her pigtails and combing her fingers through her hair, regardless of Gracie's authoritarian-style dictation.

"Gracie, you're kind of bossy, you know that?" I tease, and she shrugs her tiny shoulders at me.

"My mom tells me that all the time, Uncle Mackie." Her meaning: *You're not telling me something new.*

"And you don't think you should try to be *less* bossy?"

"No," she refutes without a second thought in her five-year-old brain. "It helps me get what I want. I like that."

A child's reasoning, ladies and gentlemen. Simple, to the point, and one hundred percent focused on her self-interest.

"Hmmm," Katy hums and glances intentionally at me out of her periphery. "I know someone else who loves to always get what they want. Must be genetic."

"Pretty sure that mind-set has positive and very *pleasurable* effects on other people too," I respond discreetly, and Katy just snorts.

Gracie, on the other hand, is too single-minded on her own wants to think twice about our exchanged words.

"Put on *The Little Mermaid*, Uncle Mackie," Gracie bosses, obviously not learning any lessons here, while Katy continues to comb her fingers through her hair. "I want to watch it while Katy does my braid."

Trust me, I know that now would be a perfect time to not give in to my niece's every want and whim in the name of helping her become less overbearing, but I'm her uncle. My role isn't to teach lessons. My role is to have fun and spoil her, consequences and future struggles that Lizzy and Tom will have to deal with be damned.

"You like *The Little Mermaid*, Katy?" Gracie asks, while a yawn makes her mouth go wide.

"I love it. It was the first movie my dad took me to when I was your age."

"Really?" Gracie yawns again. "That's so cool."

"Gracie, honey, are you sure you're going to be able to stay awake?" I question, making her small features turn up in a glare.

"Uncle Mackie, I am not tired. I want to stay up until my mom and dad get here."

My niece says this every time I watch her, and every single time, she's out like a light before ten. And since Lizzy and Tom aren't supposed to pick her up until after eleven, I'm certain the little boss isn't going to last. The proof is in multiple pudding cups, but telling her so isn't worth the argument.

I grab the remote and find the already purchased *Little Mermaid* on Prime. Despite the $10.99 cost I had to endure, we've more than gotten our use out of it. I swear, over the past year of occasionally watching Gracie on the weekends, we've seen this movie no fewer than fifty times.

As the movie starts to play, Gracie settles in closer to Katy's lap while she expertly braids her hair. I can tell by the way my niece's eyes start to look heavy that we're barely going to get "Under The Sea" before she's conked out.

Even with the adorable braid complete, Gracie doesn't leave Katy's lap. Instead, she cuddles closer to her, gently wrapping her arms around Katy's shoulders.

The sight of them cuddled up together reminds me of why Katy is such a good teacher. She's patient and kind to her students. She's supportive and reassuring while still managing to get them to work hard.

And when it comes to spending time with my niece tonight, she's been nothing but sweet to her. She's played games and joked and given in to all of her bossy little whims, just like I do. An outsider would think Gracie is Katy's niece with how tender and caring she is with her.

One day, she's going to be an amazing mother.

I don't know why, but that thought makes my chest feel tight and my heart feel oversized.

Instantly, I get up from the couch and head into the kitchen to grab some water and stretch my legs. I even manage my short break without any questions because neither one of the girls notices my departure. Both of them are too focused on Ariel swimming on the screen.

By the time I get back, my head feels a little less fucked up, but the sight of Katy and Gracie now fast asleep on my couch—still cuddled up together—makes my chest feel all tight again.

This time, though, I can tell the tightness doesn't come with any pain.

At half past eleven, three knocks sound on my door, and I hop off the sofa on quick feet to answer it.

"Hey," I greet with a whisper when I open the door and find Tom and Lizzy on the other side.

I silently gesture them into the living room, where Katy and Gracie are still sound asleep on my sofa.

"Busy night?" Lizzy asks and I nod, smiling down at the cuddle buddies.

"Pizza, ice cream sundaes, a dance party, a marathon game night, and they could only make it through half of *The Little Mermaid*."

"Sounds like quite the party," Tom comments with a grin. "I bet Gracie was in seventh heaven."

"She definitely had a good time."

"Should I try to get the little monster to the car?" Tom asks, and Lizzy nods immediately.

"I'm so tired I can hardly see straight. I'm not used to nights out anymore." She cuts hard eyes to Tom. "You'd better not wake her up."

"No pressure or anything, huh?" Tom teases and slaps an affectionate hand to my back. "Thanks for watching her, Mack."

"Anytime, man."

He heads over to the couch and carefully lifts Gracie up into his arms. Katy doesn't startle at all, and my niece only lets out a little annoyed groan before settling her head against my brother-in-law's chest.

He doesn't waste any time heading out of my apartment, and I follow his lead to the front door. Lizzy, on the other hand, stops beside me as Tom walks toward the elevator, and I look down at her in confusion.

"I thought you were so tired you had cataracts or something?"

"Oh, I am. Though, I'm not sure my vision wasn't affected even before now." Her eyes twinkle with amusement. "*Katy.*" She says her name like it's explanation enough.

"What about Katy?"

"Oh, don't be so dense, baby bro!" she whisper-yells and smacks my arm. "I've never in my life seen you invite a woman to stay in the presence of your family, and I've certainly never seen you dip into dating at work. I mean, a woman you work with?" she muses. "That's hard to get away from."

"We're coworkers and friends." And we have *a lot* of fun together.

"Right," she retorts. "I often wear nothing but an overcoat to visit my friends."

"I don't know if you want me to get into all the dirty details, sis, but yes, we also have intercourse."

She searches my eyes closely. "I can't decide if you're purposely keeping the details from me or if you're being stupid and not letting yourself realize you're, like, *really* into her."

"I'm not denying that I like Katy. Of course I do," I answer. "She's awesome. I love hanging out with her."

"This is something else. She means something to you." She reaches up to pinch my cheeks like a mother hen. "Don't be stupid with her," she says.

I roll my eyes, and she smacks the back of my hand.

"I'm serious. Don't act like an idiot, okay? You'll regret it."

"What are you even saying right now?"

"I'm saying, she's special, Mack. So don't fuck it up."

First, the billionaires, and now, my sister? What's with all these people getting so bent out of shape over me and Katy?

"Jeez, Liz. How much alcohol did you drink tonight?"

She scoffs. "Whatever. Don't listen to me. But you're going to regret it when you let her get away and then realize you've been in love with her the whole time."

I scrub a hand down my face and exhale a deep breath. "I think you're putting the cart before the horse here, sis."

She pokes me in the chest. "I guess we'll see, won't we?" She pinches my cheeks again. "Love you, baby bro. Thanks for watching Gracie."

Before I can even respond, she's offering a wave goodbye over her shoulder and scooting out my door at lightning speed.

I walk back into my living room where Katy is still sound asleep on my couch, my giant sweats hanging comically off her tiny frame.

It's so fucking sexy.

Her hair fans out across the pillow and a soft little snore escapes her lungs every other breath, so I tuck in close to press my body to hers and fall fast asleep.

And my dreams? Well, their setting looks dangerously like a wedding.

Chapter Thirty-Three

Saturday, April 9th

Katy

Dressed in only Mack's oversized sweatshirt, I walk out of his bedroom and into the kitchen, where I find him standing behind the island, flipping pancakes in a skillet.

The sweatpants got too hot while I was sleeping, but I *would've* put on underwear, had I given myself the option last night.

"You're making breakfast?" I ask, and he looks up from the stove to meet my eyes.

His brilliant smile nearly knocks me on my ass. "If I'm not, this sure is an interesting way of doing something else." I smile. "Want some pancakes?"

"My stomach is already growling at the smell of them." I snort and hop onto one of the barstools on the opposite side of the island.

"Hold up," he says, and a little frown makes his mouth crease down at the corners. "What are you doing?"

"Sitting down?"

"Without coming over here and giving Big Mack a kiss first?" He shakes his head. "Get over here, Katy Cat. Give me some sugar."

"Oh my God, you're so cheesy."

"And *kiss-less*."

When I don't make a move to get up, he sets his spatula down and raises both of his hands in the air. "These pancakes are relying on you, babe. The longer you hold out on the kiss, the more likely they are to burn."

"You can't be serious," I huff.

"Only you can save them from their fiery torture."

On another huff, I slowly push myself off the barstool and walk over toward him on purposefully heavy feet. Once we're mere inches from each other, I stare up into his green eyes and purse my lips. "You don't think you're being a little dramatic here?"

"Nope." He shakes his head, and strands of his hair shuffle across his forehead. "Now, give me that sweetness," he adds and taps his cheek again.

I stand up on my tippy-toes to press my lips to his skin, but he surprises a squeal out of me when he wraps his arms around me and lifts me up and into his arms via his big, strong hands on my bare ass.

I don't even have the ability to complain because his mouth covers mine in a slow but sweet kiss.

"You're a little trickster," I say against his lips, and he squeezes my ass as his chuckle vibrates against my chest.

"And I have zero regrets about it," he says. "How else would I have proof that you're still panty-less?"

He kisses me again, deeper this time, and I fold like a deck of cards. My lips match his lips' movement, and my tongue eagerly entwines with his.

By the time he sets me down on the counter, a safe distance away from the hot stove, I'm a little out of breath and a lot horny.

"Thank you," he says and picks the spatula back up. "Now, I can finish these pancakes."

I roll my eyes at him, but I also giggle too.

"So…I guess I kind of passed out last night, huh?" I ask, once he manages to move three fully cooked pancakes over to a plate and adds more batter to the skillet.

"Both you and Gracie fell asleep on the couch halfway through the movie."

"I don't even remember going from the couch to your bed."

He winks at me. "That's because I carried you in."

"Seriously?" I question. "You should've just woken me up."

"And missed all that adorable snoring? Hell no."

"I don't snore," I retort, and he points the spatula at me.

"You snore, babe, but it's a cute snore. A soft little snore like a kitten."

"I swear, if you start calling me Katy Kitten, I'll slap you."

"Don't tempt me," he jokes, and I reach out with my hand to shove his bicep lightheartedly.

"What can I do to help you with breakfast?" I ask, choosing to change the subject before it leads to awful nicknames and violence.

"You can set the table," he instructs as he flips the pancakes over.

I hop down off the counter and start getting plates and forks and knives from the cabinet behind him.

"I have fresh fruit and orange juice in the fridge," he calls over his shoulder. "The maple syrup and butter are in there too."

I follow his instructions and set two plates down on the long wooden table that separates the kitchen and the living room. But when I start to head back into the kitchen to grab stuff from the fridge, I stop in my tracks.

Something about seeing Mack shirtless with pajama pants and bare feet makes my heart give one of its beats to my libido. His hair looks like he just barely ran his fingers through it, and his mouth is busy singing the same Donna Summer song he played for the dolphins in Destin.

He shakes his hips a little and winks at me as he sings the chorus, and good

God, I don't think I've ever met anyone as fun as Mack. He's confident and charming and playful, and it's impossible not to feel good when you're in his presence—now that I've stopped hating him, that is.

He can make even the simplest, most mundane tasks like making breakfast and setting the table entertaining, and I never know what's going to come out of his smart mouth.

Life with Mack would be the best time.

That thought pulls me up short, and I practically trip over my own two feet when I force myself to move back toward the fridge. My cheeks feel all heated and my pits feel all sweaty, and when I open the fridge door, I let myself stand inside the cool air for a good ten seconds to calm down.

What is going on with me?

I grab the bowl of fruit, the maple syrup, and the butter and shut the fridge, my strange hot flash thankfully starting to recede.

I'm half leaned over the table, arranging the items in the middle, when I feel Mack step behind me and grab my hips.

"Babe, you're killing me," he growls and pushes himself against my backside.

He's thick and hard beneath his flannel pants, and it urges a little moan to escape my lungs.

"This ass," he says in a husky tone as he grips my bare ass cheeks beneath the oversized sweatshirt. "Fuck, it's perfect."

"Mack," I say, but it turns into a moan when I feel him pull his cock out of his pants. "What about breakfast?"

"Fuck breakfast," he says and presses the tip of himself at my now-wet entrance. "I have to be inside you."

Oh *hell.*

My pussy throbs at his words. It's been too long since I've felt us connected.

Between one pounding heartbeat and the next, Mack thrusts his cock inside me with a deliciously deep stroke of his hips.

I feel so full that it makes my eyes water, my nipples harden, and my breaths come out in erratic pants.

"Goddamn," he whispers. "Why is it always so good with you? Always so fucking good."

I could ask him the exact same question, but when he starts up a greedy, powerful rhythm that has my tits bouncing and my head falling forward, all I can do is savor the feel of him inside me.

All I can do is enjoy the ride.

Chapter
Thirty-Four

Thursday, April 14th

Mack

Since I wasn't on cafeteria duty, I ran up the street to grab a sandwich from Marty's Deli. This place has been around for years, and their turkey Reuben never disappoints.

The lunchtime rush is in full swing, but their assembly-line style setup makes moving through it a breeze.

"You get the usual, Mack?" Sally, one of the owners, asks when I step in front of her cash register.

"Yep. Turkey Reuben. Extra turkey. Chips. And a double order of pickles."

"That'll be $12.52."

I hand her my credit card, she swipes it, and hands me the receipt. "Have a good one, Mack."

"You too, Sally."

I grab my bag, shuffle through the Marty's Deli crowd, and the bell jingles as I walk out the door. This spot is only half a block from Calhoun, which gives me just enough time to get back and into my classroom so I can enjoy my lunch.

But just as I'm heading in the doors of school, my phone vibrates several times in my back pocket. I pull it out to find two new messages from Lizzy and Thatch.

Ladies first, always, I click on my sister's text.

Lizzy: Your niece won't stop talking about how much fun she had with you and Katy. She's requesting another night with you two soon. PS: How is Ms. Katy?

Even though I know Gracie *did* have an awesome night with Katy and me last weekend, I'm not a moron. This message's sole purpose is to aid my sister's urge to pry into my business.

Her nosy ass can definitely wait on a response, I think to myself as I open Thatch's message next.

Thatch: How's Ms. Dayton? You still hot for teacher?

Why does it feel like everyone is texting me about Katy? It's not that I mind it, but it's just strange.

As I step into the teachers' lounge to grab some napkins, I decide to respond to Thatch's message. Though, I pointedly choose to ignore his questions about Katy.

Me: How are Kline, Wes, and Cap? All three still alive, I hope?

Thatch: Ha. Nice deflection, Mackie. And Kline and Wes are fine. Cap is a fucker. Still alive, but a fucker.

Me: I know our last investor meeting almost turned to bloodshed over your future career as a children's book author, but I'm hoping maybe we can give it another go and quite possibly get some official investors on board with the foundation…

Thatch: All right. I'll take the bait. I guess I have time to play Santa Claus right now and bring you a bag full of good news.

Me: Are you saying what I think you're saying?

Thatch: It's looking like your little music foundation is going to have four investors, bud.

Me: You better not be fucking with me right now.

Thatch: Would I fuck with you?

Me: Yes, you would, actually. And you do all the time.

Thatch: No lube or penetration needed. I can say with certainty that all four of us are in. I'll get a meeting scheduled to finalize the details soon.

Me: HOLY FUCKING SHIT. I CAN'T BELIEVE IT.

Thatch: Congrats, McMack. Looks like your dreams are coming true.

I'm pretty much pacing the teachers' lounge by the end of our conversation, and by the time I shove my phone into my pocket, I've completely forgotten about my lunch.

"You got the shits or something, Mack?"

I look across the room to find Alma sitting at one of the tables, staring at me.

"It always happens to me after I eat cottage cheese." She gives me more info than I certainly need. "I got some Imodium in my bag, if you need it.

"Thanks, but my stomach is good, Alma," I say through a laugh and run a hand through my hair. "I just got some news that's almost too good to be true."

She shrugs and takes a bite from her sandwich, unbothered.

I grab my bagged lunch and dart out of the lounge. There's only one place I want to go, and my feet don't have any problem taking me there.

"Mr. Houston, you wanna play dodgeball with us at recess?" Bobby, one of my favorite third-grade kids, shouts toward me, but all I can offer him is a high five and the bag of potato chips in my bag.

"Sorry, dude. Gotta take a raincheck," I call over my shoulder. "Next time, I'm in!"

"Thanks for the chips, Mr. H!"

I have similar interactions with a few more kids in my classes, though I don't have any chips to pass out to them, and by the time I make it to Katy's classroom, I'm practically out of breath from having to sprint through the halls to avoid any more distractions.

"Mack? You okay?" she asks when I barrel into her empty room and shut the door behind me.

"I finally did it!" I announce and walk toward her. I drop my deli bag on her desk and pull her up and out of her chair in two seconds flat. "I got my investors, Katy," I whisper into her ear as I hug her tightly to my chest.

"That's…uh…really great, but should I know what that means?"

I laugh and force myself to step away from her before someone in the hall sees us together. "I guess an explanation would help, huh?"

She holds two of her fingers close together. "Just a little bit."

"I've been working on this for two years, babe." I let out a deep exhale and try to slow my excited heart down. "For two years, I've been trying to start this music foundation, Music in Motion. And I finally have enough investors to really do it."

"Music foundation?" she asks and tilts her head to the side.

"Yeah. I mean, you know music education is always the first thing that goes when schools have to cut budgets," I start to explain, and she nods along in understanding. "My foundation will help avoid that. The goal is to make sure every student at every school in this city will get the music education they deserve, whether there's official funding or not."

"Seriously, Mack? I had no idea you've been working on something like this." Her eyes search mine, but it's not because she's trying to find something. It's because of something else I can't quite discern. "That is…such an incredibly honorable thing."

"It's the right thing," I voice, but she surprises the hell out of me by stepping forward and pressing a gentle kiss to my lips.

"I'm so proud of you. Congratulations," she says, and I can't do anything but smile down at her.

Feeling Katy's pride for me is almost as good as having Thatch tell me they're investing. My heart celebrates with erratic, raucous beats in my chest.

I don't know why, but she kisses me again. Even deeper this time. And I lose myself a little in the kiss, sliding my hands into her hair and hungrily swallowing down the little moan that escapes her lungs.

But just as I start to get into it, she jumps away from me like my mouth is the stove and she just got burned.

"*Shoot*…I think I got a little carried away," she says, shaking her head and holding her hand to her lips.

"It's safe to say I did too."

Katy rolls her eyes at herself, glancing over my shoulder and toward the door, undoubtedly trying to make sure no one is peeking inside the window.

"Is the coast clear?" I ask, and she nudges me with her hip as she walks back to her desk to sit down.

"Yes, it is. Smartass."

"Is now the wrong time to mention that I can't seem to find any of the three pairs of spare panties you've brought to my apartment?"

"Mack!" she whisper-yells, acting all scandalized even though we're still the only two people in her room. "Talking to me about my panties is completely off-limits at school."

"But anywhere else, I can?"

"You're a pain in my ass," she grumbles. "And stop hiding them, for Pete's sake. I'm running low on my supply."

"That's kind of the point," I taunt with a smile. I step toward her desk, lean down, and whisper into her ear, "So, whose place are we sleeping at tonight? Mine or yours?"

For the past four nights, she's been in my bed, and I'm hoping to keep that glorious streak going.

She glares at me, but she also says, "Mine, you idiot."

"Can't wait." I stand back up, victorious and completely aware that I need to quit while I'm ahead. "I'd tell you I'll bring your panties back, but I doubt I'll be able to find them, so…"

She snags a pencil from her desk and throws it at me. It hits me square in the chest just as I start cracking the hell up.

I hold up both hands in innocence as I move toward her desk again. "Just getting my lunch," I say as I make a show of carefully grabbing the bag into my hands.

"Goodbye, Mr. Houston," she says, her voice anything but firm. "I'll see you later."

"Trust me, Ms. Dayton, I can't wait."

I head out of her classroom and walk into my own, catching sight of my reflection in the window of my door. For far from the first time in the last month, Katy Dayton is the cause of an all-consuming smile.

Maybe, just maybe, it's time to consider the reason this woman continues to put it there.

Chapter
Thirty-Five

Friday, April 22nd

Katy

"Ah, fuck. I missed the show," Mack says as he steps into his bathroom to find me fully dressed in my favorite nude shift dress and finishing up my hair and makeup.

"There was no way I was going to let you make me late again today."

He's also fully dressed in his typical work attire—khaki slacks, red Chuck Taylors, and a white button-up shirt. He steps up to the sink and grabs his deodorant. "*Almost* late," he corrects. "Not late. And that happened over a week ago, babe. Surely I've regained your trust by now."

"Ha!" I scoff and reach for my hair spray. "You'll never have my trust when it comes to being on time."

"But I have your trust with other things?" he questions and raises one eyebrow as he runs a comb through his hair. "I think we both know you can always rely on me and my cock to make you come."

I almost say, *and your mouth too*, but I refuse to give his ego that much of a boost at six thirty in the morning.

"I thought you were going to the gym before work?"

"Your horny little ass kept me up until two last night. I needed my beauty sleep." He shrugs as he spritzes on some cologne. It makes the bathroom smell like the softest vanilla and cedar and him. It threatens to go to my head.

"*I* kept you up?" I nudge him with my hip. "Pretty sure you have that all wrong."

I fell asleep after we'd engaged in a little sexual fun, but *he's* the one who woke me up for round two via his mouth on my vahooch.

"Yes, you," he retorts and moves his body to stand directly behind me while I'm leaning forward to put on some lipstick. "If you wouldn't have been all naked in my bed, I would've gone to sleep. But nooo, you just had to have your perfect pussy out to tempt me."

"Your reasoning could be classified as gaslighting right now, Big Mack. Which is seriously deranged, considering the circumstances for this discussion."

He waggles his brows at me in the mirror as he slides his hands under my dress to grip my ass through my panties. "There's something about that nickname that I thoroughly enjoy," he says as he presses his half-hard cock against me. "It feels right, you know?"

"Oh my God!" I retort on a laugh and turn around to push him and his grabby hands away from me. "You need to leave this bathroom right now, mister. I refuse to let you pull me into your perverted sex web! I have a busy day today, and I am not going to be late."

"Fine." Mack just laughs it off and puts his hands behind his back like he's going to be handcuffed any minute. "I certainly don't want to be the reason you're late today, of all days."

I quirk a brow at him.

"Career Day," he answers my silent question, and I am shocked when I realize he's completely right.

Today is the big Career Day that I've been planning for the past several weeks. And I pretty much forgot about it.

How in the hell did that happen?

It probably has something to do with that sex web you mentioned.

"I guess I'll let you finish getting ready," he states and leans down to press a kiss to my lips. He doesn't care when he sees that some of my lipstick finds its way onto his face. He just smiles at the discovery in the mirror before swiping it off with his hand. "I'll make myself useful and prep us a quick to-go breakfast. Sound good?"

"Sounds like the first rational thing you've said all morning."

I can hear his responding chuckles down the hall as he heads out of the bathroom and into the main area of his apartment.

I spend the next ten minutes putting the finishing touches on my hair and applying some blush, eye shadow, and mascara. By the time I meet him in the kitchen, he's at the stove, moving slices of freshly cooked bacon onto a plate.

Normally, I'd be all in for some bacon, but when the smell hits my nostrils, it's entirely grosser than I'm expecting. It's potent and intense, and instantly, my stomach gives its best impression of Lurch from the Addams Family.

"A little bacon, egg, and cheese breakfast sandwich sound good to you?" Mack asks, but I'm already covering my mouth and nose with my hand and shaking my head.

"That bacon smells so bad. I think something is wrong with it."

"What?" His eyes go wide in outrage. "Are you kidding me? It smells fucking fantastic. And I just bought it two days ago."

"I don't know, Mack. It's literally making me want to puke."

"I take it you don't want the sandwich, then?" he questions, and I laugh.

"Definitely not." I head over to the pantry, and when I spot a box of granola bars, I snag one from it without a second thought. "I'll eat this instead."

"You sure you don't want me to make you something else?"

"No thank you." While pinching my nose, I close the distance between us and place a gentle kiss to his cheek. "I'll see you at school, okay?"

"What? You're leaving without me?"

"Uh, yeah." I walk around the island and grab my bags. "You know the routine. We can't show up together."

Of course, I only make it halfway to the door before Mack jogs up behind me and spins me around to face him. This is pretty much the drill every morning too.

"Just one more kiss before you go," he says and presses his mouth to mine. The kiss lingers a little longer than it probably should, and when he finally pulls away, I can see remnants of my lipstick on his lips again. "Have a good day at school today, honey," he adds with a sexy little smirk. "I can't wait until tonight."

"What's tonight exactly?"

"You're going to stay at my place again."

I snort. "I've been here the past three nights, Mack. I have to stay at my place."

"Okay, fine." He shrugs. "Then, I'll stay at your place."

"I'll think about it." I press one final kiss to his lips and make a point to wipe the lipstick off his mouth. "*Goodbye, Mack.*"

"Bye, Katy." He waggles his brows, and as I turn around to head for the door, he gives my butt a gentle slap.

I swear, that man, he's so much trouble.

Thing is, I'm beginning to think I'm made for trouble.

The auditorium is filling up by the second, and I'm basically running around like a lunatic trying to get all my ducks in a row for the Career Day presentations.

I've been here ever since I dropped my kids off at lunch around 11:30, and I still don't feel like I have it all together. But since it's now nearing 12:30, and soon, the event is supposed to start, I kick it into high gear.

Two of our speakers are already here, but I've yet to speak with either of them about what they're going to say and what types of questions we'll be taking from our students.

This has to be the least prepared you've ever been.

With students beginning to file into the auditorium in class-sized groups, I'm obviously going to have to save the berating myself for later. I hurriedly head over to where all three speakers stand.

This should be a total fangirl moment for me right now as I prepare myself to meet my favorite author Brooke Baker, but I'm too busy internally freaking out over my lack of organization to even give in to the urge to talk about her books and how much I love them.

She sits on the stage in one of the chairs I set up just minutes ago. I've seen her in interviews and on TV, but she's even more beautiful in person. She's also very pregnant—which I didn't know—and her German shepherd service dog lies by her feet. He's dressed in a Batman costume and has a vest on his back that's labeled with "Service Dog" and "Do not pet me, please."

"Hi, Brooke. I'm Katy Dayton. I want to thank you for coming in today to talk to our students," I greet and realize I'm talking *way* too fast. I'm also pretty sure I'm sweating at this point. My pits certainly feel a little damp beneath my dress. "Do you…" I pause and force myself to slow the heck down. "Have everything you need?"

"Hi, Katy. It's really nice to meet you," she says with a smile that doesn't seem too terrified by my most likely frazzled introduction. "This is my buddy, Benji," she adds, scratching her dog between the ears. "And I think I have everything? I hope?" Her laugh is downright adorable. "I've been told I'm just supposed to talk about my career as a writer and answer any questions the kids might have…?"

In this moment, it's more than apparent that I didn't do my job as the planner of this event. My speakers should feel confident in what's expected of them. Not completely uncertain about what the heck they're supposed to do.

Way to really drop the ball.

"Yes," I say and nod three times too many. "This is all very relaxed. No pressure. Any insight into your career and the path you took to get there will be beneficial for our students. Also, they'd probably love to hear about Benji's role in your life too."

Brooke smiles. "I can definitely do that."

"I really love your books, by the way," I blurt out, and she offers an awkward little giggle. "Sorry. You probably hear that all the time, but it's the truth. I'm a big fan of yours."

"Oh, I'll never get tired of hearing people tell me they like me," she comments with a wink. "It's appreciated, and any future compliments you have for me, do not hesitate to send them my way."

I can't do anything but smile at how relatable she is. It's wild. This woman is an incredibly successful writer, and yet, talking to her feels like talking to an old friend.

"Also, directions to the nearest bathroom would be nice to have too," she adds and rubs at her rounded belly. "Seven months pregnant and my bladder tends to give very little notice. I certainly don't want to scare the kids by peeing on the stage."

The mere sight of her pregnant belly and the affectionate way she rubs her hand over it gives me the strangest emotional jolt. It's like I could cry at how beautiful she looks right now. It's a wildly weird response to have toward someone I barely know, and I swallow past the ball in my throat to give her quick instructions on the closest bathroom.

Thankfully, there's one just off the left of the stage.

Once I feel like she's pretty well prepared, I move to my next speaker who sits beside Brooke, the anesthesiologist that Sammy Baker helped me book.

Though, she didn't tell me he's good-looking enough to play a hot doc on *Grey's Anatomy*. Honestly, if this were an auditorium full of high school kids, the girls would probably have a hell of a time concentrating on anything but him.

"Dr. Philips?" I ask and hold out my hand to shake his.

"That's me," he says with a smile. "But please, you can call me Noah."

"It's really nice to meet you, Noah. I'm Katy Dayton."

He nods. "Nice to meet you too, Katy."

"Thank you for coming in to talk to our students. Do you have any questions for me?"

"Nah." He shakes his head and offers a handsome but slightly self-deprecating smile. "I was listening in on your conversation with Brooke, so I think I'm good. No reason to make you give the speech twice."

Brooke cackles. "Oh, so I'm not the only one eavesdropping because my sister signed us up to do this but gave us very little information on what to do?" she teases.

"Definitely not," Noah responds with a big smile.

Instantly, I feel like the worst planner ever. "I'm really sorry you guys feel like you're being put on the spot without any instructions. That's probably my fault. I hope—"

"No," Brooke cuts me off with a reassuring smile. She reaches out to squeeze my hand gently. "You have to understand that Noah and I have jobs that keep us pretty introverted. I mean, I'm a writer—definitely a reclusive career—and all of Noah's patients can't speak because they're sedated. We're both happy to be here. Just feeling like fish out of water because it's not our normal gig to speak in front of a lot of people."

"Definitely happy to be here," Noah agrees. "And I feel like I know what to do, Katy. I'll talk about how I became a doctor and give the kids some funny stories on what it's like being an anesthesiologist."

"Are you guys sure you're good?"

"Positive," Noah states and Brooke nods.

"We got this so good, Katy, we're going to convince every one of these kids to become writers and doctors at the same time. Watch out, world, there's about to be an oversaturation in two career markets."

If there's one thing I'm certain of, it's that Brooke Baker is just as funny in person as her characters are in her books.

She offers me two thumbs up. "It's going to be great, Katy."

"Ms. Dayton?" someone calls from behind me, and I turn around to find Principal Dana standing stage right.

I excuse myself from Brooke and Noah and head over to her.

"You think you're ready to get this show on the road?" she asks, glancing at the watch on her wrist pointedly. "All the kids are here, and any minute, they're going to start getting antsy. We can only make them listen to the *Frozen* soundtrack over the speakers so many times, you know?"

"Yep. Yep. Yep." I nod and dart my eyes around the room in search of Mack. His speaker is the only speaker I haven't talked to yet. "I just need to find Mr. Houston, and we should be all set."

As if I conjured him to existence myself, I spot him walking in through the back auditorium doors.

"Looks like he's here," I announce and don't even bother saying anything else. Instead, I haul ass down the stairs and close the distance between us.

"Hey, where's your speaker?" I forgo a greeting and get right to the nuts and bolts of the matter.

"He's running just a few minutes late," he says, and when my eyes go wide, he quickly rests both hands on my shoulders. "It's all good," he reassures. "Your two speakers can start, and once he's here, I'll get him up on the stage without interruption."

"But is he prepared?" I ask, and Mack squeezes my shoulders.

"It's going to be fine, Katy. Promise. Thatcher Kelly knows how to work a crowd."

I can't refute that the man he's referring to is a larger-than-life kind of guy. He's the father of one of my students, Gunnar Kelly, and every time I've had a conversation with him, I've always walked away laughing or smiling.

"Okay," I agree, and my feet are already heading back toward the stage. Once I walk up the steps, I look toward Brooke and Noah.

"Looks like we're about to start. You guys ready?"

They both nod their agreement, and I step behind the stage to switch off the *Frozen* music and switch on the microphone.

A moment later, I'm standing at the podium and grabbing the attention of our students. "Good afternoon, everyone!"

"Good afternoon, Ms. Dayton," a lot of them respond back.

"Today, we have three amazing speakers who have taken time out of their busy schedules to come in and talk to you about their careers," I explain and feel like most of the kids are paying attention. "I expect that you'll all be quiet and well-behaved while they're speaking. And when it's time to take some questions, you need to raise your hand to be called on, okay?"

Most of the kids nod, and I move along to introducing our first speaker.

"I'd like to introduce you to Brooke Baker," I continue and look onto the stage where Brooke sits with her dog, Benji. "Brooke is a number one *New York Times* best-selling author. She is loved by many readers, and Netflix recently made a series based on her books. Please give her a round of applause as she comes up here."

The students clap their hands, and Brooke makes her way to the podium. I note that Benji follows her very closely, and once she's settled behind the podium, he lies right at her feet again.

"Good morning, students," Brooke greets into the microphone. Her voice is a little shaky, but her smile is downright lovable. "I am so excited to be here with you guys today."

"That's my aunt Brooke!" a child's voice yells from the crowd, and I look over to see that it's Seth Brown, and he's now standing up on his chair. "She's awesome!"

"Thanks, Seth," Brooke says into the microphone on a laugh.

"Seth Brown, you need to sit down," Principal Dana whisper-yells, already slowly moving toward him, but Seth just keeps talking.

"She writes books that have s-e-x in them! My mom says I can't read them, but I've heard my mom talking about them!"

"Oh God," Brooke mutters, but it's right into the microphone, and her words echo throughout the entire auditorium.

"I don't know much about s-e-x, but my aunt Brooke does because that's how you get a baby in your belly!"

"Seth Brown! Sit down!" Principal Dana is practically climbing over kids to reach him at this point.

"I think I need a minute," Brooke Baker announces into the mic, and when I look back at her, I see she's as pale as a ghost. Her dog Benji is on his feet, nudging her legs persistently with his snout, and Dr. Noah is already moving toward her with concern on his face.

"You okay, Brooke?" I hear him ask her, and all she can do is shake her head.

So slowly, it feels like I'm watching a car crash, I see Brooke's knees buckle, and Noah just barely reaches her before she faints. He catches her in his arms and gently lays her on her back, and I'm already running across the stage to help.

Principal Dana has finally reached Seth Brown, but it's too late. The damage is already done.

"Oh my God, she's died!" one student yells, and that makes the rest of them scream in horror.

The entire auditorium turns into complete chaos, and I'm left standing in the middle, powerless to stop it at all.

Chapter
Thirty-Six

Mack

"Call a doctor!" Bobby Carol yells at the top of his lungs.

"I think that man is a doctor!" another student shouts.

A bomb of fear and terror explodes in the auditorium as more kids start shouting from their seats, and teachers bounce around the room like pinballs trying to calm them down.

"Call 9-1-1!"

"Call my mom! I want to go home!"

"I'm so scared! I've never seen a dead woman before!"

"You think they're gonna make us look at the body?"

"I'll puke!"

"My mom loves to listen to smodcasts about people dying!"

See, the thing about having nearly three hundred elementary students in one room at the same time while something unexpected is happening is that there's almost nothing in the world that could or would calm them down.

Their minds are a filterless abyss of commentary and conclusions.

"Damn, cuz," Thatch says from right behind me, startling me completely.

Apparently, he's arrived just in time to see the shitshow. "I don't know if I can follow this act," he says. "I was just planning on talking about finances and shit."

"How about you do something to help? Go manage your kid and the ones around him," I order as I take off for Principal Dana and a group of other teachers to try to get a game plan.

I can't see much from my vantage point, but it looks like Brooke's eyes are opened again, and her service dog isn't as amped up as he was mere minutes ago.

"Everything is going to be fine," I announce to the rows of students closest to me. "Brooke Baker is going to be okay."

"She's not dead?!"

"No," I tell second grader Landon Evans and gesture for everyone to sit back in their seats. "She's okay, Landon."

"Well, then what happened?"

"Yeah, what happened?"

"And why is her dress all wet now? Did she pee her pants?" Mary Thomas, one of my second graders questions. "I stopped peeing my pants in preschool!"

When more kids start to chime in about peeing their pants, I realize that things have gotten really out of control. I look toward the stage again, where Brooke Baker is now sitting upright, but Katy looks…really bad. Her face is ashen, and in a split second, she goes from kneeling down toward Brooke to shooting up to standing and walking quickly toward the stage stairs.

I follow her the entire time, and when she reaches the auditorium floor, she's at a full run with one hand on her stomach and the other pumping wildly in an attempt to pick up the pace.

Instinctually, I take three steps in her direction, the urge to chase after her crashing over me like a wave. But an old memory of her scolding me for scapegoating all the responsibility in work assignments like this one makes me pause.

The queen of organization is no doubt mortified by the chaotic scene, and the best favor I can do for her—the best way to prove to her that she can always trust me, no matter what—is to deal with the fallout and make things right.

We both own the responsibility of this Career Day, and I'll be damned if I leave her hanging high and dry.

My eyes move back to Principal Dana and find that she, along with Anna and Barry, is still struggling to gain control of the students.

"The ambulance guys are here!" one little girl comments, and I look toward the stage to see that someone must've called 911, and three paramedics have arrived.

"Is Career Day over?" one boy shouts, and another follows with, "Maybe we're supposed to be watching those 911 guys do their job?"

I choose to ignore their comments and focus on restoring elementary law and order. When a damn ambulance has to arrive and students fear that someone has died, it's safe to say someone needs to take action and shut shit down.

With two fingers to my lips, I let out a loud whistle, and it's piercing enough that most of the students look in my direction. "Everyone needs to be quiet right now!" I announce. "I need each class to stand up from their seats and get in your single-file line immediately!"

Since Mr. Houston never shouts, it doesn't take a second try for them to follow orders. Kids hop up and over the seats—which Principal Dana eyes with disdain—but find their way into their lines quickly and even begin organizing themselves.

Teachers begin to lead their classes out of the auditorium, and finally, some tiny semblance of order starts to return.

I spot Thatch talking to his son Gunnar, who just so happens to be one of the kids in my current class. When Thatch meets my eyes, he gives me an incredulous smile.

"I guess I'm taking a rain check on my speech?"

"Looks that way."

"Maybe next time you can give me some notice."

"I've got you on my speed dial."

"My dad has my mom's tits on his—"

"Son," Thatch barks, his beefy hand finding Gunnar's shoulder and shaking. "I think the good students of Calhoun Elementary have been scarred enough for one day."

"He really is your mini me, huh?" I say with a soft laugh.

I start to guide my students to the main aisle in a single-file line, but Thatch calls out after me. "Hey. I almost forgot to ask. Can you make it to breakfast tomorrow morning?"

"Does this breakfast include three other men with deep pockets?" I ask, and he gives me a big old smirk.

Hell yes.

"I think I can make it."

"I'll text you the details," Thatch updates before giving Gunnar a hug goodbye and heading for the door.

The now-excited-for-another-investor-meeting part of me almost forgets about what just went down, but it only takes one glance to the stage to be starkly reminded. Katy is still MIA, and Brooke appears to be doing well but is still being assessed by the paramedics and the physician.

God, I hope Katy is okay.

Knowing her, she's probably blaming herself for what happened here, even though it was completely out of her control. If I didn't have a class of students to get out of the auditorium, I'd already be scavenging the halls and bathrooms for her.

All I can do is slide my phone out of my pocket and send her a quick, "Are you okay?" text message before returning my focus to my class.

I don't get a response, but I don't exactly expect one.

But you can bet your ass once I finish my dismissal duty, she is my number one priority.

Chapter
Thirty-Seven

Katy

You've failed your students and Brooke Baker and yourself.

Honestly, this might be the biggest catastrophe you've ever had as an educator.

I am in full-on beratement mode as I swiftly walk toward the nearest subway stop.

A deep sigh escapes my lungs, and it's loud enough to earn a few curious stares from my fellow pedestrians. All I can do is briefly shut my eyes and wonder how everything got so messed up.

I'm a do-er. An achiever. I'm organized and always stay on top of my responsibilities.

And I'm a planner. A thorough planner who doesn't leave anything up to chance.

Yet, today's big Career Day for the students that I was in charge of was an absolute disaster.

You only have yourself to blame.

I can't deny that. I didn't put in the time and effort to know each guest who was there to speak today. I should've been aware that Brooke Baker has a service dog because of a medical condition that makes her a risk for passing out. Not to mention, she's *very* pregnant. In her third trimester, actually.

I should've made sure she had a chair to sit down in while speaking. I should've had the school nurse available at the assembly in case anything went wrong.

Luckily, she's okay and nothing tragic happened, but I can't help but carry most of the weight of today's chaos on my shoulders. I mean, one of my speakers passed out on stage, peed herself, and had to be assessed by paramedics all because I took zero precautions to prevent it.

If that isn't an outright failure on my part, I don't know what is.

Not to mention, Career Day isn't the only thing I've been failing in lately. I have about two weeks' worth of papers to grade. My lesson plans are the opposite of planned. And my students have had the sad reality of a distracted teacher ever since I got back from Destin.

I'm dropping the ball. Actually, scratch that. I am the ball, and I am wrecking every-freaking-thing. Instead of being focused on my career and the well-being of my students, I've been too busy thinking about Mack and our hot sex.

Ever since my whirlwind vacation, I've been anything but myself.

Three days ago, I got frisky with him on school grounds, for goodness' sake! In a place of education, I did everything but climb up him like a flagpole and hump his brains out. Last week, I sent him dirty text messages while my students took a pop quiz!

I did everything but what a teacher should be doing.

Goodness, I knew this wasn't a good idea, engaging in some kind of fling with Mack Houston. I knew it, and yet, I willingly drove down his highway of fun at a hundred miles per hour, ignoring every giant red flag I sped by.

You certainly let your heart get a little involved, that's for dang sure.

What did I think was going to happen? That our sexy fling was going to turn serious, and we were going to fall in love and get married and have some kind of happily ever after?

Mack Houston isn't that kind of guy.

Is he fun and sexy and exciting? Yes, I can't deny that.

But he's not the guy you settle down with. He's the equivalent of playing with fire, and you get burned. Hell, the man has a history of notating women in his phone by the places he's met them because of how many women he's dated in the past.

I inhale a sharp breath through my nose. *Way to go, Katy.*

My phone pings as I'm heading down the stairs of the subway station, and I pull it out to check the screen.

Mack: I just got to your classroom after I finished dismissal duty, and you're already gone. Why'd you leave in such a rush today, babe? Are you okay?

This is the third text message he's sent me since the Career Day disaster went down, and I'm too busy licking my wounds of embarrassment to text him back.

Am I okay? No, I'm not okay.

I fear that my students are traumatized, and they all went home from school today thinking about anything but their future careers. At one point, half the students were convinced Brooke Baker died on the stage. Thankfully, she only passed out, and the paramedics even cleared her to go home.

Though, I didn't get to witness that because I was too busy puking up what little I ate today in the restroom. Truth be told, I'm still nauseated as hell from what I'm assuming is the utter failure I provided.

And Mack is right. I did leave school in a hurry. Once the bell rang and I successfully ensured all of my students were packed up and heading down the hallway, I grabbed my purse, locked up my classroom, and left before I had to talk to anyone.

I can only imagine the earful I'm going to get from Principal Dana Monday morning in our faculty meeting. She's most certainly going to ream my ass for what went down in the auditorium this afternoon.

Even though I don't have much to say to him right now, I know it'd be unfair to go radio silent. So, I type out a quick text message and hit send.

Me: I'm okay. Just not feeling so well. I'll call you later.

Before I can shove my phone back into my purse, it pings with another notification. I expect it to be Mack, but it's a reminder from Murck, a healthcare company I use for medication delivery.

Murck: Good news! Your next birth control shipment is on the way! Estimated delivery date is Wednesday, April 27th.

Out of pure habit, I open my calendar app to leave myself a reminder to look out for my shipment, but I pause when I see the familiar red devil emoji I use to mark the first day of my period, and I marked it over five weeks ago.

That has *to be wrong.*

I scroll through the dates, checking my previous periods from the past three months, and see that Aunt Flo is consistent in her every twenty-eight days schedule...except this time. I'm a week late.

Instantly, my stomach gives the familiar lurch of nausea it's been plaguing me with all day, and realization and outright panic set in.

No. *No way.* I take my pill every morning at nearly the same time. I *never* miss one. And I haven't been on any medication like antibiotics or anything else that would make it inactive—*oh shit. Did they give me antibiotics at the hospital?*

Oh my God. I was so out of it, I don't even remember. But my boobs certainly hurt and I'm nauseated and I puked today and I got emotional over the sight of Brooke Baker's hand on her pregnant belly and I've definitely been having unprotected sex with Mack Houston...

Oh my God.

I feel so scatterbrained and confused and shocked over the possibility of the P word that I almost miss hopping on my train when it arrives. Luckily, a lady with an oversized purse knocking into me on her way to the entrance doors snaps me out of my trance, and I manage to step on to the train just in time.

I slide into the seat on the subway car and tuck my purse into my lap like a little old lady in a bad neighborhood. I don't have anything of real value in there—I'm a teacher, for Pete's sake—but right now, with the way I'm feeling, this old knockoff Chanel is the blankie I never had as a kid.

I just…don't know how I could have spiraled so far—how I could have let Mack Houston bring me so far out of my normal routine—that there's an honest-to-goodness chance I'm…with child.

Holy cannoli. Just the thought in my head is almost enough to send me into an intense medical episode right here on this train car for the good people of New York to deal with.

And the more nauseated I continue to get, the more I start hoping this car I couldn't wait to get on will stop already. I have to get off this thing, breathe air, stare at the sun and burn my retinas…something, *anything.*

An older woman watches me unabashedly as the car jostles back and forth and the lights flicker on and off. Something snaps inside me, and I stare right back at her. With the way I'm feeling, it only takes three seconds for her to break the eye contact first.

I know I must look like I could do anything at any moment because, quite frankly, that's the way I feel. Like I could explode all over the place at any second with little to no help from an outside catalyst.

You're going to have to figure this out ASAP.

When the subway stops and the doors open, I jump up and exit with no regard for my fellow passengers or even the location of this stop. It's New York City, so I know there's bound to be a convenience or drug store within a block or two, no matter what, and I'm going to be in it toot sweet.

Truth be told, I never really understood that saying enough to use it, but I'm fifty percent sure I've just done it correctly.

My legs churn so hard up the stairs out of the subway station that a numbness tingles in my thighs. I frantically search the street around me for a Duane Reade or Walgreens, spinning in circles and jogging at the same time. People move out of my way—the same way I do when I'm confronted with an erratic stranger on the sidewalk—and I funnel through their holes without pause.

The beacon of Walgreens' red-and-white sign is dead ahead, and nothing can stop me from answering its call. I need to know if I'm pregnant, and I need to know it right now.

Of course, I don't realize until I'm stepping inside that I'm completely devoid of *nature's call*. How in the hell am I going to pee on a stick if I'm this dehydrated?

I pull out my phone as the welcome bing on the Walgreens door greets me, and I dart into the first aisle so I'm out of the way. Thanks to my millennial-dom, I have Google up and running quickly and my query typed in in no time.

What liquid makes you need to pee quickly?

The Goog is swift with its response, but the first two answers on the list are nothing but a disappointment.

1. **Alcohol.**

2. **Caffeine.**

I don't know crapola about pregnancy, but I'm pretty sure those are two of the main things you're supposed to avoid.

I'm one second short of a petulant foot stomp when the third option saves me.

3. **Acidic juice**

I can definitely slam down some orange juice, so I head for the cooler in the back corner in a rush to grab a half gallon.

A good two minutes later, I check out with a pregnancy test and the fluid I need to take one.

And I don't even bother leaving the establishment to do it. Instead, I head straight for the bathroom and guzzle down as much orange juice as I can on my way. To everyone around me, I probably look like I'm on the edge of a nervous breakdown, but I don't care.

I have to know if I really am pregnant.

By the time I lock myself in the stall, I've managed to drink so much orange juice my stomach hurts and peeing on the stick is a breeze. The instructions say to wait three minutes, but there's no way it's been that long, and it's already showcasing the word **pregnant** on the digital screen.

What the hell?

Clearly, it's malfunctioned. Pretty sure three seconds isn't enough time for this test to really know if I've got a baby growing inside my uterus.

I barely give myself time to wash my hands before I head back out of the bathroom and go straight for the feminine products aisle where two rows of pregnancy tests sit. I grab one at first, but figure four more is better, all made by different brands, just in case I get another one that's broken.

Once I have a receipt and I'm sixty dollars poorer, I head back to the bathroom, guzzling more orange juice as I go.

Locked in the stall again, I grab the first box out of my bag, rip it open like a heathen, and pee on it. When I realize that my bladder is still practically bursting full, I hold my stream briefly, tear open the other four boxes, and pee on those too.

I avert my eyes as I wipe and pull up my underwear, but once I'm dry and covered, I look down at the opened bag, where all five pregnancy tests sit.

The first two each showcase two bright pink lines.

And the other three say **Pregnant.**

Pregnant.

Pregnant.

Oh my God. I think I might be pregnant.

You think?

Six pregnancy tests say you are.

🍎

My shoulders sag as I hop off the subway when it reaches my stop, and those shoulders stay hunched forward as I trek the two blocks to my building.

I'm pregnant? It's all I can think. Over and over and over again. *I'm pregnant?*

I'M PREGNANT?

I have no idea what time it is or if the sidewalk is crowded or even what the weather is like right now. I can barely see anything but the way the word pregnant looked on four of those digital tests.

When I walk into my building, I can barely muster a smile for my doorman, Terry, and by the time I ride the elevator seven flights to my apartment, I feel like I'm carrying the weight of the universe on my back.

Though, that weight doesn't get any lighter when I step inside my apartment, and I'm faced with the sounds of rock music blaring from my Bluetooth speakers like someone has decided to throw a party without my presence.

What the…?

"Katy!" my dad bellows over the noise the instant the door clicks shut behind me. He's made himself comfortable on my sofa, and my mother sits on the ottoman across from him. They're both sharing a bag of Doritos that I guess they found in my pantry.

"Honey!" my mother greets, but it mostly just sounds like she's screaming at the top of her lungs so I can hear her over the music.

My nerves feel frazzled as it is, so I immediately head over to my speakers and turn the volume down.

"Ah, man!" my dad groans. "Zeppelin was just about to hit my favorite part in 'Stairway to Heaven'!"

"How did you guys get in here?"

"Your mom got a key made when you were in Savannah over Christmas."

This is the first time I've heard this. Normally, I'd focus on how that is not an appropriate thing to do behind my back, but with the way this day has already gone, I don't have the brainpower for scolding my parents.

"What are you doing here?"

"What do you mean?" my mom asks. "Sunday is the big day. Gran is going to spread Granddad's ashes on the Staten Island Ferry. Anniversary of the day they met and all." When I don't respond she adds, "Surely you didn't forget?"

Oh, but I did, because evidently, these days, I'm a woman who has spent the last several weeks practically shacking up with Mack Houston so much so that she just so happens to be pregnant by him and is, for all intents and purposes, a complete mess.

I ignore that thought like my life depends on it.

"Of course I didn't forget," I offer a little white lie. The last thing I want to do is let the current drama of my life bleed into what should be a very emotional and poignant weekend for my family. My gran's been planning this since two days after my granddad died eight months ago. I guess when you're married for sixty years, doing the right thing by your partner is important to you even after they're dead. "Where's Gran?"

"She's at the hotel taking a nap."

Both my mom and dad stand up to give me big hugs, and I try my darndest to look like a daughter who is happy to see them and make myself smile through my current mental discomfort.

"It's so good to see you, Katy," my mom whispers into my ear. "I've missed you."

"Missed you too, Mom."

"Glad to see ya, Katybug." My dad grips my shoulders in his big hands and playfully jostles me back and forth before giving me a kiss on the forehead.

"Ditto, Dad."

"So…" My dad pauses long enough to plop back down on my sofa and grab a few Doritos from the open bag. "What's new in your world, sweetheart?" he asks, popping one chip into his mouth.

And it's that very question that makes my entire world spin so hard, the nauseous feeling I've had all day becomes so strong that I can't ignore it.

"Not much," I say through gritted teeth. "Uh…just gonna run to the bathroom real quick. Be right back."

"Can we turn the music back on?"

"Yes!" I call over my shoulder as I jog into the bathroom connected to my bedroom.

And for the first time in my life, as I'm throwing up all that orange juice I made myself drink at Walgreens, I'm thankful that my dad likes to listen to his music at rock-concert-style levels.

Led Zeppelin drowns out my vomit noises, and I can hear my parents loudly laugh and chat with each other as I hurl a few more times.

By the time my puking session is finished, I wash my hands, brush my teeth, and stare at myself in the mirror, wondering how in the hell I'm going to spend a weekend with my parents and Gran after having six pregnancy tests tell me that I'm knocked up with Mack's baby.

Now might be a good time to find an OB doctor who has Saturday hours…

Chapter
Thirty-Eight

Saturday, April 23rd

Mack

I haven't heard from Katy since yesterday, and it was brief at that. Just a short text telling me she wasn't feeling well and that she'd call me later.

But the entire rest of the day and night passed without any call.

I'm trying not to worry, but I've already attempted to call her twice this morning without an answer.

I'm supposed to have another investors' meeting with Thatch and the guys this morning at George's for breakfast, but I can't bring myself to go there without at least stopping by Katy's place first. Her apartment isn't on the way to the Financial District, but I don't care. I even leave an extra hour early just to give myself enough time.

Her building is only one subway stop and a two-block walk away from my place, and I manage it at record-breaking speed.

When I walk into her building, I offer Terry, her doorman, a friendly wave. He's busy talking to a man with a Pomeranian on a leash, but since I've been here so many times in the past month we're on a first-name basis, he doesn't hesitate to give me an approving nod as I head to the elevators.

But just as I'm taking a step toward the next available cart as it opens its doors, the woman I came here for is walking off it.

"Katy?"

She stops on a dime, and her expression is a combination of outright surprise and kid-who-just-got-caught-with-their-hand-in-the-cookie-jar. And she's not put-together like she normally prefers when she goes out. Her hair is in a messy bun, and she's currently wearing sweatpants and a hooded jacket.

"Uh…hi," she says, but her voice matches her odd appearance. It's all off, and if I weren't standing right in front of her, I'd question if the words even came from her mouth. "What are you doing here?"

"I came to check on you."

"Oh."

Oh?

"You never called me yesterday, and I wanted to make sure you were okay," I explain and step closer to her. The instant the scent of her familiar flowery perfume hits my nose, the urge to hug her becomes too strong to resist. "Babe, I was worried about you," I whisper into her hair. "Are you okay?"

"I'm fine," she answers and ends the hug with a pointed step away from me. "I'm just…kind of in a rush right now."

"Are you going somewhere?"

"Yeah…" She pauses again and stares down at her sandal-covered feet. "I… uh…have somewhere I need to be."

"Where are you going?"

"I just have somewhere to be," she repeats her earlier explanation, which is no explanation at all.

"What's going on, Katy?"

"What do you mean?" she tosses back, her voice snapping softly like the edge of a barely jerked whip.

I don't know what's going on, but I certainly don't like the feeling I have standing here with a Katy I can't even recognize. She's flighty and nervous and makes me feel like she wants to be anywhere but next to me. Hell, back when she couldn't stand me, she'd at least make eye contact with me.

But right now, her eyes look every which way but at my face.

"Katy…you're acting strange."

"I'm *acting strange* because you stopped by unannounced, and I don't have time to sit here and chat because I have somewhere I need to be." She is on the defensive, which is crazy, because I didn't realize we were in a battle.

"Let me get this straight…you're pissed at me for stopping by?"

"A little heads-up would've been nice."

"I tried to call you three times this morning. You didn't answer," I counter. "Kinda hard to tell you anything when you don't pick up the phone."

"I was busy," she snaps, completely losing patience with me. "I don't know why you even care so much. It's not like we're in a relationship, Mack. I don't owe you any explanations."

It feels like her words dive-bomb straight to my chest and cut me wide open.

The way the word relationship falls from her tongue makes it feel like being in a relationship with me is the very last thing she'd ever want to do.

All I can do is laugh, but it's harsh and rough and not out of humor at all. "Well, sorry I was worried about you," I retort and run a frustrated hand through my hair. "I'll try to worry about someone else next time."

The instant the words leave my lips, I regret them.

But she doesn't give me any room to apologize.

"Okay, then," she mutters and is already stepping around me to head for the door.

"Katy, wait, I—"

"Whatever, Mack. See you around."

And just like that, she leaves me standing there by her elevators, and all I can do is watch her head out the door and hop into an awaiting cab.

What in the fuck is going on?

There are so many things wrong with this situation, I don't even know where to begin.

I don't know how long I stand there, trying to understand how my coming to check on her ended in some kind of fight, but eventually, I find the strength to head back out of her building and toward the Financial District for my breakfast meeting with a head full of confusion and a heart that feels sliced in two.

What a great fucking start to the day. I'd rather have eaten a live frog.

Chapter
Thirty-Nine

Katy

It's not every day you get to spend your Saturday morning spread-eagled and in stirrups, but it's also not every Friday that you get six positive pregnancy tests.

Dr. Wethers is a physician in Upper Manhattan who not only had Saturday hours but could fit me in on short notice. And by short notice, I mean I called her office first thing this morning and begged her receptionist to fit me in until she was nearly in tears. Poor Carla probably didn't feel like she had a choice, and for all I know, overbooked the good doctor on account of preventing me from having a breakdown on the phone.

Thankfully, Dr. Wethers hasn't made me feel like she's upset about my addition to her schedule. She's been friendly and informative, and once I peed in a cup and she asked me some questions, I was instructed by her nurse to get undressed so the doctor could perform an ultrasound.

Which leads me to my current situation—all spread out in this small exam room.

"Katy, since you're most likely very early along, I'm going to have to do a vaginal ultrasound," Dr. Wethers says as she puts on a pair of gloves. "This ultrasound will be able to give us a little more info and confirm if you're pregnant."

Confirm if I'm pregnant. Here goes nothing…

More like everything.

Unbidden, a visual of Mack's concerned face pops into my head. It's the look he had when I ran into him near my elevators this morning. He said he was worried about me since I never called him after I left school yesterday, and I was nothing short of a bitch to him.

It's like the stress and fear of this appointment and not knowing what is going on inside my uterus and not knowing if I'm about to be a mother to Mack's child turned me into someone I didn't even recognize.

A bubble of emotion lodges in my throat, and I have to strong-arm myself to stop thinking about that conversation or I just might start sobbing before the doctor even starts my ultrasound.

The nurse turns off the lights in the room and switches on a spotlight that's pointed right at where my legs are currently in stirrups and a paper sheet is spread over my thighs.

My body is shaking, and I try to control the tremors by gripping the edge of the table, but it does nothing to calm my anxiety. Needless to say, I'm nervous as hell as I lie here, waiting to find out if the rest of my life is about to change in the most drastic of ways.

"You're going to feel a little pressure as I insert the wand, but it shouldn't feel painful, okay?" Dr. Wethers updates, meeting my eyes briefly with a reassuring smile on her face.

I can't smile back, but I do manage an "Mm-hmm."

She covers the wand with something that looks like an oversized condom, squirts some kind of clear, gooey liquid on it, and the instant it touches my skin, my hips jolt.

And she's not wrong about the pressure, but it's tolerable as she puts the ultrasound device inside me.

"Here are your ovaries," she says, and my eyes stay fixated on the screen above her head. I can't make anything out; it's just a mishmash of black and white splotches to my untrained medical eyes.

"And here's your uterus." She continues describing what she's seeing, but still, she could be showing me the inside of my kitchen pipes and I wouldn't know the difference.

"And this little bean right here is your baby."

White noise pierces my ears and time stands still as I silently repeat the words *your baby* in my head.

My baby? My uterus really has a baby inside it?

I strain my eyes, trying to understand what I'm seeing, but all I can make out is the tiny bean shape she's pointing at.

"And that little flutter right there is your baby's heartbeat," she announces with a soft smile. The nurse steps forward to click something on the machine, and just like that, the sounds of a galloping horse echo inside the small exam room. "One-hundred-and-fifty beats per minute. Perfect."

That's my baby. Tears threaten to prick my eyes, but I blink past the emotion and stare at the little fluttering spot inside the tiny bean.

"Congratulations, Katy. I'd say you're about six weeks along."

"*Six* weeks?"

"This baby was probably conceived somewhere around March twenty-third, give or take two or three days," she adds, and *that's* when the dates make sense.

Holy moly. I might've gotten pregnant the first time I had sex with Mack?

What are the odds? I mean, I'm on freaking birth control!

Seeing as there's a whole-ass baby in your uterus, the odds appear pretty good.

Suddenly, my mouth feels like it has way too much saliva, and the urge to vomit is stronger than I'd like while I'm spread-eagled in stirrups with an ultrasound wand shoved up my hoohah.

I try to stay strong, breathing through the sensation that is my rumbling stomach, but when it feels like saliva floods my mouth, I know I don't have much more time.

"I think I'm going to be sick," is all I can manage, and luckily, the nurse moves quickly and holds a trash can near my face.

Seconds later, I'm puking in said trash can while the doctor finishes up my ultrasound.

Thankfully, the rest of my appointment is sped along—probably because they don't want me to cover their office with chunks of vomit—and I'm walking out the door with ultrasound photos of my baby in my hand and a packet labeled "Healthy Pregnancy" that the nurse instructed me to read before my next appointment in a month.

Yes, my next appointment for my pregnancy. Because I'm *pregnant*.

If I weren't so emotional, I'd probably laugh over the insanity that is my current situation, but all I can do is sob as I walk down the sidewalk toward the subway.

My reaction makes me feel super guilty. There's an innocent little baby growing inside me, and all I can do is cry about it.

Most women would feel happy and excited, but most women don't get pregnant by Mack Houston the first time they have sex with him. Most women are probably also in an actual relationship, but I don't even know what to call what Mack and I are doing.

Though, it probably doesn't matter anyway. After the way I treated him this morning when I was rushing to get to this last-minute appointment, I have a feeling Mack is going to run for the hills when I find the courage to tell him I'm preggo.

It's too bad you're in love with your baby daddy. That certainly doesn't make it any easier.

That thought only makes me cry harder.

"Just get home," I mutter to myself, completely ignoring if any of my fellow pedestrians can hear me, as I swipe a rough hand down my face. "Just pull it together and get home."

Oh yeah, get home, so you can start the big weekend with your parents and Gran and pretend like you're not a constantly nauseated pregnant woman who just found out she's knocked up by the man she l-o-v-e-s, even though she was a total bitch to him mere hours ago and has zero hopes that he's going to be on board with saying goodbye to his happy bachelor life to become a family of three.

Sweet Lucifer. I almost forgot about my family.

Dear Universe,

You really know how to stack a deck, don't you?

Chapter Forty

Mack

I'm pretty sure George's is a really nice restaurant, but fuck if I can even notice anything around me. I can barely register what Thatch and Kline and Wes and Cap are talking about as our server sets our plated orders in front of each of us as it is.

Hell, I don't even remember ordering the pancakes and sausage that now sit in front of me, but that's probably because all I can do is think how badly things went with Katy this morning.

She looked upset and scared, and all I did was add fuel to the flames.

You are going to have to get it together, man, my mind reminds me. *You're in the middle of an investors' meeting, for fuck's sake.*

"Well, boys, should we give him the good news?" Thatch questions around a bite of his omelet. "Or should we wait until after we eat?"

"Nah," Cap refutes, even flashing a wink my direction. "No need for suspense and drama. I think we should tell him now."

"All right, Mackie," Thatch announces as he pulls a check out of his jacket pocket and slides it to me. "You officially have four investors for your music foundation."

Kline, Wes, and Cap follow suit, all sliding over a check of their own. And from what I can tell, between the four of them, I have over a million dollars in investment money for Music in Motion.

I should be over the fucking moon. I should be jumping out of my seat and shouting my excitement from the rooftop of this restaurant. But it feels like a Herculean effort to even give them a smile when I say, "Thanks, guys. This means a lot."

For fuck's sake, dude, pull your head out of your ass and stop thinking about Katy!

"We're happy to be a part of this, man," Kline says.

"Congrats, Mack-a-lack!" Thatch exclaims and slaps a hand to my back. "You can finally fulfill your music foundation dreams."

"Wow," I say, clearing my throat to try to cut some of the roughness in it. "This means a lot. I really appreciate your support."

"Uh…" Thatch snorts and turns in his seat to look at me. "Don't take this the wrong way, Mackadamion nut, but I'd hate to see what you're like during the big O. We dudes just handed you a milly, and you look like my cat took a shit in your pocket."

"You have a cat?" Cap asks, to which Kline shakes his head and puts a finger to his mouth.

Shit.

"I am. Really." I try to force a little oomph in my voice, but I mostly just sound like a monotone puppet. "Very excited. Very thankful. I…well, I—"

Good grief, any second, they're going to be taking their checks back, bro.

"Hold on…" Cap pauses, and I can feel his scrutinizing gaze on me. "Holy shit, guys. He's got that look."

"What look?" Wes asks.

"The *look*," Cap repeats. "The look we've all had before. The look that can only involve one thing."

"Oh shit!" Thatch bellows. "He does have the look. I can't believe I missed it."

"I don't have a look," I insist, shaking my head pathetically. "There's no look."

"Yeah, you do, Mackie," Thatch counters. "You have the look of a man who is so far deep in love with a woman, he can't tell the difference between his mouth and his asshole."

"That's an incredibly specific look," I retort, even though a big part of me is shocked at how close to the truth they've gotten.

"I bet it's that teacher he went on spring break with," Cap suggests, and I kind of want to pick up one of the sausages on my plate and throw it at his big fucking head.

"Oh, for sure, but I think it's more than that," Kline adds. "I think something has happened, and he doesn't quite know how to solve it."

Kline's words draw everyone's attention back to my face.

"You're right, you wise motherfluffer," Thatch says, and immediately, he pats a big hand to my back again. "C'mon, Mack, you're in the circle of trust, bro. You can tell us anything, and we won't judge."

"Normally, I don't condone Thatch's bullshit, but he's right, Mack," Wes concurs. "You gotta tell us what's up. Group support is the only way to fix whatever problem you've created. Trust me."

I look around the table, noting that everyone's attention is still on me. But more than that, these four men don't look like they want to razz me or give me any crap. They mostly just look genuine in their offer to give me some advice.

And boy do you need some fucking advice right now.

"I think I might be in love with Katy, and I feel like I've managed to fuck it up somehow." The words are out of my mouth before I can stop them. It's like these bastards have hypnotized me or some shit.

I wait for their outlandish reaction, preparing myself for them to shout things like "I told you so" and "If you'd have listened to us…" But it never comes.

"I know you won't believe me right now, but I'm telling you, dude. This *always* happens."

Kline and Wes nod in agreement with Thatch, their faces serious.

"Have no fear," Cap states. "We got your back, bro."

"First things first," Thatch announces and puts two elbows to the table. "You're going to have to lay out all the facts. All the details on your current situation and how it came to be. We're certified deep divers, but even we can't make it back up from depth without the proper equipment."

Cap, Wes, and Kline all nod in agreement.

"What?" I drop my head into my hands. "Truth be told, guys, I'm so fucked in the head, I don't even think I understand your question."

"This might be worse than I thought," Kline muses, taking out his phone to text his wife. "I'll text Georgia and tell her I'm going to be a little while."

Before I know it, all three other men are following suit.

And just like that, this investor meeting turns into me talking about Katy Dayton. I tell them everything.

How she used to hate me, our Destin trip and how she had to go to the ER, how we ended up having sex, and how I gave up my flight to drive her back to New York.

I tell them how we started a little fling once we got back from Florida, but how it's turned into an almost nightly thing of us hanging out and having sleepovers, and how she's the most beautiful, interesting, and amazing woman I've ever known. Our night with Gracie and the Career Day disaster. And how today, I ran over to her place to see if she was okay and she was acting weird, and somehow, everything went to shit.

Most importantly, I tell them that I'm ass over head in love with the woman, and there's nothing more I want in the world than to spend the rest of my life with her.

By the time I'm done, all four men are staring at me with stupid grins on their faces.

"What?" I ask, and Thatch is the first to comment.

"The story of love never gets old."

I don't have a response to that, and Cap is the next to speak.

"And the male leads never get any quicker on the uptake either. Seems like you've been in love with her for a really long time, my guy."

"Just so you know, now isn't the time to avoid it," Kline says. "Now is the time to face it head on."

I look at him, and then I look down at my hands. I think about Katy and everything we've been through and how I've never felt this way about anyone. How I feel like I'd walk through fucking fire just to make her mine.

"I love her," I admit out loud again. "I'm madly in love with her, and I'll do anything to make her mine."

"Bingo bango!" Thatch exclaims. "You need a plan, dude. A big romantic gesture kind of plan."

"What do you mean?"

"I mean, you need to show Katy that you're not the impulsive, inconsiderate, anticommitment bastard she once thought you were," he explains. "You need to show her that, when it comes to her, you're all-motherfluffing-in. A man who wants to commit to the woman he loves."

"Hell yeah, you do!" Cap exclaims. "Otherwise, Ms. Katy will continue to think you just want some kind of meaningless fling with her. Talk is cheap. You need to show her that she's it for you. She's the one. She's your lady, and you are not only in love with her, but you see a future with her."

I see a future with her, all right. This woman has become *the one*. The end game. The *everything*.

I don't want to wake up without her lying beside me. And don't want to go to bed without kissing her good night. I don't want a future without her in it.

When I look around the table, all four men are looking at me like I've just told them I can make them one trillion dollars in the next five minutes.

"You're on the right path," Kline states. "It's written all over your face."

"Fluffing right, Special K," Thatch agrees. "You just need to take one more giant leap forward and figure out how you're going to show her how you feel."

In an instant, like a crashing waterfall, it all comes together in my mind.

And there's only one man who can help me pull it off.

Immediately, I pull my phone out of my pocket and type out a text—*I need your help with something REALLY important. The most important thing of my life, actually.*

An answer comes back immediately. And my plan is officially in motion.

Chapter Forty-One

Sunday, April 24th

Katy

The Staten Island Ferry crowd is bigger than I'd expect for a Sunday afternoon, and my mass-gathering claustrophobia is amped up to an eleven thanks to the hot flashes I've been having all morning.

But my role today is to be the dutiful daughter and granddaughter, so without complaint, I follow my parents and Gran down the stairs as she leads us toward the very spot on the bottom deck where she and my granddad first met.

As hard as today is for me, given my current—*still secret*—with-child condition, I can't even imagine how hard it is for Gran.

She looks so small and fragile with the urn in her hands, and the emotion is almost too much for me to bear. Tears are already pricking my eyes, and we haven't even started yet.

Just breathe, I coach myself, afraid that I'm going to have the kind of hormonal meltdown that will show my pregnancy cards to my family. *Your granddad's burial at sea is not the time to reveal this kind of news.*

Obviously, I'm going to have to tell my family at some point—when the risk of thunder-stealing my gran is off the table—but, even then, it feels wrong to do so without first talking to Mack.

My stomach turns.

The mere thought of how he might react and the fear that's involved in that sours the breakfast I just ate with my family at Sarabeth's and threatens to bring it back for a second showing.

I swallow hard against the nausea that won't quit and shuffle around a group of tourists who already have their cameras out and are snapping photos.

"This is it!" Gran shouts as she steps through the doors and onto the outside deck. She stops right in front of a bench that's smack-dab in the middle.

The ferry horn honks, indicating its imminent departure, and my mom and dad and I come to a stop right beside Gran.

But instead of focusing on this emotional moment with his mother, my dad decides now is the time to pull his cell out of his pocket. His fingers type furiously across the screen, and my mother nudges him with her elbow. "Kai," she whispers. "Put your phone away."

"In a minute, sweets," he states but doesn't lift his eyes away from the screen.

The boat's engine roars to life as we leave the harbor, and my gran steps toward the deck railing with my granddad's urn in her petite hands. My mother and I follow her, but when I glance over my shoulder, I see my dad is still busy with his stupid device.

Are you freaking kidding me?

"Dad." I join my mother's quiet outrage. "Come up here."

"Just a sec, Katybug."

My gran is too busy thinking about her beloved husband, but my mom's eyes now look like they might make an actual departure from her face.

"*Kai.*"

"Almost done," he says, and I honestly think my mom might toss him and his phone in the water before Gran has a chance to dump the urn.

But a moment later, he's shoving it back into his pocket with a smile and looking over his shoulder toward the doors that lead back inside the ferry.

What on earth is he doing?

"Harry, I loved you my whole life," Gran starts to announce toward the water, and I'm torn between listening to her emotional words and trying to understand why my dad is acting like such a fool. "For sixty years, you were my everything. For sixty years, I was madly in love with your laugh and your smile—"

"There he is!" my dad shouts, making Gran stop midsentence and practically trampling all over her memories of her beloved husband.

I expect her to yell or smack him right in the kisser at the very least, but before she can even raise an arm to dole a blow, she's staring behind me right along with him.

I turn around, anger and indignation instantly taking a back seat to confusion, only to find the one man in the universe who continually shows up where I'm not expecting him—my baby daddy, Mack Houston.

He looks painfully beautiful as he strides out onto the deck in jeans and a white T-shirt and his red Chuck Taylors. His gorgeous hair blows in the wind, and a part of me feels like he's some kind of mirage my brain has conjured up from all the stress and emotion I've endured over the past forty-eight hours.

"Who is that?" Gran asks from behind me, her voice almost inexplicably loud.

"It's Mack, Mom," my dad explains at a normal volume. "Katy's boyfriend."

Boyfriend?

My head jerks back to my family at the misnomer, and Gran is all smiles as she greets him excitedly. "Oh! Hi, honey. I'm so happy you made it."

So happy you *made it?* Was she expecting him or something? What the hell is going on here?

"And I'm happy I get to be here," Mack says as he steps up to give my sweet gran a hug and a kiss on the cheek.

"My Harry would've loved to have met you," she says and squeezes the urn tightly to her chest.

"He certainly would've, Mom," my dad agrees, wrapping his arms around my mom's shoulders. All I can do is stand there, slack-jawed, silently wondering if all these pregnancy hormones that are running rampant inside my body have given me brain damage.

Because unless I've been in a *While You Were Sleeping*-style coma for a couple of days, Mack showing up at this family dumping of a charred relative should be surprising someone other than me.

"Harry, my love…" My gran turns back toward the water. "Now that the whole family is here, it's time, honey. It's time to say goodbye."

The *whole* family? *Jerry Springer on a Sunday afternoon, did I miss a paternity test announcement?* Since when is Mack a member of the Daytons?

It's on the tip of my tongue to question it, but when my gran starts speaking again, Mack moves closer…and I have to admit, it feels good.

"You were my everything for sixty years," she says through a trembling voice, her love for my granddad so obvious, all of us can feel it.

Mack's at my side now, and I can't stop myself from looking up and into his eyes.

"What are you doing here?" I whisper, even though I shouldn't be busy with anything but my gran right now.

"I didn't want to be anywhere else, babe, besides right here, with you, on this very important day." He just smiles down at me and puts his arm around my shoulders, tucking me close to his side and kissing the top of my head.

It's like yesterday's fight didn't even happen, and I don't know how to comprehend it. Everything about today feels very *Freaky Friday*, and I look nothing like Lindsay Lohan or Jamie Lee Curtis.

Still, Mack's presence is a comfort. That part is undeniable.

A rush of unexpected tears forms in my eyes. I have no control over them as they spill down my cheeks, and my gran's following words don't do anything but create more.

"Harry, I love you," she says as she opens the urn. "I'll always love you. This isn't goodbye forever, honey. It's just goodbye for now. I'll see you on the other side."

I'm a mess at this point, basically sobbing, as my little gran starts to lift the urn toward the water.

"Ma'am!" a loud voice booms from behind us. "Put the urn down!"

All five of us, including Gran, look away from the water and toward the security guard who's now jogging toward us.

"Ma'am, you can't do that yet! We have to be three miles away from the coast!"

Gran isn't having it, though. "No!" she shouts and turns back toward the water with the urn. "This is the exact spot where I met my Harry! It has to be here!"

"No! Don't do it! Put the urn down!" the security guard shouts, but Gran is already letting my granddad's ashes fly into the air. They leave the urn in a brilliant heap as they head off the deck and onto the water below.

"That is illegal!" the security guard shouts as he reaches my gran and tries to remove the urn from her hands.

They're in a struggle, my dad trying to both help my gran and keep her from committing assault, but eventually, my gran wins and just throws the whole dang urn into the water.

"Ma'am, you really shouldn't have done that," the security guard says through a heavy sigh.

"I don't care!" Gran shouts victoriously and turns around to put her arms behind her back. "Arrest me! Take me to the slammer! I did it all out of love for my Harry, and I don't regret it!"

"*What?*" my mom shouts. "You're going to arrest her?"

"You better not touch my mother!" my father joins in.

I'm still sobbing, mind you, and the fear I now have for my sweet little grandmother feels like too much for my current emotional state.

The rubber band of tension inside me breaks with a snap.

"You can't arrest her!" I yell at the top of my lungs. "I'm with child! It'd be a crime to take a pregnant woman's grandmother away from her!"

The security guard looks downright confused, and like a whip, four faces turn to look at me at once, and I realize the words that just came out of my mouth.

Oh shit, what have I done?

Chapter Forty-Two

Mack

I almost don't believe my ears, but when I look down at the woman beside me and see big, fat tears falling from her face, all that comes out of my mouth is "*Katy?*"

"You're pregnant?" Melissa shouts.

"Katybug?" Kai looks like he just swallowed his tongue.

But Gran, well, even though she continues to stand there with her hands behind her back, the look on her face is outright elation. "Oh, happy day! I'm going to be a great-grandmother!" she cheers like a woman who didn't just battle over an urn with a security guard.

"I…I…" Katy's lip trembles through her tears. "I…yes…I'm pregnant." She looks up at me, and my heart wants to break over the uncertainty I see within her blue eyes. "Mack, I'm pregnant."

"You're pregnant?" I ask dumbly.

She nods, tears still falling down her cheeks. "I'm pregnant with your baby. Our baby."

Holy fucking shit. Katy is pregnant with my baby?

Katy is pregnant with my baby!

Old Mack would be freaking the fuck out, but I'm not the old Mack anymore. I'm the Mack who's been forever changed since falling in love with Katy, and I can't do anything but feel happy over this news.

Sure, it's the last fucking thing I expected to hear come from Katy's lips, but now it's all making sense. Her running out of the auditorium on Friday and the way she looked yesterday.

She's pregnant. With my child.

I feel like someone has put a shot of adrenaline in my veins, and I almost don't know what to do with myself. I want to run. I want to shout the news from the rooftops. I want to kiss Katy like she's never been kissed before. I want to do a million things right now, but her next words pull me up short.

"I'm sorry," she says, like she's supposed to apologize to me for the best fucking news I think I've ever heard. "I know things didn't end well yesterday and I know I was a bitch to you, and I understand if you need some time to think about this..."

What?

"I know this was just supposed to be a fun fling between us and this isn't at all what you had in mind, but I—"

"Katy." I say her name to get her to stop talking nonsense. "I love you," I tell her and reach down to gently hold her face in my hands. "I love you," I repeat so she doesn't misunderstand what I'm saying.

"You...you love me?" Her voice is so small that I know with certainty there is so much more she needs to hear me say.

"Katy, I am so far deep in love with you that there is no going back for me. And I came here today because I don't want to be anywhere else but with you."

"You love me?"

"Yeah, Katy, I love you. More than words. More than anything."

More tears spill from her eyes. "You love me?"

"He loves you, Katybug!" Kai shouts from behind us.

"But…you're not freaked out?" she asks, and I shake my head.

"Honestly? I'm the opposite of freaked out. I'm all in, babe." I smile as I pointedly place my hand on her belly. "I want you and I want this baby and I want our future together. It's all you, Katy Cat. Just you, babe. It's all I want and need."

Her eyes search mine for the longest moment, but then, like the heavens themselves open up just for me, she says the three words I didn't realize I've been longing to hear from her. "I love you."

"Yeah?"

"Yeah." She nods. More tears slip down her cheeks. "I love you, Mack. So much."

Between one breath and the next, she's in my arms and my lips are on hers. I kiss her with everything I have. I kiss her with everything that I am. And I kiss her with everything that I know we're going to be together.

"Hell yeah!" I can just barely hear Kai cheer in the background.

"I'm going to be a grandmother!" Melissa exclaims.

"I know my Harry isn't here with us, but he's certainly looking down at us from heaven, smiling that big, handsome smile of his!" Gran calls out. "Oh, and Kai, I think you need to try to get some bail money, dear."

"Ma'am, you're not under arrest," a voice I'm not familiar with announces with a laugh. "You don't need to have your hands behind your back."

And it's that voice that has Katy and me ending the kiss to see what's going on.

"You're not going to take me to the slammer?" Gran questions, and the security guard is smiling down at her.

"No," he says. "But just so you know, you need to be three miles away from the coast when you spread ashes into the water, okay?"

"Okay," Gran says with a shrug and not a single ounce of regret. She's also quick to move her attention back to Katy and me. "So, do I get to witness a proposal on this ferry too?"

Katy laughs outright. "How about we take this one step at a time, Gran?"

"Honey, just so you know, it usually goes marriage first, then baby."

"Yeah, well," Katy comments and smiles up at me, "Mack and I never seem to do things in the typical way."

"Well, Katy, that's normally true. But today, it's not." I step back from her a bit and then sink down onto one knee. I pull the ring box out of my pocket and click open the lid, my smile broad and brilliant.

"Katy Dayton, would you do me the honor of marrying me?"

A titter rings out as the crowd catches wind, and every romantic bone in my body sings with the satisfaction that I've done exactly what the billionaires suggested.

Grand gesture moment, here I come.

"You've got to be kidding me," Katy replies unexpectedly, immediately dissolving into tears and shocked laughter. "My gran just chucked my granddad overboard, and I just found out we're pregnant less than twenty-four hours ago. Do you think you could give me a little time just to get my bearings first before you freaking propose?"

I stand up as the crowd wavers, completely clueless as to what to do now.

Thankfully, I'm not clueless. Because I know my girl. And I know, despite this shitshow of a grand gesture, she loves me.

I chuckle and pull her up and into my arms until her legs are wrapped around my waist. "Just so you know," I say and rub my nose against hers, "one day, very soon, I'm going to propose again. And that time, you're going to say yes."

"And what if I decide to say no again?"

"Then I'll keep asking until your answer changes. Big Mack's worn you down before, Katy Cat. I've got no doubt I can do it again."

Her responding giggle and smile are all I need.

"Love you," I whisper and brush my lips against hers.

"Love you too," she whispers back, just before placing a soft kiss to my lips.

Happily ever after, here we fucking come.

Epilogue

Thirty-two weeks later...

Katy

My sixth-period class of third graders is far more boisterous than I'd like, but that's usually how it goes on Fridays. Not only are they all hyped up after recess, but they're also excited for the weekend to begin.

"Everyone, settle down," I announce and stand in front of the big whiteboard at the front of the room. "I know Fridays are hard to focus after recess, but I also know that you guys are all great kids who are capable of giving me your attention right now so we can go over fractions."

I hear a few moans of annoyance, but mostly, my students listen.

But just as I'm lifting my marker to the board, the baby decides it's a good time to rearrange my organs, and my stomach tightens in discomfort.

Ouch. That hurts.

"You okay, Ms. Dayton?" Caroline Matthews asks, and I force a smile to my lips.

"Yep. I am."

"Is it your baby?" Seth Brown questions. "When my aunt Brooke was pregnant, her baby was a wild child! Always moving around. Sometimes, she'd curse because of it!"

I can certainly relate to that sentiment.

"The baby is definitely moving a little, Seth, but it's okay," I answer, but it's like the baby can hear me and has decided my words pose a challenge. After another bout of kicks and rolls, my stomach contracts so hard it takes the breath right out of my lungs.

Son of a bitch.

At thirty-eight weeks today, I know I still have at least two weeks until this baby will officially come, so I'm trying like hell to push through the pain. That doesn't mean that some days aren't harder than others, though.

Surely I just need to rest for a moment and drink some water.

"You know what?" I announce through slightly gritted teeth. "How about you guys pull out the worksheet we were working on yesterday and finish those last three problems on your own? Just try your best and solve the problems how you think, and then, in about fifteen minutes, we'll go over them together."

I don't normally shuffle my teaching responsibilities like this, but damn, today is not a great pregnant day.

Thankfully, my students follow my instructions, and I head over to my desk to sit down and sip some water from my giant Yeti cup that's become my best friend for the past several months.

I don't know what it is about pregnancy, but it's like I can't ever put enough food or water in my body. It's like I'm either starving or so thirsty I feel like I just spent three days walking through the Sahara.

I snag my phone from my top desk drawer to set a fifteen-minute timer, but as I do, I note a missed text message from someone who always manages to bring a smile to my face, even when he's being a pain in my ass.

Mack: My sweet, beautiful, gorgeous fiancée who accepted my marriage proposal, how are you feeling this afternoon?

Three months ago, after Mack had proposed to me on no fewer than ten different occasions, I finally said yes to him, and he still won't stop reminding me of that fact.

Me: Like I'm very, very pregnant.

His instant response surprises me, but then I remember it's his free period, and he's probably just in his classroom working on lesson plans or something.

Mack: You want me to come over and give you a break? Surely I can teach some math. Or pretend to teach some math. LOL.

I snort.

Me: I appreciate the offer, honey, but I've got it covered. But I wouldn't mind a good foot massage tonight when we get home…

Mack: Your wish is my command.

About two months after I dropped the pregnancy bomb on him in the middle of the Staten Island Ferry, we found an apartment and moved in together. And honestly, it's been nothing but bliss ever since.

Sure, Mack likes to purposefully get on my nerves sometimes, but the man is so damn thoughtful, so damn caring, that I don't know what I'd do without him. He's my rock. My everything.

Me: I love you.

Mack: I love you more.

Pfft. Doubtful, but I refuse to go down that rabbit hole that is the back-and-forth of the who-loves-whom-the-most discussion he always tries to pull me into.

Once I put my phone back in my desk drawer, I stand to my feet and head back to the whiteboard with the intention of writing out the first problem on the worksheet to make it easier to go over with my students.

But halfway to the board, I feel this intense popping sensation, and then, warm fluid gushes down my legs.

Oh no.

I look down at my feet and see a puddle of clear liquid.

Holy hell. I think my water just broke.

"Ms. Dayton?" Seth Brown's voice fills my ears. "I don't want to embarrass you, but I think you just peed your pants."

I open my mouth to offer some kind of explanation that won't freak out my whole class, but my stomach turns hard as a rock as an insanely intense contraction rolls through my body.

Goodness, I don't think this is a Braxton-Hicks…

"Holy schnikes!" I groan and have to brace my hand on the board to stabilize myself as I breathe through it.

"Ms. Dayton?" Seth Brown's voice is back. "Are you okay?"

"Mmmhmm."

"I don't think you're okay," he continues. "You look like my aunt Brooke did before she had to go to the hospital to have her baby."

"Oh my goodness!" another student calls out. "You're going to have your baby, Ms. Dayton!"

"Are you going to have your baby right now?"

"But someone has to be here to catch your baby!"

"I can catch a baseball really good!"

"Anyone got a glove?"

My class is in shambles now, but all I can do is shuffle over to my desk and pull out my phone again.

Help, I text to the one person I need right now.

And I swear, not even ten seconds later, Mack comes bursting through my classroom door like Cosmo Kramer on *Seinfeld*.

"Katy?"

"My water broke," I manage to breathe out while another contraction starts to roll through my body.

He's at my side and wrapping his arm around my waist. "We need to get a move on it, babe," he whispers quietly into my ear. "Looks like we're going to have our baby today."

All I can do is nod through gritted teeth.

Holy moly. I'm about to have a baby.

Mack

"You can do it, babe," I coach as Katy pushes with a contraction. "You got this."

She grabs the backs of her thighs, and her face strains as she pushes with all of her might. My girl has been in labor for the past sixteen hours, and she's been pushing for the past two. I know she's tired, but I also know that she's getting close. I can actually see the baby's head at this point.

"You're almost done, Katy," Dr. Wethers encourages. "The head is right there. I think with the next contraction, the baby will be here."

Katy looks up at me, her breaths slowing during the short break.

"You okay?" I ask her and she nods.

"Just ready to meet our baby."

"I'm so proud of you," I say and kiss her forehead. "Strongest woman I know."

She smiles up at me, and I don't think she's ever looked more beautiful than she does in this moment. Sure, she's sweaty and her hair is a mess, but she's having our baby. Right now, Katy is delivering our child into the world. Nothing could ever be more beautiful than that.

"Okay, Katy, here it is," Dr. Wethers announces. "Give me another big push with this contraction, and I think we'll have a baby."

Katy takes a big inhale of oxygen, grips the backs of her thighs, and pushes with everything inside her.

"That's it," Dr. Wethers says with a smile. "Keep going. Keep going."

I watch as our baby leaves Katy's body. And then, I hear the most beautiful sound I've ever heard—our baby's first cry.

"You did it!" Dr. Wethers cheers. And the two nurses in the room do the same.

"Good job, Katy!"

"Way to go, Katy!"

"And it's a girl!" Dr. Wethers announces as she clutches our baby in her hands. "Congratulations, Mom and Dad, you have a daughter."

I have a daughter? Holy shit, I have a daughter!

"You ready to cut the umbilical cord, Dad?" the doctor asks as she smiles up at me.

But I don't even know what to say as I stand there, looking down at Katy's and my daughter. All I can do is nod.

One nurse hands me surgical scissors, while the other holds the umbilical cord with a gloved hand. "Just right there, Dad. Right between my fingers."

I feel like I'm having an out-of-body experience as I cut my daughter's umbilical cord, and a moment later, Dr. Wethers places our baby on Katy's chest.

And I can't fight the tears of joy carving paths down my cheeks.

"She's so beautiful," Katy whispers as she stares down at the tiny, precious little face.

"She's perfect," I say and lean down to kiss Katy's forehead. "You're perfect. I love you so much."

"I love you too."

"Do you have a name?" one of the nurses asks, and Katy looks up at me with a soft smile on her face.

The name game. Man oh man, that's been a difficult one for us. For the past six months, we've been trying hard to figure out a name for our baby. We have lists of boy and girl names, but we never actually decided on anything.

"She looks like a Hannah to me," Katy says, and for some crazy reason, I couldn't agree more. I guess, like everything else for us, the timing just had to be right.

"Hannah," I say out loud. "Hannah Houston."

"Yeah?" Katy asks and I nod.

"Yeah, babe. It's the perfect name for our perfect girl." I kiss both of them on the forehead. "Hannah Banana, we love you so much."

"Oh no," Katy says through a laugh that makes my heart melt. "A nickname already?"

I grin. "Katy Cat, it's only right, you know?"

"Yeah, Big Mack," Katy replies with a big smile. "It's only right."

"Dad, I think I need to let you know that you have a room full of impatient family members in the waiting room," a staff member updates as she walks into the room. "I've had several people come up to the desk for updates."

Katy laughs. "I think you need to go out there, Mack. Otherwise, my dad might stage a riot."

I don't want to leave my girls, but I give Katy and Hannah one more kiss to their foreheads. "Be right back."

Out of Katy's delivery room and down the hall, I make my way to the waiting room. The instant I walk through the swinging doors, I spot our crew of family and friends.

My parents and my sister and Tom and Gracie.

Kai and Melissa and Gran, who somehow managed the drive from Savanah in record time.

Thatch and Kline and Wes and Cap, who have become some of my closest friends since I started Music in Motion.

Anna and Kimmie and a few of our close friends from Calhoun—even Alma.

It feels like everyone we know and love is here, and I don't think my heart could be any fuller than it is right now.

"Is the baby here?" Gracie exclaims when she spots me first, and everyone looks toward me with excited eyes.

"The baby is here," I announce. "Hannah Houston, our daughter, is here."

The room erupts in cheers and hoots and hollers and happy tears.

And in this moment, I know with certainty, because of Katy, I'm the luckiest man who's ever walked the face of this earth.

Best of enemies, best of frenemies, best of friends. Whatever stage we're in, Katy and I are in it together. *Forever.*

THE END

Loved being inside Mack and Katy's world? Well, we have good news! You can read about how famous author Brooke Baker fell in love in *Accidental Attachment!*

There's nothing like sending your editor—*and secret crush*—the wrong manuscript. Instead of the book that was due, Brooke accidentally sends dreamboat Chase Dawson the secret romance book she wrote about her crush...*on him.*

And for everyone waiting on Sammy and Noah's book...

Cluelessly Yours is coming up next!

Need EVEN MORE Max Monroe while you wait for Sammy and Noah's book?

Never fear, we have a list of nearly FORTY other titles to keep you busy for as long as your little reading heart desires! Check them out at our website: *www.authormaxmonroe.com*

COMPLETELY NEW TO MAX MONROE AND DON'T KNOW WHERE TO START?

Check out our Suggested Reading Order on our website!
www.authormaxmonroe.com/max-monroe-suggested-reading-order

WHAT'S NEXT FROM MAX MONROE?

Stay up-to-date with our characters and our upcoming releases by signing up for our newsletter on our website: *www.authormaxmonroe.com/ newsletter!*

You may live to regret much, but we promise it won't be subscribing to our newsletter.

Seriously, we make it fun! Character conversations about royal babies, parenting woes, embarrassing moments, and shitty horoscopes are just the beginning! If you're already signed up, consider sending us a message to tell us how much you love us. We really like that. ;)

Follow us online here:

Facebook: www.facebook.com/authormaxmonroe

Reader Group: www.facebook.com/groups/1561640154166388

Twitter: www.twitter.com/authormaxmonroe

Instagram: www.instagram.com/authormaxmonroe

TikTok: www.tiktok.com/@authormaxmonroe

Goodreads: https://goo.gl/8VUIz2

Acknowledgments

First of all, THANK YOU for reading. That goes for anyone who has bought a copy, read an ARC, helped us beta, edited, or found time in their busy schedule just to make sure we stayed on track. Thank you for supporting us, for talking about our books, and for just being so unbelievably loving and supportive of our characters. You've made this our MOST favorite adventure thus far.

THANK YOU to each other. Monroe is thanking Max. Max is thanking Monroe. We always do this, and it's because we *love* writing books together.

THANK YOU, Lisa, for being an editing Queen (please, don't edit the Q to lowercase because you very much deserve the capital) whom we can't live without. We love you to infinity and beyond. Or even farther. Did we get that right? (P.S. We added farther after edits, so if it really is wrong, we're sorry.)

THANK YOU, Stacey, for always making the inside of our books so pretty! And for being so dang flexible with our last-minute asses. We couldn't survive without you!

THANK YOU, Peter for working your ass off on this cover and making it everything we wanted and need it to be!

THANK YOU, Mel for taking the giant leap to join on our team! We're so excited that you're here!

THANK YOU to every blogger and influencer who has read, reviewed, posted, shared, and supported us. Your enthusiasm, support, and hard work do not go unnoticed. We love youuuuuuuuuuuuu!

THANK YOU to the people who love us—our family. You are our biggest supporters and motivators. We couldn't do this without you.

THANK YOU to our Awesome ARC-ers. We love and appreciate you guys so much.

THANK YOU to our Camp Love Yourself friends! We love you. You always find a way to make us smile and laugh every single freaking day. You're the best.

As always, all our love.

XOXO,

Max & Monroe

Made in the USA
Middletown, DE
24 October 2023